Upstate Downstate

By Jeff Ward

Contents

Chapter 1
Moving On

The milk company was going to leave Long Island, New York, after 89 years. Seems like they can do business in New Jersey for half the cost. NEW JERSEY STINKS, figuratively and literally. Sometimes they send some of their stinks right to New York. Gas tanks, billowing smoke stacks, and the dumbest roadways in the country. Thank goodness we had Robert Moses to structure our roadways, as congested as they are. In Jersey, you can't make a left-hand turn. First, you have to make a right turn then a U-turn to go left. And don't miss that turn or you'll have to go 20 miles to the next exit before you can make another right/left turn. I guess they had Grandma Moses do their roads. And what's with this Bruce Springsteen character anyway? He ain't no Billy Joel that's for sure. New Jersey can't even get their own sports teams. They steal ours. Giants, Jets, and Nets. Despicable!

The company, "Cows" of Elmont told their employees they were relocating the company to New Jersey. Any employee willing to follow them to Jersey could retain their jobs.

NO THANKS! I'd rather move to Siberia than move to Jersey. 25 YEARS of hard work DOWN THE DRAIN. Now what?

After a few days of brooding, I decided to get off Long Island and head upstate New York. When we were kids my parents would take us to a cabin on Summit Lake in the town of Summit. Swimming, fishing, and boating. We loved every minute. The ride up was always so picturesque. The mountains were so big and beautiful. The biggest thing you can view on Long Island is the Nassau Medical Center. Oh yeah, we also have Bald Hill in Suffolk County. If nature cooperated and left a foot of snow on the ground you could ski this MONSTER slope. Top to bottom took about 30 seconds if you could avoid the thousands of kids

1

sprawled all over the place. Then to get back to the "PEAK" you had to hold a towrope (a mechanically pulled rope) and ski your way up the slope holding on for dear life. Oh, the good old days.

I decided I would pack up and leave the following morning. I chose to take Taconic Parkway, which is a prettier ride than the N.Y. State Thruway. Also, there are no tolls and I *am* unemployed. On the ride up I had a real brain fart. I have a class-A license, I drove tractor-trailers for Cows, and maybe I could get a job driving a truck upstate! The cost of living on the Island is getting out of control and at my age, I wasn't going to get a job making the same salary I made at the milk company. I could probably find a cheap house upstate and I wouldn't have to make as much to afford it. Brilliant.

As I was nearing Summit I went thru the town of Stamford. I stopped at the local real estate, Mountain Realtor, and spoke with an agent named Lorretta Tillis. I told her of my new plan and asked if she had any cheap places." We've got whatever you want. I can show you some now, do you have the time?"

"Let me look at my appointment book and see. I'm joking I have nothing but time.".

"Good, then let's jump in my car," she said. Off we went to find my new life.

"I'll show you this handyman special I have on 2 acres for 25 grand."

We pulled up to a one-room shack. I follow her in (no lock on the door, not necessary) and I took a look around the place. Now I'm not the handiest guy around but to fix this place you would need a degree in architecture. No heat. No kitchen and worst of all no indoor bathroom as you'll find out later, bathrooms are an important part of my existence. I was hoping she didn't show me the best one first.

"So how do you like it? The owner is motivated (no shit) You could probably get it for a steal." (I've seen homeless people with better places)

"No, I'm not crazy about the drapes, maybe you can show me something a little bigger."

2

The second place we go to was a little bigger than the first. It had a separate bedroom and an indoor toilet. The only problem was it was free-standing in the corner of the room, out in the open. Tough to have company over that way.

We're off to see house #3 The best thing about driving around up here is the surrounding beauty of the place. Majestic mountains, cows grassing, horses galloping. After living on Long Island my whole life, and the Island is a beautiful place to live, you can't believe that you are still in the state of New York. You would think you were somewhere out west.

"The next place we'll see is on 2 acres and it has a little pond on it." Loretta explained, "It's within walking distance to a small town called Jefferson. We'll be passing through it in a minute."

It didn't even take a minute to pass the town. It ran for 2 blocks. There was a bed and breakfast, a small eatery, a church, and a place I remember my dad used to frequent. The local gin mill, The Jailhouse Rock Inn. The home of the one-pound hamburger. On his deathbed, dad swore that burger had something to do with his demise.

She pulled into a dirt driveway and there it was. Compared to the others it was like the Taj Mahal. It was a modular home, and the door even had a lock on it, though no one locked their doors here. Inside it was all right! A separate bedroom, separate kitchen, and living room. Best of all a real bathroom, which I was way overdue for so I excused myself and said I was going to test the plumbing. All the plumbing worked, including mine. Thank God for little things.

"How much are they asking?" I said.

"$49,900, good buy." She stated in her best realities.

She didn't realize she was dealing with a shrewd businessman. "I'll give them $45,000 and not a penny more!"

"Let's go back to the office and I'll give them a jingle." She said.

We were back at the office in 2 shakes of a lamb's tail. She shuffled to her desk and got the phone number. The office was small and it had only one phone, off to the side behind a partition. I don't hear well but I can hear her telling the owner.

"Sue, I have a man here who just offered $45,000 for your dad's place. Yeah $45,000, do you believe it? Some downstater...you can say that again. I'll call you later with the details." With a large smile on her face (or was it a grin) Loretta said you have a deal.

"I'm going to need a mortgage," I said.

"No problem. Directly across the way is a bank. Ask for Harvey I'm sure he will help you" she said.

Out the front door, I went, not quite as happy as I was a couple of minutes ago. I felt like I was at the supermarket and forgot the coupons at home.

I opened the door of THE FIRST (and only I'm sure) NATIONAL BANK OF STAMFORD...Inside the place was pretty empty. There were no bars on the teller windows and the door to the teller counter was open. Bonnie and Clyde would have loved this joint. Arriving from behind a rear door came an elderly neatly dressed man.

"May I help you?" he inquired.

"Yes, I'm looking for Harvey. Loretta from the real estate sent me". "I'm Harvey, Harvey Kean, bank manager, loan official and with Marge out today teller. And you are?"

"Patrick Hunnewell, glad to meet you."

"Same here. Looking for a mortgage I assume since Loretta sent you." "Yes, I just made an offer on a place in Jefferson."

"Nice town, you'll love it there. Do you have the paperwork?". "Yes, it's right here".

Harvey checks the paperwork and raises his eyebrows. That's Jeb Potter's old place. Nice guy. Shame what happened to him". He reads on a little farther down the page. "$45,000!!!Wow seems like only yesterday he bought the place for $750. I gave him the mortgage. $45,000!! Kids could sure use the money! Can I see your driver's license?"

"Sure, here"

He looks it over and writes down some information. "Any money down?"

"How much do you need?"

"$50".

"I guess I can do that.". ($50 wow)

"Congratulations, the place is yours."

A couple of hours ago I was on my way for a little r&r and now I live here!

Harvey said that it was all right with her if I moved in today. Unbelievable!

After leaving the bank I realized I would be needing some things. The gas station had a sign HAPPY HOUR EVERY M-F 4-7 GENESEE BEER 30 PACK $9.99. I checked my watch and it was 4:05. It must be my lucky day. I usually drink Bud, but at that price, I figured I would help the local economy and my pocket. I grabbed a 30-pack from the glass-encased fridge. I noticed on the side of the case a mail-in coupon for "$4.00 off a t30 pack and $8.00 off on 2". I now hold in my hands 60 beers for $12.00. I think I'm going to like this place. You can't buy bottled water downstate that cheap, and water won't even give you a buzz.

Boy, I was wrong about bottled water. I never figured people would buy something they have flowing out of their tap, practically free. And why does water have an expiration date on it anyway?

I put the beers on the counter and I say to the clerk," A little I nippy out there for June?"

"You're not from around here are ya?" he says.

"Yes, I am I have a house in Jefferson. I've been living here a whole 5 minutes".

He looked at me strangely mumbling something under his breath, then told me the amount. I don't think I should be a wise guy until I've been here a little longer. After all, this guy looks like he just crawled out of a cave (nice shave).

I grabbed my beer and walked out of the store with a shit-eating grin on my face. This might just work out!

The town of Stamford is not a small town, but also not a big town. It has a True Value Hardware store, a Radio Shack (all right, in the same store), and a couple of eateries including a Chinese joint and a pizza joint. It has everything a town can have, even a supermarket. A Grand Union. Maybe I shouldn't call it a supermarket like the colossal stores on the Island. (And shouldn't it be pronounced Grand Onion).

I stopped in the Grand Onion and got the necessities, one of which was a small hibachi and some charcoal. I can't live without a grill. One last stop at the liquor store for some pirate-loving rum! I grabbed the cheapest stuff they had, Ensign Morgan, and was on my way" home".

On the ride back, I put on the radio and The Beatles (the best group ever) are singing, "The Two of Us", with the line WE'RE ON OUR WAY HOME, and I guess I am.

I pull into the driveway and just take in the scenery. Mount Jefferson looms large directly behind my house. It is saturated with evergreens and assorted other trees and shrubs, with an occasional house carved into an open clearing. I get out of the car and venture into the backyard I'd never seen before. It drops off into a valley, where I got the first glimpse of the pond. MY POND! It was about thirty feet by fifty feet. I can't wait to drop a fishing line into it!

After absorbing the breathtaking beauty, I head back to the car to retrieve my goodies and head into the house. I need to keep the beers cold because it's almost time to imbibe.

The refrigerator seems like it's from the fifties. The freezer does not have a separate door. When you open the refrigerator, the freezer is on top with a pull-down door. I don't think it was called a freezer when this thing was made. They called it an ice box, and if I remember correctly, after a few days it was an ice box, surrounded by ice needing to be defrosted.

I peer behind the fridge and see the cord lying dustily on the floor. I blow the dust off the cord and dare to plug it in. I gingerly place it in the outlet expecting to get electrocuted (as if putting it in gingerly will save me.) I get the plug into the outlet and nothing happens. Silence. I guess I need a fridge. Then I hear it. A faint humming, like the sound of a cell phone, vibrating. Little by little the sound increases. Within minutes the humming turned into the thundering sound of the Space

Shuttle taking off. The floors started vibrating and I thought the house was going to take off and slide down into the pond. As I reached behind to pull the plug, I the sound was opening the fridge door and I am amazed to see the light is working. I feel a slight bit of coldness in the air. In goes thirty-pack and the food. Good enough for me.

I cleaned the place up a bit. I checked my watch and noticed it was ten minutes to seven. The New York Mets game will be starting in a couple of minutes. The Mets were in 1st place and were about to begin a three-game series with the hated Atlanta Braves, who were in 2nd place. My dilemma was that I had neither a radio nor T.V. I pondered my situation and realized I would have to listen to the game on the car radio. I grabbed a couple of beers and some snacks and headed for the stadium (my car). It was then I learned another inconvenience of living out of the Metropolitan area, poor radio reception. The sound coming out of the radio was either the crowd cheering or static. It brought back memories of my childhood listening to a transistor radio. It sucked then and it sucks now! I quickly found that by repositioning my car, I could get better reception. I spent the whole game driving my car to different parts of the property to hear the game. I'm sure if my next-door neighbors caught any of this act, they would have to think a lunatic must have moved in next to them.

It was worth all the work! Johan Santana pitches eight strong innings, Carlos Beltran hits a homer and Francisco Rodrigues gets the save, but not before giving up a run and leaving the bases loaded. And I thought John Franco was bad!

It had been a long day, plus eight beers and I was feeling a little groggy. I closed my eyes for a minute, or so I thought. The next time I open my eyes it is already light out and I'm freezing my ass off. Quite the first day of my new life.

Chapter 2
Maybe a New Tomorrow

After finalizing the deal, the NEXT DAY, (I gave Harvey 50 bucks, and signed some paperwork without the need for a lawyer) I had to plan my move from downstate to upstate. I had an apartment in North Babylon, Long Island. I had the usual junk to move, T.V., bed, dressers, etc. I will rent a U-Haul, load it up and set it back off for Summit. I hadn't even told family or friends about any of this. I figured they would call me an asshole for making such an abrupt move (they would be right.) and they would try to talk me out of it. I wanted to give it a try first and then drop a bombshell on them. They'll understand. NOT!

The ride back takes about 4 hours. I try to go as fast as I can without getting a ticket, which is 12 or so miles over the speed limit, but today I was anxious to get my new life underway so I was pushing my chances. The speed limit on the N.Y.S. Thruway is 65 mph and I was doing 83 mph. After a while I noticed a strange trend starting to take place behind me. Every lane change I make 2 cars behind me mimic every move. To make sure I'm not crazy I make a couple of unorthodox moves and sure enough, they follow the leader. Now I get it! They know they can go as fast as me because the cops will always get the 1st car on the radar, so I decide it's time to play a game of ticket tag. I pull over into the far-right lane and slow down to appear as if I'm going to get off the next exit. Sensing these the other 2 cars (a Cadillac Escalade and a Ford Mustang) take off, the Cadillac in the lead. They get a distance ahead and I start trailing them. After 10 miles or so they realize the game is on, so we all play. The Caddy slows down and drops behind me so the next 10 miles it's the Mustang's turn. The game goes on for about 2 hours but the Caddy is about to pay the price. The Mustang and I trail the Caddy by about ¼ miles when out of nowhere a state trooper pulls behind him, lights flashing. Game over! As we crawl past the scene both the Mustang guy and me wave a thank you, and in return, we get a shoulder shrug from the poor bastard. Hopefully, the guy has a get-out-of-jail-free card (PBA card).

The rest of the ride is uneventful and the trip winds up only taking 3 ½ hours.

I got back to my apartment and started to gather my belongings. I packed the rental to its fullest. I get a good night's sleep and looked forward to my move tomorrow.

I hit the L.I. Expressway at around 10 in the morning, dragging the U-Haul behind. It's about a 3-hour ride with the trailer in tow. I have to take the N.Y. State Throughway because you can't take trailers or trucks on the Taconic. It always puzzles me why they bother to put up speed limits because nobody except me (if a state trooper is reading this) does it anyway. The speed limit on the Expressway (rte,495) is posted at 55 mph. If you do 55 mph you will get so many middle fingers at you that you'll think Rosanne Barr was driving every car. At 70 miles an hour, you'll just be keeping up with traffic. When you hit the thruway the speed limit goes up to 65mph, which means everybody does 80. They should just make it like the autobahn and have no speed limit, but then what would the highway patrol do with their day?

I backed the U haul into the driveway and opened the rear door. I grabbed the most important thing, the T.V., and lugged it into the house. Next, I took the TV Stand in and set it up in the corner of the living room. I plugged it in and turned it on. All I got on the screen was snow, every channel. We ain't in Kansas anymore Toto, I thought to myself. There are no cable wires in here like on the island. Now what?

I emptied some of the smaller things and started to put things away. When I entered one of the closets, I came upon some things left behind by poor old Jeb. There was an old heavy-duty frying pan, an old pair of skis from the 1920s, and a familiar old friend from my childhood. Rabbit ears! For those of you who are unfamiliar with them, they are used to getting TV reception when there's no antenna on the roof, or, in today's language, cable wires. The rich people back in the day had an antenna on the roof and would get fine reception. The rest of us had rabbit ears. You attach 2 wires from the ears to the rear of the TV and then the fun begins. The antennas are similar to those on an automobile and are attached to a round ball. They can be manipulated around. Changing the direction or moving the whole base around you try to get the best picture on the TV. When you were the youngest in the family you would draw this duty. "Hold it right there, no move a little right, a little to the left. That's it. Don't move. You would hear these commands all night long, while not being able to watch the stupid TV. Sometimes, you would move the ears just to the right spot and everyone would scream "THAT'S IT!" Then you would leave to sit down so you can watch, but when you let go of the antenna, the picture would get bad. You knew this was going to be trouble because they were going to make you hold this as long as the picture was clear. (Did I say I found an old friend?)

I decided to give it the old college try. I hooked it up, turned the TV on, and tried to get a station, any station. I was spinning and turning so much that I felt like I was involved in a game of Twister Lo, and behold I heard a voice, then I got a picture. I could vaguely see the outlines of people. It was like watching a show that was caught in a snowstorm. Then I saw a guy throw a punch at another guy and I knew I was watching The Jerry Springer show. It's at least a start.

Later that evening I decided to take a walk to the Jailhouse Rock Inn. It was only around the block which would bode well for avoiding d.w.i's The" Rock" had a satellite dish on top so I figured I could catch the Met game. They were playing the Phillies, who were in third place. They had that damned Pat Borough (?) who would be in the Hall of Fame if he played the Mets every game.

I got to the front door [it was two flapping doors like in the old west] and could hear the noisy goings-on inside the bar. I heard them yelling at the T.V. complaining about a bad strike three calls. Great! A place I can come watch the game with my new friends. I split the doors and enter my new home away from home! What I entered was the Twilight Zone. The place got as quiet as a library. The "Patrons of the bar" all stopped what they were doing and stared at me as if I had three heads. I didn't know whether to run or feign a heart attack to gain sympathy [the only sympathy this crowd would give is if their pickup truck was in an accident]. I decide to make myself to the bar and asked the bartender [Maryjane I would find out later] for a Genesee on tap. I figured it would make fit in with the crowd. After placing my order, I heard a lot of snickering. After only one sip I could tell the beer was flat. No one had ordered Genny in months. They were Bud drinkers. The beer was flat but it only cost a dollar a pint!

A YANKEE BAR! A-Rod just hit his 30th homer of the year [it's only June] and the place erupts with high fives. I shake could get used to this joint.

The focus of the bar shifted back to the game on the tube. Then, worse than the silent treatment I received, was the real killer. It's my head at my bad luck. "Man, that guy can hit ", I pipe in.

"Yeah, but last week he struck out with the bases loaded and cost us a game," Mike said (Alex can do no right for the Yankee fan).

"I saw that. Against Boston."

Yeah, Boston.

Mike was a tall guy with a ponytail. He had a can of Bud wrapped in a cooler sleeve. He seemed to be enjoying the game as well as the beer." Why did you order that shit?" he asks me.

"When in Rome," I said. He squints his eyes and shakes his head.

Maryjane, give this guy a real beer. She hands me a can of bud. "Take it from her," he tells Maryjane, pointing to his cash on the bar.

"Thanks, I'm Patrick."

"I know, bought Jeb Potters house for$ 45,000. Too bad about Jeb"

I knew this was a small town but shit travels pretty fast here.

"You plan on sleeping in the car every night?" He said. "Just . the nights I drink. Yeah, every night."

Mike and a bunch of guys around start cracking up. "You'll fit in here just fine." Michael, Mike's brother says. His brother is about a foot shorter with darker hair. There's no way the same man fathered both of these dudes.

"But I'm a Met fan," I said.

'Too bad for you. 26 rings and counting. I always wondered why the Yankee fans felt the right to claim championships before they started rooting for the team, nevertheless before they were born".

"We have 2." The place roars in laughter. At least I saw the 2.

The Jailhouse Rock Inn was the kind of local bar you would find in most neighborhoods. There was a pool table, dart board, and some tables for dining. It had the usual local characters hanging around. You had the drunk, who started drinking when the doors opened and were trashed by 5 pm. Thank God he lived five doors away and didn't have to drive home. He would stumble all the way home, but would never fall.

Then you had the jolly drunk, Michael, who was jolly till he got drunk. Then he became nasty. Wants to hit anything and anyone that gets in his way. He is just about at his limit right now. Luckily, his brother Mike is here, and he coaxes his brother out the door and drags him home. I have a feeling this is not the last I will see of him.

It was only eight o'clock (A little too early for me to eat.), but those chicken wings everyone was eating sure looked good. I ordered a dozen wings and a Genesee from Maryjane. She was a pretty woman. Her breasts were large and she wasn't shy about showing them. She came over and placed my beer on the bar, leaning over to show me just enough.

"How do you like them?" she asks.

My jaw drops, and I am thinking of a thousand responses. I'm just about to do something stupid she asks …

"Hot, medium, or mild?"

"I like them hot."

She gave me a cute little smile and headed back to the kitchen with my order. I gulped down my beer, just so she would bring me another and I can get a second look at those mounds. I think I'm going to like this town.

Mary Jane brought my order of wings to the bar and place them in front of me. They were the biggest wings I've ever seen. They look more like turkey wings than chicken wings. On top of that, they were only 25¢ apiece. They were hot but not too hot.

The Yankee game was in the fifth inning, and they were leading seven to one. The Yankee announcers gave the scores around the league. The Mets were trailing two to one after four innings. I was about to bring the wings with me and go listen to the game in my car when I noticed another TV in the back of the bar. It looked like it was from 1950. I ask Mary Jane if it still worked and she said yes and it's also hooked up to cable. Bingo! Could you please put the Met game on so I can watch it? She said she didn't know which Channel it was on. She asked around the bar and someone told her to try channel 71. She flicked on the TV and there were my beloved Mets. Carlos Beltran is on third and only one out, but as usual Mathieu Schneider pops up to the second baseman and Louis Castillo strikes out. End of the inning 2-1 Phillies. Then the old TV starts to flutter. The picture starts rotating horizontally first slowly then it starts to pick up speed. I look the TV over and I notice there are dials on the side, one which says horizontal. I remember these from the TVs I had as a kid I start turning the dial, first Clockwise then counterclockwise and it rotated even faster. But the rotation started slowing as I turned the dial clockwise. It got it to the point where it would only turn about once every 30 seconds. It still beats sitting in a car trying to get the game on the radio.

After another couple of beers [I switched back to Genesee, it was good] I noticed the crowd thinning out. The Yankee's game was over. Ten to one was the final score. The Mets game was going to, the bottom of the ninth still trailing two to one. They loaded the basis with two out but Carlos Beltran struck out looking at a pitch two feet off the plate. I was holding in all my cussing and screaming till I get back to the house. I guess the umpire had a hot date tonight, probably with a bowl of pasta, that big fat basted.

The next morning, I was lying in bed with my eyes shut. I could feel a warm breeze on me and although my eyes were closed, I could feel it was a bright sunny day. When I open my eyes a feeling of disorientation came over me. I didn't know where I was. It took me a couple of seconds as I looked around the room to realize I was at my new home in Summit. How did it ever come to this? If a fortune teller had told me three years ago that I would not be working for Cows, I would be divorced, and I would be living in a new house in upstate New York I would've asked her for my money back. That could never possibly happen. But here I am.

Chapter 3
It Is What It Is

I married a rather large woman to put it nicely. She weighed about 180 lbs when I met her and she grew steadily throughout the fifteen years of marriage. I was never a chub chaser, but one of the philosophies I'd preached to friends was that before you get married you should do a white woman, black woman, Spanish woman, Asian woman, and a fat broad. The last one got me in trouble. Her name was Michelle. She had a very pretty face and was very pleasant to talk to. She was a secretary at Cows. Something about her grew on me, but at the same time, her size frightened me. I finally decided what the heck and asked her out to a movie. I know I was being a bit of a "Shallow Hal," but I figured in a dark movie no one would see me. I thought maybe after the movie I could bang her and scratch a fat one off my list. Instead, I found her to be nicer and even sweeter than I thought. As they say, the rest is history.

We married and had three daughters, The first and third, Betty and Margaret turned out just like her. The middle one, Pamela, took after me. After the birth of each child, she put on fifteen extra pounds that never came off. She was a good mother and a good cook but she overfed the children. I'm is sure that her mother, also a very large woman, did the same to her as a child. She always spoke of losing weight but walked around the house with a bag of Wise potato chips strapped to her face like a feed bag. She would go on one diet and not lose weight. I would find bags of cookies in the linen closet under towels. She would swear she had no idea how they got there.

" Must be that burglar heard about that's breaking into houses in leaving food behind", I told her.

It wasn't just the weight that bothered me, she began getting lazier and lazier. The house was becoming a mess, and she showered less and less frequently. But this is the woman I chose, so I was going to stick it out to the end. Then one day I came home from work early because I was feeling sickly, and to my surprise, I found my wife in bed with the butcher, a 300 Pound man himself. It was an awful site but if I had my video camera handy, it probably would have ranked the number one viewed video on YouTube. I closed the door, walked away, and never came back. I knew this was the end because after seeing them and then seeing me, they never stopped. I should have had a clue when we started eating beautiful steaks and chops every night and the food bill hadn't increased. So here I am.

I dragged myself out of bed and went into the kitchen to get myself a cup of tea. I opened the refrigerator door and realized it was time for me to go get the necessities of life milk, eggs, butter, bread, and beer. I also needed to fix some things around the house. I could use some nails, some spackle, and some paint. I hopped in my car and went to the corner gas station. I put $10.00 worth of gas in that car and went into pay. There was a skinny kind of cute teenage girl behind the counter. Her name tag said, Peggy. I gave her the money and asked her if she knew anywhere, I can get some nails and paint and food. She said 'not too far from here they opened up a Walmart. It's the best place in the whole world. They have everything. I even get jeans there. Ten bucks. It only opened a little while ago and everybody goes there at least once a week. '

I said, "that sounds fine but I also need to get some food too".

She said, "The Walmart in Cobleskill has a whole supermarket in it". "That's great". I spoke. Can you give me directions to get there?"

She said "Take route ten till it comes to an end. Make a right on route seven and take that about 10 miles. Then you'll see the Walmart on your left side."

"I thought you said that was close."

"It is," she said, "about a half an hour away"

I guess I'm just going to have to get used to what is considered nearby in upstate New York.

I followed her directions and a half hour later found myself in front of Walmart. I've seen Walmarts before on the Island but you can fit 4 of those Walmarts in this one. It would be a $5.00 cab ride to go from one end of the store to the other. As I approached the front door, I noticed soda machines on the side. 25¢ for a soda! Wow! I wasn't thirsty but I bought one anyway. I cannot pass up a bargain like that. I walked through the front door and was amazed when I saw it. The store is so large I figure I had better find my way to the sporting goods department, so I can buy a compass to help me find my way out of there later. Fresh vegetables, fresh meat, steaks, chops, chicken, this place had it all. Frozen foods, a cold-cut department, just like a regular supermarket. And it hardly took up 1/10 of the store.

I grabbed my shopping cart and went to work. A couple of rib eyes, some sausage, Johnson Ville beer bratwurst, and a chicken. I was grabbing food like I hadn't eaten in a month. I made my way through the whole store and get everything I needed. The cashier checked me out. $250.00. No wonder they are the number one department store in the world. And at least the soda was only 25¢.

I packed the car and headed back home. What a beautiful place it is to drive your car. Beautiful majestic mountains everywhere you turn. Rows and rows of corn growing on farms as far as the eye can see. Cows, horses, sheep. Barns, silos, some brand-new others that look like a good wind would blow them down. Route ten is a 2-lane road one lane going in each way. You're lucky if you see a car every five minutes. Just like good old Long Island. Not. Downstate to turn out of my driveway takes five minutes. Then I head towards the Expressway which should be a five-minute ride but it takes fifteen. Once on the Expressway [which is anything but an expressway] I pulled into the first lane and wait. It used to be that rush hour went from seven to 9:00. Now it starts at six and you're lucky if it's over by ten. And then to add to the road rage they have what's called HOV Lane which stands for High Occupancy Vehicles. It is a lane that to drive in, you must have more than one person in the car. While you're sitting there, barely moving cars are whipping by you. It makes you nuts to see people in the HOV Lane in their SUVs on the LIE, watching HBO on their TV talking on a cell phone and eating, all while doing 70 miles an hour. I certainly won't be missing that.

I pull into my driveway after enjoying the ride home so much that I guess I'll take a ride to nowhere later.

It's time to rise and shine and greet another beautiful day. Another day another dollar, not true. Not if you don't have a job. Maybe I should look for a job today. Ah, maybe tomorrow. Instead of looking for a job, I'll look into unemployment insurance. I take a stroll down to the local gas station; my favorite cashier Peggy is there again.

"Good morning Peggy how is everything?" I enquire.

"Fine she says Did you find the Walmart yesterday," she asked

"Yes actually. that's why I'm back here today. Your directions were so good yesterday and I decided to come back and ask for some more. Do you have any idea where the State Unemployment office could be?"

"Yeah, it's in Albany." She said.

"Since I'm too cheap to buy a Hansom map can you give me directions?" "Sure. Take Route Ten north, again. When you got to route seven yesterday, did you notice a big highway sign?" She asked. "Yeah, I did."

"That would be 88. Take that west and look for signs from Albany ".

"Thanks, I owe you one. If I were twenty years younger, all right 30 years younger I would take you out to lunch."

"Oh, you don't look that old. But I'm sure if my dads saw me eating lunch with you, he would bring a shotgun out."

"Does that mean we would have a shotgun wedding?" "No, it just means that you'd be dead."

"In that case, I'll just stick to the directions. Maybe I'll see you tomorrow."

"Okay, but don't let those unemployed people push you around. Every time my dad goes, they give him crap."

"Thanks for the advice. See ya."

I've never been unemployed before but I was about to become a statistic. I guess I've earned the right to collect unemployment being that I've been working steadily since the age of sixteen.

I jumped in my car and off I go. Just another beautiful day in the country.

I put on the radio and hit seek. It stops at a classic rock station and they're playing Graham Nash's" Chicago and he's singing We can change the world "The song is 40 years old but things still need to be changed in this world. We are still looking to change the world as we have for every generation since mankind was on this earth. Graham Nash is one of my favorites, whether he is by himself or with Cosby, Stills, and Young. Not so much the Hollies'. I hit - 88 And headed west young man. I've never been to Albany, the state capital, and I'm curious about how big that town will be. I know the New York Football Giants will be starting their preseason training there soon. I follow the signs for Albany and next thing you know I'm in the state capital. It's a nice town but not as big as I thought it would be. I decided to find a parking space then find my way around the town, and hopefully, find the unemployment office that way. I asked the first policeman I saw but he didn't know where the office was. Then he gave me a look that said "get a job, you lazy bastard." I wandered around the streets checking out all the little shops along the way. Then I saw someone I knew who would know where the unemployment office was, the postman, or in this case the post lady. Whenever you're lost I can always trust most people. They know where everything is. Of course, this sweet post lady tells me exactly where to go. No, not what you're thinking. She tells me the way to the unemployment office.

Chapter 4
What's Not to Celebrate

It was only about five city blocks away so I started putting one 1 foot. in front of the other and headed toward hopefully my next paycheck. I walked in the front door and went to the information desk. The lady gave me some forms to fill out, which I did, and I handed them back to her. She looked them over quickly and said I should be hearing from them within the week I asked "do you think I'll get anything?"

"Looks like it is no problem she says. You should get the maximum$ 405 a week," she said.

"And for how long can I collect this?" "Six months," she says.

"Thank you, "I said. I walked out of there and felt like a kid on the last day of school before summer vacation." Six months wow. I haven't had more than two weeks off in a row in about 30 years. Everything seems to be going my way!

I decided to celebrate my employment insurance by going to the Jailhouse Rock Inn for an ice-cold Genny. It was the usual crowd Mike and his brother Michael were there and a couple of new faces. I strolled up to the bar and ordered a Genny on tap from Mary Jane. I told her to back up Mike, whatever he wants.

"Thanks, dude, Mike says.

"I owed you," I replied. "Besides I'm here to celebrate today. I just got back from Albany and have been OK'd for unemployment insurance. They said I could collect for up to six months. That wouldn't be too hard to take.

"You lucky dog. I think I'm going to get fired tomorrow So I can collect some too." Mike says.

"Sometimes you don't get unemployment when you get fired. Be careful." I said.

Then from across the room, a new county was heard from. "Is there something wrong with you boy that you can't work?" The voice says.

"No, I just get laid off from the job that I worked 30 years for. They left me cold and dry so I decided to try for unemployment insurance." I told him. "And you are?"

"My name's Bill, the last name is Koe. And I think you should find a job. You stealing money from the government with that welfare stuff. Money wasted on people like you could go into up troops overseas to protect them and send them the best equipment. Instead, the money goes to lazy-ass draft dodgers like you." He yelped.

"Hey Koe, calm down. He's a new neighbor, at least wait a week before you break his balls." Said Mike. "He just bought the...."

"I know, Jeb Potters place. Damn shame what happened to him," Koe said.

Bill Koe, I find out later, with a drill sergeant for 25 years in the army. If they were casting the part for a movie, he would get it. He had the exact look that they portray in movies and on TV. He had the big giant head attached directly to his shoulders. He had a flat-top crew cut. The top of his head was so big it looked like a helicopter landing strip. And I'm sure if the army asked him to lead the helicopter on his head, I'm sure he would be proud to do it for his country. He has been out of the army for about two years now and runs an appliance repair shop. He will get your washing machine fixed, but they may be a part of it from a 57 Studebaker. He's never been married, except to the army, and no one's ever seen him with a woman, not that I'm implying anything nor would I say that out loud lest he shoves my right arm up my asshole been taken out and beat me over the head with it.

"I ain't no draft dodger," I tell him.

"Oh, then my apologies." he says "Which branch of the service did you serve in?"

"I didn't serve in any of the branches. When it was my turn to be drafted, they changed the system in your draft order was picked by a lottery based on your birthday numbers. One through

a hundred would be drafted. My number was 327. They never called."

"I knew you weren't in the service. They take no panty-wearing wimps like you. He challenged.

I'm not the type to go looking for flights, but when someone challenges my manhood, I will stand up for myself. I know I'm still a stranger in a new bar but I'm not gonna take any shit from him. I've kicked ass on bigger guys than him, and have gotten my ass kicked by guys the size of Joe Pesci. I stand up from my stool and start to make my way over to the sarge when Mike and Michael get in front of me.

"Come on Koe, that's

enough," Mike says.

"Aw, I just wanted to see if he had any balls. I think I might get to like the panty wearer. Welcome to the neighborhood. Buy him a drink on me, Mary." He says.

The bar roars and starts saying hell must be freezing over if Koe's buying.

Truth is, I think I would have made a good soldier. I love my country and would do all I could to defend her, but given the choice of having to get shot at or not, I'll take the not. I have the utmost respect for our armed forces and you need guys like sergeant Bill. There can never be enough John Waynes around.

After this whole incident, I start to feel a little guilty about this U.I. Maybe I should start looking for a job. Maybe tomorrow, Nah. I go back to my Genny and notice it's time for the Mets game. They have won 2 in a row and are playing the lowly Washington Nationals in a four-game series at home. The Nat's have lost 8 in a row. Being a Met fan, I know we will be lucky to win one. Sure enough, the leadoff batter for the Nat's hits a homer on the first pitch from Oliver Perez. Either he's great or he sucks, so I can see where this one is heading. The rest of the night goes nicely, except for the Mets. they lose 12-1 figures. Time to head home. I wonder if I'm on the clock now?

I woke up the next morning to another beautiful day. The sun is shining; it's 75 degrees and I have a date with a golf course. Last night at the Jail House not only did I meet the sergeant but I also met another guy, Angelo Generally. He was a local insurance salesman who owns his own business. He didn't have a large clientele, he told me, just mostly local people, enough to put food on the table and a little left over for golf. He was a member of the local country club, Buck Farms Golf Club. Being a member of a country club upstate is a lot different than joining one downstate. Downstate you need to take out a mortgage loan to be able to afford to do a country club. At Buck Farms CC it costs $750.00 for a year, unlimited play. He asked if I played golf, and I said yeah if you call it that. He told me about the course; how it was a lot different playing in the mountains. You'll have to play the course a couple of times before you learn all the little idiosyncrasies of it. He asked if I would like to play with him tomorrow around 11 a.m. I told him I'll look at my schedule; of course, I have the time, see you at eleven.

The course was only ten minutes from my house and again it was a beautiful ride there. I can't get enough of farms, cows, horses, and hay. I start heading up the mountain to the Country Club. About three-quarters of the way up the mountain, the entrance to the golf course appears on my right. I pull into the parking lot and park my car. I often wondered why they had handicapped parking at a golf course. Every golfer should be allowed to park there because they all have handicaps. Mine is about fourteen. I pop my trunk and get out my clubs. I pause for a while to take a good look at this beautiful course in the mountains. God knew what he was doing, except for giving us the game of golf. I've played every sport imaginable and could hold my own against most, but no sport drives me nuts as golf. You can be playing and do no wrong for fourteen holes, approximately three hours, and then yank one drive to the left out of bounds, retee another ball, of course, hit it so far right you're still no closer to the hole, hack a couple more to the green, three-putt and ruin everything you've done for the last three hours. What am I doing here?

Angelo pulls up next to me a couple of minutes later. It's a beautiful day to be on the golf course. Then again, any day is a beautiful day to be on the golf course. I find out playing with him today and other times in the future that if he hits two balls in a row that get airborne, he has an orgasm. Angelo is about 30 handicapped on a good day, but he enjoys golf ten times more than I do. If I played like him, I would throw my clubs in the lake. Come to think of it I may have done that once or twice.

We head to the pro shop. It was a small pro shop, compared to the one downstate. A couple of drivers for sale, two sets of clubs, a couple of putters, five boxes of shoes three size sevens, a thirteen and fifteen. We walked up to the counter and Angelo introduced me to the man behind the counter, the club pro, Ben Hogue. He's about 80 years old and looks very fit for his age. He's been here since the club opened in 1972 and has never left. People say he could've made it on the tour but he loved his little town and never wanted to leave. Angelo says there was more to it than that, but he never volunteered any more information.

"Glad to meet you, Patrick. And welcome to our town. I hear you bought Jeb Potter's place. Too bad about what happened to him."

"And it's a pleasure to meet you, Ben," I said.

"Any questions about the course?" he asked.

"Yeah, where is the first hole, and what's the course record?" I joked. "The course record is 62, held by Arnold Palmer. He used to have a place up here. Said it reminded him a lot of where he grew up in Pennsylvania. Shot 29 on the front. I played with him that day and shot a 65 myself. Yanked one out of bounds on the fifteenth. I took him for a couple of dollars that day. To this day he still shakes his head, shot the course record, and loses ten bucks."

Just then I see a picture of him and Arnie standing on the first hole. On the bottom of the framed picture is a $10.00 bill signed by Arnold.

We make our way to the first hole, usually a par three, 215 yards downhill.

I grabbed my five wood and tee a ball. I notice Angelo smirking as I'm about to hit the ball. I hit a beauty right at the flag. By the time the ball came down, it was thirty yards past the hole, into the woods.

"Oh, I forgot to tell you the ball travels farther up here in the mountains," he said.

"Thanks for the advice, one swing too late," I said.

"Ben asked you if you wanted any advice on the course, and you just said that dumb ass thing about the first-course record," he said

"From here on in I'll take any advice you would like to give," I said sheepishly.

Angelo took out a four-iron and dribbled one about halfway there. I noticed he didn't even carry any wood in his bag. Said he can't hit 'em. He told me I'd better hit another one, that I'll never find that ball. I re-teed, this time with a 4 iron, and hit one to the front edge of the green. We jumped into our cart and away we went. I double-bogey the hole and cussed under my breath about hitting two good balls and doubling the hole. Angelo pumped his fist with satisfaction after dropping in its 3-foot putt for a double bogey. If only I could enjoy the game that way.

The course is in great shape and the greens are very fast. The first tip he gives me is that every putt will break towards Mt. Ute, which was in the distance right behind us. It took me three holes to believe him, but he was right. No matter which way the ball looked like it was going to break, it broke toward Mt. Ute.

We are standing on the tee box of the fourth hole, a long par 5, 565 yards. On the green behind us, I see a hot-looking chick roll in a fifteen-foot putt. When she bends down to get her ball out, I notice she has a great ass. I get Angelo's attention and nod toward the lady.

"Oh, that's Mary Jane the bartender." He says.

I take a closer look and sure enough, it is. First time I'd seen her in the light. She looks great but there is something different about her. As she gets closer, I see what the change is about her. It's her smile.

She has all of her teeth and she looks hot. It seems her bridge fell out and she just needed time to get to the dentist to repair it. I was ready to tee off as she was making her way to the tee.

"Hi Maryjane," I said. "Do you want to play through us or you can join us if you'd like?" I said.

"I wouldn't mind playing with you guys, if you don't mind, Angelo?" she said. "Why sure Mary, just don't kick my butt too bad," he said.

"Oh, you guys just take it easy on me. Go ahead and hit Patrick."

The ball was teed up already so I went thru my routine and was ready to hit the ball but I was as nervous as a grammar school kid asking a girl to roller skate for the first time. I wanted to impress her and didn't want to dribble one off the tee. I took a deep breath and spanked one right down the middle.

"Nice shot', she said and Angie said the same. "Thanks," I said "just lucky."

"That's not luck, you have a nice swing." I just nod and give her a little smile. Angie gets up and rolls one down the fairway about 100 yards.

"I hope you didn't kill any worms with that shot," Mary says.

Wow, beautiful and has a sense of humor. Mary tees her ball up as I stand behind her [great ass in those shorts, I think to myself] and she cracks one down the middle with a smooth swing.

"You have a nice (I have to be careful here) swing," I said.

"Thanks. Let's go chase 'em. She says. When she bends over to get her tee I sneak another peak at her ass, only this time I get busted as she glances behind her while taking the tee out. She just gives me a cute little smile and says nothing.

Mary Jane Withanee was married right out of school to a local golf pro, James Withanee. They were married for 15 years and had 2 boys. She has been divorced and on her own for the last 10 years. Both of her boys have aspirations to be tour players. The oldest, James Jr, 22, is going to Stanford on a golf scholarship. The youngest, Pete,18, is hoping to follow in his footsteps. When they were married, he was the head pro of the Hobart cc, the youngest they ever had. He made a good salary and supplemented his income handsomely by giving lessons. He would take you to the range and watch you swing the club for half an hour, giving tips and videotaping your swing. The next half an hour you would go back to his spacious and very private office to analyze your swing.

Apparently, thru the years, he would take some of his female students back to the office and analyze everything but their swings. His antics were legendary, sometimes 2 or 3 times a day the moans and groans coming from his office were earth-shattering. Then he would go home and still have some left for Maryjane this went on for many years but when you are as blatant as he was, sooner or later the shit will hit the fan. He made so many gals pregnant that he started writing checks to the abortion clinic. Finally, one of the gals shows up on Maryjane's doorstep pregnant and with no plans of giving it up. When James gets home for the day, she confronts him with the details. At first, he denies knowing anything about it but then fesses up to it. He says it was a one-time thing that would never happen again. After the hurt and shock wear off, she decides to give him another chance, only this time she would keep a closer eye on him. Of course, after a short time, she catches him red-handed, showing up unexpectedly at his office. This time it was over. He cried and pleaded for forgiveness; he did love her but he loved his penis more. She raised the children and was now on her own.

We made our way thru the next couple of holes, a couple of pars for me and MJ, and a couple of triples and doubles for Angelo. On the eighth tee box, Angie gets a call on his cell phone. It's an elderly client of his. She tells him her husband had passed away this morning and could he come by to help her with the arrangements. This is what makes Angelo the good businessman and good person he is. He grabs his clubs, apologizes to us, and heads his way to his car to help this lady.

Now it's just the 2 of us for 11 more holes. It's one of my most enjoyable times on a golf course. I was playing pretty well, as was she. Everywhere I looked there was beauty, the flowers, the trees, the mountains, the sky, and Maryjane. We finished the round in what felt like two minutes but it was four o'clock when we were done. I asked if she wanted to go for a drink but she declined, stating she had to work the bar at six and she needed to shower and rest a while before her shift.

"Are you going to stop by tonight?" she asked me. "Sure, I wouldn't miss it.'

She went her way and I went mine. You couldn't take the smile off my face with a jackhammer. I put on my radio and a Beatles song was playing "I've Just Seen a Face." with Paul singing it and me harmonizing with him. I had just seen a face.

I skipped my way to the front door and went inside. I had such a good time on the golf course I even forgot what I shot. All right I didn't forget what I shot. I shot 87 Maryjane shot 91 and Angelo was already at 48 when he left after the seventh hole. I was gonna take a shower and grab a quick bite. When. I'm taking a shower I will have sex with Maryjane. She won't be with me in the shower but I will be having sex with her. After today I have to release some of this or it will explode. When I'm all done, I will head over to the Rock for Friday night happy hour.

Chapter 5
Same ol' same ol'

I spiffy myself up put on a little C. K. one and head over to the Jailhouse Rock Inn. I think I might get lucky tonight. I make my way through the front door and the place is pretty packed and noisy. I'm still getting acquainted with the place so I see a lot of new faces. At the far end of the bar, there's a big guy about 6ft. four. It's only 6:15 and he's already hammered. He's yakking away at two people who don't seem to be paying attention to him. He yells to Mary to bring another Jack and Coke and she just gives him a dirty look. He then says he wants another one NOW and she brings one over to him. When she places it on the bar in front of him, I notice there already are two full ones there. He continues gabbing away and yells to Mary to bring in another Jack and Coke, even though he hasn't touched the other three yet. He has that dumb, aw-shucks look on his face, the same look as the New York Giants Eli Manning has on his face after throwing an interception.

'If it isn't the old golf stud. Mike says to me. I hear you and Mary Jane was banging some balls around today.'

'Hey, hey, hey, watch what you say. Don't be spreading any rumors around.' I said. Mary glances over and smiles at me.

'She says you hit the ball pretty well he said 'I hit it OK. Do you play?'

'Nah, walking up and down hills and chasing the little white ball doesn't sound like fun to me.' He replied.

'Yeah, but you can drink beer when you're playing.' I said.

'Or I could just sit here and drink beer and not chase a white ball. I hear we're eyeballing up Mary Jane pretty good on the course.' He noted.

'She is a pretty cute gal now that you mentioned it.' I said

'Well before you start snuggling up with her, I think you'll want to know that the guy at the end of the bar is her fiancé'. He's a pretty big boy too. His name is Brad.'

Fiancée? I feel like I've been kicked in the gut. She'd made no mention of Brad on a golf course, But then why would she? It's not like I asked her out or anything.

His name is Brad Winston the third. Brad is about ten years younger than Mary Jane. He was the starting quarterback on his Roxbury high school team, the same team his father brought to the state championship as the quarterback. Brad's team went six and five. His dad pulled some strings and got him a partial football scholarship to Yale, the college his dad was a star at and he was a big alumni booster. But Bradie boy pouted that he wanted to go to Notre Dame and be the star quarterback there. His father knew he couldn't carry the water bucket there, so he went ahead and enrolled him at Yale anyway.

This wasn't easy since Brad's grades weren't up to par, but money always talks.

His dad was a lawyer and he took over the firm from his father. The firm of Winston and Winston was very successful. His father hoped that Brad would come into the firm and one day takes over. He was an only child so his dad was banking on him. But his father also knew that sometimes you don't luck out with the right gene pool, and Brad takes after his mother. His mom was a cheerleader for the college football team. She was beautiful and built like a brick shit house. His father flipped for her but she was as dumb as a rock. He couldn't see passed a pair of tits so he married her. She gave him the son he always wanted. Who know he would look like dad but have mom's brain

Halfway through his second year in college he dropped out and came home. His dad then set him up in a local community college, which is like thirteenth grade. Brad barely got his degree and had been working with dad ever since making a hefty salary, but learning nothing.

'You didn't think Maryjane would go for somebody on welfare did you chimed in my good buddy the sarge,'

'I'm not on welfare and what makes you think I wanted to go out with her anyway.' I said

'Probably the way your jaw dropped when I told you she had a fiancé' Mike said putting his 2¢ in.'

'She's pretty I'll give you that, smart and a good golfer but there are plenty more women out there like her.' I told them as my heart was breaking.

'Not up here,' Mike says. Unfortunately, I know he's right.

I awake the next morning to the tapping of rain on my window. It's a dreary day, just like last night was a dreary night. The whole night's a bit foggy to me, I drank too much and don't remember much after finding out that Mary was engaged. Oh yeah, I do remember The Mets lost to the Nationals, twelve to three. John Maine only lasted 2/3 of an inning giving up seven hits and three walks. I knew this was gonna happen.

I weigh my options. Should I get up and look for a job, should I get up and clean the house or should I go back to sleep for another hour? I choose the latter.

Two hours later I start all over again, instead this time the sun is starting to peak through. I get up to make myself a cup of tea and contemplate what's next. I look out the back window and all I see is high grass for as far as the eye can see. I noticed a shed in the back and I decide to go to check it out. There's an old rusty lock on it that requires a skeleton key to open. I'm sure if I go back into the house and look around, I will find the key, but this lock is useless. I search a round for rock and find one a foot away. Rocks are aplenty upstate. One good swing of the rock and not only does the lock break but the door falls. There are some tools in the shed. I know this is a tool shed because there are tools in it but something tells me it had another purpose originally. On the back wall is a boxed-in bench with a hole in the middle. This is the original outhouse. Boy am I glad I didn't live in those days. The amount of time I spend in the bathroom they probably would have found me frozen to death out here one day. I find in the shed/outhouse a pick, a rake, a sled hammer, and the original weed whacker. It has a broom-like handle and the blade comes off the bottom in an L shape. You swing it like a golf club to knock down the weeds. I figure this is a great way to work on my golf swing and hacked down some weeds. I grab it and take a couple of practice swings with it in the yard. This gets me in the mood to play real golf. Screw this yard stuff, Let me call Angelo and see if he wants to play.' All right I'll work on the yard,' I answer to the mother part of my brain saying to finish your chores before you go play.

The first hole is 427yd.s par four. I take out my driver and hit one right down the middle. I cleared an area of weeds about 3ft. wide with that first swing. Hey, maybe this can be fun. I keep hacking away until an area about 20ft. by 20ft. is clear.

Now that wasn't so hard. I keep wailing away and now I get a nice clearing in my backyard. The only problem is I'm huffing and puffing and already getting calluses on my hand. I figure that's all for today, don't wanna ruin my golf game. As I'm leaning on the hacker trying to catch my breath I noticed something up ahead in the weeds I hack my way to it I can see it's an old ice box. I've seen these in books and old movies but never in person I decide to open up to see what's in there when a weird thought crossed my mind. What if Jeb Potter was in there, dead or alive? I opened it slowly and to my delight, there were no Jeb surprises in there. All that was in there was a milk bottle. The distinctive shape of the milk bottle brought me back to my childhood. I recalled the days when there used to be milkmen that delivered to your house. When I started working for the milk company, these types of deliveries were just coming to an end. These milkmen used to work very early in the morning. You would be laying in bed and you would hear the clanking of the milk bottles as he was putting them in your box on your front porch.

My dad used to order the milk with the funny-shaped bubble on the neck of the bottle that had cream floating in it on top of the milk. They would also deliver milk and eggs if you wanted. Back in those days they even had a bakery that delivered. It was called Dugans and they had the best crumb cake of anyone. There was nothing like waking up in the morning and having your milk and cake waiting on your front porch. Then later on in the day, another man would come by with your soda and beer. The coming of supermarkets priced these guys out of business. Maybe it's time to bring these delivery guys back. With the hustle and bustle of today, it would be nice to open your front door in the morning to find milk, cake, and beer. What better start to a day than that? [If anybody steals this idea I'm going to want ten percent of the gross].

I guess I'll stop here, enough calluses and adventure for one day. And I'm afraid if I keep hacking I might find a model T. Ford somewhere back there. Or maybe I should grade that pick and whack it into the ground and strike an oil well, black

gold, Texas tea, like good old Jed Clampett did. Ah, maybe tomorrow.

I head into the house to grab a bite to eat. I have some cold cuts in the refrigerator and a roll to put them on. Cold cuts are great. Boars Head makes the best. I believe they have an 11 o'clock mass tomorrow. Why would you waste time on that whole fairy tale stuff anyway.'

' At the end, if you're right neither of us will know. But if I'm right we'll both know. Doesn't mean I won't be down there with you looking up, or maybe you'll be up there looking down at me, but we'll know.' I said

'Well before you go whining away on me Maryjane went to the Waterfall steakhouse with Brad.' he says. Best steak in town, but expensive. Brad can afford it, he digs me.

'Never entered my mind' I bullshitted and he knew.

There were a lot of new faces at the bar tonight. A heavy-set guy was sitting at the far corner of the bar. He was a real Italian-looking guy, with dark hair, and dark skin, and was wearing a suit jacket over an unbuttoned white collared shirt. He was eating clams on the half shell one after another and was making a slurping noise you could hear from miles around. Everyone at the bar seems to know him.

' That's Donald Nonstick Mike says. He's the owner of this joint.' Bought the place above five years ago. He's not here very often, usually just stays at his place in Howard Beach. downstate. He's a real nice guy when you get to know him but you would not want to be on his wrong side.'

' Why is that,' I inquire "Just don't, he says

The music playing on the jukebox was a mixture of country western and classic rock. The bartender seem to be the only one putting any money in the jukebox, but as soon as she did five people would walk up and try to tell her what songs to play. The pool table was in constant use. It was 25¢ a game and if you wish to play you needed to place a quarter on top of the table in proper order. I threw a quarter up there behind the other 14 quarters. I guess I'll be playing somewhere around midnight. Donald, the owner never played, but he always told everyone what shot to take. He seemed to enjoy every shot taken when they were made or missed. He bellows after every stroke, sometimes coughing uncontrollably, due to the three packs of Camels he smoked daily. The bartender was playing in this game. Donald pointed out a shot in which she could sink two balls at one time. He got up from a seat and waddled all over to the table to point at the spot on the ball way she should hit it. She listened to him and knocked in both balls with one shot. He laughed and coughed so hard I thought he was going to have a heart attack. When he finally caught his breath he yelled out 'Drinks on the house for everyone.' I think I'm going to like this guy.

'Donald Nonstick grew up in Brooklyn near the Verrazzano Bridge. His dad, Luigi, was a barber and his mom did what moms did in those days, stay home, cook, and have children. She was very good at the latter having ten children, nine boys, and a girl in the space of eleven years. Luigi senior came home from the barbershop and did a lot of trimming of moms bush. Donald was the youngest. The first one was his brother Luigi junior. Junior, hated to be called that although everyone in the family knew him only as Junior, started off running numbers and was now the area's bookie.

Donald was ten years old at the time and Junior had a job for him. He would send him around to the local pool halls and other gathering places to pick up envelopes, filled with cash. He figured the police would never look for a little kid and he was right, all most. He told Donald that if he ever noticed the police or anyone else following him, he should run and look for garbage to throw the money in and remember which one it was and continue running. One day he noticed a policeman getting closer and closer to him and picking up speed. He took off at once and made a quick left turn down the next alleyway and threw the money into a dumpster and continued. The problem was the alleyway he took was a dead end. He ducked into a doorway breathing heavily and heard the footsteps of the policeman approaching. He heard the policeman stop and then heard him open the dumpster which he had put the money into. Donald took a quick peek and saw the police officer, Joe Bolden, with the bag of money in his hand. Donald again hid in the doorway awaiting the approach of the officer scared out of his mind. The next thing he heard was three gunshots fired and then a thud. He was shaking uncontrollably until the heard the sound of Junior telling him to come out of hiding in let's get the hell out of here. He peeked out and saw Junior standing in the middle of the alleyway. He immediately started running toward him and as he approached him he noticed officer Joe lying in a pool of his blood. He jumped over the police officer, splattered a little blood then started running like crazy with his brother.

Junior, or Lou as he liked to be called, had been keeping an eye on officer Joe for a while. He had been extorting money from Junior and many of the local businesses, including his father's barbershop. He had been making money at the expense of poor, hard-working shop owners with the law on his side. No one knew that there was an internal investigation going on at the police station. They were about to arrest him when they found him lying in the alleyway. Officer Joe was a loner he had no family.

Rather than give a black eye to the police department they scooped him up and gave him a quiet burial.

Word of what Lou had done spread quickly through the neighborhood. He now ran the neighborhood and in the following years, Donald would become his right-hand man. Now, and now everyone called him Lou, of course except his family. Donald called him Lou.

My quarter finally makes its way to the front of the line and it's my turn to shoot pool. 9:30 is not too bad. I've been watching the Mets game, Pedro is twirling a beauty, with six innings one hit and no walks seven strikeouts Mets are leading two to nothing. I was pretty good at shooting pool, especially on these small barroom tables. I rack up the balls and introduced myself to my opponent, Mitch. He had won five games in a row, despite the help from Donald, but around here that doesn't mean much. Stevie Wonder could probably win five games in a row here. He grabs the cue ball and hammers it into the rack. The ball is flying all over and the eight ball goes in the side pocket. I lose. I place another quarter at the end of the line shake my head, congratulate Mitch, and go back to my barstool to wait for my next chance, probably around 12.

Mitch was a weathered 50-year-old, with long hair thinning at the top and a Vandyke goatee. He was an artist and had a gallery in town displaying his work. I enjoy his paintings but some people view them the same way people viewed Picasso's work in the beginning. Unlike Picasso's work where noses, mouths, and eyes were scattered, Mitch's work scattered many things, furniture, stars, books, and other things in strange shapes. He was a talented man in many ways. He had some fine works of sculpture and in the rear of the gallery, he had a baby grand piano. He played beautifully and made the taste buds in my ear jump for joy. His dad Arthur Henderson, was a Wall Street tycoon who'd never forgiven Mitch for not following in his footsteps. His dad wanted him to attend the Wharton school of business. Instead, Mitchell went to the Julliard School of Music. He excelled there and graduated Magna cum Lada but his dad never attended the graduation. After graduation, he enrolled in a college of art. There he studied for the master's for four more years and graduated at the top of his class again. Again his dad was a no-show, but at least he was footing all the bills. Mitch sold a couple of his paintings early on and composed a well-received concerto, his one-hit wonder, before the thing you dried up.

That is when he realized how difficult it would be to make it in either of these fields. He was 35 years old and got an apartment/ gallery in Manhattan, Bedford Stuyvesant, the only place he can afford He worked day and night on his paintings He couldn't even afford the paint since his dad had cut him off from the money. He started doing etchings, and of course was very good at that, too. Then one time to try to get money for paint and food, he brought his sketching pad to midtown Manhattan, set up on a street corner, and started drawing caricatures of people for five bucks apiece. It was in the middle of one of these drawings that he realized this wasn't what he wanted to do with his life. He reached out and grabbed the sheet of paper he was drawing a caricature on and crumpled it up and threw it on the ground, screaming out something unintelligible. He folded his easel and huffed away, as the stunned, confused patron just sat there." Crazy bastard" he said. got up and went on his way.

Mitch walked easel and all to the building his father worked at in the Wall Street section of the city, quite a haul from where he was. He went up to his father's office, which had a stunning view of the city, and ask the receptionist if he could see Mr. Henderson.

'Whom shall I say is asking for him' she asks.

'His son, I say. A bewildered look came over her face and she contemplated calling security.

' Are you sure? I didn't even know you had a son.'

' In his mind, he doesn't, but here I am. Could you please buzz him for me?'

' And your name?' 'Mitch'

' Mr. Henderson, there's a man here, his name is Mitch, who says he's your son. Should I let him in?'

There's a long silence since I haven't seen or spoken to my dad in five years. Then dad peaks out through the blinds to make sure it was me.' Send him in.'

' So I see you're still alive. How much money is it that you want?' he says ' I came here for the job. Are you hiring?

At first, a stunned look came over his face. Then he seemed to think he had it figured out. I didn't want a job he just wanted money and this is my way of getting it.

' What is it you want?'

' I'm serious. You were right, it's impossible to make it as an artist.' He said

' If you're serious I have a job for you. Don't think you'll be starting at the top. You'll start at the bottom just like everyone else does and earn your way to the top. Still want the job?'

'Yes.'

His dad gets up with and I told you so looks on his face and shakes Mitchs' hand. I'll see you Monday morning. I'll. expect you to be cleaned up a bit.'

Once again Mitch excelled at the job. He moved quickly to the top. Within two years he was making $200,000.00 a year. Two years after that he quit and bought the gallery upstate, to do what he wanted to do all along. At first, this infuriated his dad, but in the end, his dad was proud of what he accomplished in the short time he was there. He knew his son could do it and now he would let him be to do what he wanted to do. Art.

At 12:15 my quarter finally comes up again. I easily win the next five games, but then again so would Stevie Wonder. The night is starting to wind down. Mitch tells me he's going to have a band come down to his art gallery next Saturday, and he would like for me to come and join them. He tells me he's trying to make his place somewhere local artists and musicians can come and strut their stuff. I told him it sounds like fun and I'll be there. I finish up my last beer and notice I still have $3.00 from the $10.00 bill I started the night with, added a couple more bucks to it, and was on my way to that short stroll home. Drink all night for ten bucks, imagine that!

Chapter 6
Sunday Ventures

I wake up on Sunday morning at around 10:30, take a shower, and I'm on my way to church. The church, Saint Peter's, is a small church that can hold about 100 people. It says on the sign in front of the church that this is the first Catholic Church in the Catskill region. It was built in 1820. The church still is very sturdy.

This is one of the things that surprises me most about the upstate region. Homes that were built 200 years ago are still standing strong. Back on Long Island, there are whole communities built by contractors twenty to 30 years ago that are falling apart. With all the new tools, machinery, and technology, how could they not build a better house now? I guess we all know the answer to that, money and greed. Contractors build these houses to make money not to make them last. It wasn't long ago that American automobile companies were doing the same thing. You bought a car and once it hit 50,000mi. things started going wrong with it. You were lucky to have a car that was still running at 100,000mi. Then along came the Japanese companies which almost put the American auto companies out of business. The Japanese cars would run 150 to 200,000mi. no problem. At least now the American auto industry is making better cars and taking more pride in what they put out. Maybe, home builders should take notice of this.

I walk through the large front doors of the church at around 11:05. I'm always late for everything. The mass has already begun. There are approximately twenty people in the church. The priest is of Korean descent. It seems there are more and more foreigners becoming priests than Americans. There are very few young to middle-aged people going to church anymore. I hope this trend will change because I wonder what's going to happen to the church in the next 50 years or so. Maybe people just wait till they get older, closer to the end so to speak, and start going to church just in case.

It was a very nice mass and of course, everyone seemed to know each other. They welcome me to the church, said an impromptu prayer for Jeb Potter, and continued with the liturgy. I felt a closeness and a feeling of belonging that I hadn't felt in church for a long time. The churches on the Island were very big, and sometimes you just got lost in the crowd. Although I attended the same mass every Sunday on the Island I hardly knew anyone by name and only a few by face. I have a feeling it will be different here.

It was another gorgeous summer day and as I was leaving the church I headed directly to the local bakery. This was a family tradition on Sunday morning. go to church, get rolls or bagels, and head home for bacon and eggs. I look forward to this as a child and still do as an adult. Sometimes we would even have pancakes or French toast. It was always one of my favorite meals of the week.

I went into the bakery and ordered a couple of bagels. On my way to the car, I could tell by the feel of the bagels in the bag that they were not gonna be good bagels. I still can't figure out why when you leave New York City and the surrounding area you can't get a good bagel are a good slice of pizza. This never made any sense to me. The one common excuse I hear from people from different areas of the country is that it has something to do with the water. If the water is the only difference between a good bagel and could slice of pizza outside of the city, then why don't they just ship water from New York City to their stores so they could make better bagels and pizza? Hey wait, that's a great idea. If you steal this idea I want 20 percent of the profits.

The week went by enjoyably but at the slow pace of upstate. I looked at the want-to ads in the papers once for about three seconds until I saw the funnies on the other side of the paper. One of these days I'll look for a job. It was Saturday and I was looking forward to local artists and musicians who would be showing up at Mitch's art gallery tonight. The gallery is in Stamford about a ten-minute ride from my house. My church is only a couple blocks away from the gallery so I decided to go to the 5:00 PM mass on Saturday have a bite to eat in town and then go to the gallery which is supposed to start at seven.

I make it to the church and 5:05, late as usual, and get smiles as I walk into the church from the parishioners. [Maybe they figured I was just one of those once-in-a-while people who go to church.] It's another spiritually fulfilling mass with all the people holding hands while saying the Lord's Prayer. I am touched by the closeness I feel in the church but due to my bad hearing, I find it very hard to understand the priest. I have trouble hearing in general but when someone speaks with an accent it makes it ten times harder. The priest's name is Father Joe. I wondered to myself how many other Joe's there are in Korea, besides the GI ones. Not only does he speak with an accent, but he speaks very softly. I'm sure he's saying wonderful things about God because everyone is smiling and nodding as he speaks. People often ask me why I don't just get a hearing aid, but I never liked the look of that thing sticking out of my ear. People who wear them always get stared at and looked at as if they're some kind of cripple.[I wonder if I can get a handicap sticker if I wore one] Nowadays what people looked at with disdain has become a trendy thing. Everywhere you look People are walking around with these big things growing out of their ears. They are called Blue Tooth and they let you speak hands-free when you're on your cell phone. When I was young and people would walk down the street talking to themselves, you would try to find a straitjacket for them. Now all those same nutty people fit right in with everyone else walking down the block talking to themselves. How are we ever going to distinguish between nutty people and sane people or maybe we're all nuts!

Leaving the church I exchange handshakes and greetings with every one of the parishioners and the priest. I decide to stroll around town to see what there is to eat. I find what is my favorite thing to eat out, Chinese food, in a small take-out joint. I wonder if getting Chinese food upstate is going to be the same thing as eating a bagel up here. I stroll into the joint and order a number one which is chicken chow mein, fried rice, and an egg roll. The guy behind the counter tells me ten minutes and welcomes me to the town.

He says Glad to meet you, my name is John.[I wonder how many John's there are in China].

Glad to meet you John my name is…

' Patrick I know. Bought Jeb Potter's house. He always ordered moo goo gai pan but could never pronounce it properly.

It was nice to have someone speak good English at a Chinese restaurant I felt it very refreshing to hear counter person in a Chinese restaurant that can speak good English. Usually, especially on a call in order, I'm so confused that I don't even know what I ordered. If you order anything that's not a number, good luck. To my surprise, it was the best chow mein I have ever had. I told John how much I loved it and he was very appreciative. I told him to join me at the gallery to have some fun but he had to work late. The gala at the gallery was a bring your bottle [byob] party. I stopped at the local Stewarts [which is the upstate version of 7-11.] Bought a 12-pack of Genny Cream Ale and headed to the gallery. The band was setting up their equipment when I arrived. A crowd of about 20 people was settling in on the rows of folding chairs set up in the gallery. I was meandering around checking out Mitch's work. He was not only a good painter but he had some cool-looking sculptors and busts around. I was checking a particular one of a large rear end when Mitch came up behind me.

' Glad you could make it he said.

'Wouldn't have missed it for the world.' We'll have a lot of fun. You can put your beer in the cooler over there.'

'Thanks. Pretty good crowd.'

' Yeah, this band rocks. They call themselves Honor. Do you like that sculpture? A couple grand and it's yours!'

'Couple grand, I said. I would have to sit on my couch for 2 months to make that kind of money on unemployment.' He laughed and patted me on the back.

'Who's got it better than you ?' he stated.

It was a mixed bag of a crowd. Some with long hair, some with short hair, and some with none. There were a few women in the crowd, a couple of leftover hippie broads from the sixties, tie-dye and all. Talking to the band near a side door were a couple of groups of good-looking chicks. One of the band members motioned for Mitch to come over.

He made his way to them and after a little dialogue they departed out the side door, groupies and all. I made my way to a chair and waited for the music to begin. After a short time the band members, Mitch, and the chicks returned through the side door bringing back with them the sweet odor of marijuana. Pot, ganja, herb. It has been years since I have partaken in smoking the bud. I was never a big smoker but I did like to partake now and then. The reason for the years of abstinence was not by choice.

The DMV, the Department of Motor Vehicles decided that all professional truckers would be subject to random drug testing, so that was the end of weed for me. Since I am unemployed maybe hmm?

My mother did a good job of scaring the bejebus out of me to keep me drug-free as a youngster. The horror stories about drug use she would read me from the Daily News, New York City's largest-selling newspaper, were enough to keep me clean for most of my early teens. Then one day my best friend, Ron, told me he had tried weed and it was great I had read that my favorite band of all time, The Beatles, had tried weed, given to them by Robert Zimmerman, better known as Bob Dylan. If my best friend and my favorite group were doing it then so would I. The opportunity came the following weekend to hang out with Ron and a couple of buddies. We started the night as we usually did drinking 40-ounce bottles of Balentine beer. About halfway through one of these, we would be pretty snookered, and I was feeling no pain this night. That's when one of our older friends 17-year-old Pat showed up with the goods. I had never even seen or smelled marijuana before this. He pulled out a doobie and proceeded to light it up. He took a poke and passed it around, first to the veteran first-timers from last week, and then handed it to me. I was already smoking cigarettes so how bad could this be? Well, it didn't take long for the paranoia to settle in. Everyone else seemed to be enjoying themselves, but all I could think of was all the stories my mom read to me about drugs. I told the guys I was tired and was going to go home. I lived about 2 miles from the hangout spot [the Catholic Church parking lot of all the unlikely places] so the walk home was both long and strange. I felt a kind of good feeling of floating along but at the same time, I could hear the voice of my mom saying 'I warned you I walked in the back door of my house and was glad no one was home. I went straight to the bathroom and barfed my brains up, swearing if I ever made it through this horror, I would never do any kind of drugs again.

That promise lasted until the next weekend, the same scenario, and I tried it again. The reason I tried it again was that Ron told me that the same thing happened to him the week before during his first try [of course he didn't tell me this before I tried it] He told me the second time he relaxed a bit more and loved it. Then I used the logic that I didn't like sweet air [nitrous oxide] the first time my dentist tried to make me high, and now I love it. I even make him give it to me when I get a check-up. I wonder how many kids got their first high from a dentist? The Beatles got their first taste of LSD from their dentist, Dr. Roberts, who even wrote a song about it. Well, Ron was right although the part about relaxing wasn't as easy as he made it sound. I fought the same thoughts of what am I doing again until someone told a joke about a prostitute and a blind man. We all laughed so hard. This shit is pretty good. Sorry, mom.

Chapter 7
Worth a try, eh?

I settle into my seat and it was then I saw her standing there. One of the groupies was not a groupie at all, it was Mary Jane. She looked better than ever. A tight-fitting pair of jeans, a button-down white silky blouse, and the pair of f-me pumps. She was talking with the band members and they all seem to be enjoying themselves away too much. Must be good stuff.

I was going to get up and go over to see her, but she saw me first, smiled, and came over to me.

'I didn't know you came to these things, She said.

'This is my first time. Mitch invited me the other day at the bar. This is a pretty cool place' I said

'He does these about once a month. They're lots of fun and the bands are pretty good. A couple of drinks and just enjoy.

'And sometimes a little more than just a couple of drinks I said. By the scent of things, I detect a little weed.' I said

'You would be right there. Pretty good stuff. Like to try some.' 'It's been quite a while since I've done any but what the heck.'

'We'll smoke when the band gets done with this first set.' She says 'By the way, where's Brad', I ask.

'Oh, him, away on some business I guess.' She says I asked no more.

We sit down and the band starts playing. They are pretty good. They play some of their stuff and mix in a little Lynard Skynard, Marshal Tucker, and The Band. We were on our feet dancing around and clapping by the time the band came to defeat their first break. Now it was time.

The band starts unstrapping their guitars. Mary Jane grabs me by the hand and pulls me up towards the stage where the bands playing.

'Hey, I want you to meet a good friend of mine, Patrick. Patrick this is the band.'

'You guys are good you play tight.' I said as I put my hand out to shake.'

The lead singer sticks out his hand,' Hi I'm Nailer,' he says' Thanks for coming. He points to the drummer, 'That's Hax, and over there in a corner with his back to us, that's Joe. Hax grabs my hand and says hello, while Joe, the quiet one just grunts something.

The band starts setting out the door to go smoke a doob. They moved over to Mitch to follow them, which he does.

'Do you guys mind if Patrick joined us? Maryjane asks Nailer. "Sure, bring him along," he says.

'He's no cop, is he?' Hax asks

'Yeah, He's working undercover to bust this big drug cartel. We must have at least a quarter ounce of Pot among us.' Says Mitch.

'Just being safe' Hax replies.

The last time I smoked it was a rolled-up Dube. Sometimes we smoke from a pipe and other times from a bong. But Nailer pulled out a cigar.

I whisper to M.J. "What's that?"

'They call it a Blunt. It's a cigar that they bore out the center and fill with marijuana. This way you can smoke in public and no one will know.' She says.

I remember my days of smoking cigarettes and cigars. That there was a cigar called a Phillie Blunt and that's what they were using. They lit it up and started passing it around. When it got to me, I explain to them how I hadn't smoked in a while and then proceeded to take a big hit. I held in the smoke for a while and then the choking started. It reminded me of the first time I smoked a cigarette. I was thirteen years old and a cousin of mine, Jerry, came to stay at the house for a while. We went out to take a walk and the next thing I know he was pulling a cigarette out of a pack. He hands one to me and starts to light them up.

I started choking like crazy then too, but that didn't stop me from having a 30-year love affair with cigarettes. The only reason I quit smoking was that I told the Lord that if he would let the New York Rangers win the Stanley Cup, something they hadn't done since 1940, I would quit smoking the night they won the Stanley Cup. I had my last cigarette on June 14, 1994.

'Hey you all right over there, Nailer asks me.

'Great stuff,' I say, between the hacking and choking. Can't wait for my next hit.

They all start cracking up.

But when the blunt reached me for the second time I was a little smarter. This time I took a much smaller hit and was able to hold it in for a while, no choking this time. I started to feel the effects after the second hit. I already had four beers so I had a little buzz going from that, but this was much different. It was a feeling I haven't had for a while and I can't describe it but I could feel a smirk on my face. And I looked over to Mary Jane and she was looking at me with that I know how you feel look. Even her smile looked prettier when I was high (stop thinking like she's engaged). The blunt made its way around one more time and I was getting higher by the minute.

Everyone made their way inside, and the band started setting up again. I made my way back to the same seat I was sitting in earlier and Mary Jane returned there also. She snuggled up to me and whispered in my ear that she was having a great time. I smiled at her and told her I was having a great time too.

The band started the second set off with Lynard Skynard's Free Bird, one of the great all-time songs. It sounded better than it ever. I started to recall my days of smoking marijuana and remembered music always sounded better and food tasted better.

The band rocked on through the night for two more sets, and two more passings of the blunt. I met a bunch more friendly people, drank some more beers, and it was time to leave. Mary Jane also had too much to drink. One of Mary's friends Gary noticed that both of us had too much to drink and should not be driving. He lived nearby and offered to have us stay at his house that night rather than drive home. I had just met Gary that night but Mary seemed to know him very well. She looked at me and said we should take him up on his offer, which we did.

On the short ride back to his home crazy paranoid thoughts were getting into my head. What if this was a setup and these are two crazy people who are gonna hack me to death with an ax tonight? Then I realized it's probably better for me to get hacked up by an ax tonight than to drive home and kill somebody because I'm drunk.

We are at his house before you know it and Gary shows us around the place. He lives alone at the place, and he shows us a spare room and a convertible couch in the living room. He says he's exhausted and is going to sleep.

'Make yourself at home and help yourself to anything.' He says 'Thanks a lot 'we both say.

Gary disappears upstairs into his bedroom.

'I still have a couple of beers left in the cooler if you'd like one.' I tell Mary Jane.

'Sure, I'm still wide awake she says.

I popped off a couple of beers. We make our way to the couch sit down and start gabbing away about different things. The whole time we are talking we're looking into each other's eyes. I can tell things are starting to heat up but I know it's not right. Then she leans over and gives me a nice soft kiss, that practically melts me. We start to hug a little harder and hold each other tighter and tighter. I mumble something about her being engaged and she mumbles something about how she was gonna break it up with Brad soon. That's good enough for me.

We made our way into the spare bedroom. I gently unbuttoned her silky blouse.

I reached around back and unfastened her bra with one snap. Off it fell and exposed her beautiful breasts. They were large and aroused. Her nipples were sticking out like mini–Tootsie Rolls. As I was staring at her breast, she started to pull my shirt over my head. We took off each other's pants and underwear and we fell onto the bed. I was fully aroused.

She climbed on top of me and I realized this was the first time in years I had a woman on top of me and was still able to breathe. We rolled over a couple of more times. I was on top now and started sucking her excited teats. I was making my way south to the promised land, the land of my favorite tree, the country. Her bush was neatly trimmed and she had a pleasant musk. I placed my head between her legs and started kissing and licking her. She was groaning and writhing in pleasure. Before long she was shrieking and having an orgasm. It was the longest orgasm I had ever heard. She calmed down a bit and I made my way back to her breasts, fondling and kissing them gently. Before long I was making my way south for round two. When I reached my destination, she whispered that I shouldn't bother. She said she never has multiple orgasms. I asked if she would mind if I tried and she said go ahead but you're wasting your time. After her fourth orgasm, she was lying on the bed and looked like someone that fallen off the top of a building. One arm was this way, one leg that way. Her mouth was wide open, her tongue hanging out. She mumbled 'I can't move. How'd you do that?

After a while, she started coming around. "Now it's your turn," she said. She kissed her way from my neck down to my manhood. It didn't take long before it was all over, figuratively and literally. At least if she is still engaged, I didn't have sex with her according to President Clinton.

After the cleanup, she suggested that maybe I should sleep on the sofa bed so Gary wouldn't get the wrong idea. I said sure but either Gary is a deep sleeper or he's probably upstairs playing with himself now.

Chapter 8
Light's Out

It was Sunday morning so that meant bacon and eggs and maybe another lousy bagel. I go to the supermarket and get my needs along with some Pillsbury buttermilk biscuits. I grab the local newspaper, The Ute, and head home. Another beautiful day of my new life.

I whip up breakfast, the biscuits are great and I eat eight of them smothered in butter to go with my eggs and bacon and a cup of joe. It's a wonder how my heart can even pump with all this healthy food in me. Oh, I did have a glass of o.j.

There's a knock on my front door and I open it to find an elderly couple with a cake box in the lady's hand.

'Hi! We're your next-door neighbors, Frank and Molly Barton. We brought you a crumb cake from Reinhoffs bakery in Cobleskill, the best in the state." Frank says.

'Thanks very much, won't you come in and have a seat? There are only the kitchen chairs right now so grab one and I'll make some coffee or tea if you'd like.'

'We wouldn't want to disturb you ' says Molly.

'Nonsense, come right in, besides, I have no life.'

I said   Oh, I bet that's not true, a handsome lad like you probably gets all the gals.' Molly says.

' Aw your just too kind, especially coming from a beautiful lady like you.' She blushes and giggles.

'It looks like I'm gonna have to keep my eyes on you two.' says Frank. "Will it be coffee or tea? I inquire.

"Tea sounds fine for both of us,

thanks.' Frank says.

'So how do you like it up here so far?' A big change for a flatlander like you. Nice place you got here .'

'You've never seen this place before? I said.

'Nah, that Potter som bitch, and I never saw eye to eye about anything. [couldn't have happened to a nicer guy] he mutters sarcastically under his breath.

'Watch your language in front of our new friend!' Molly exclaims.

'That's all right Mrs. Barton if you hear me during a Mets game you'll think you live next door to Eddie Murphy,' I say

'Eddie who? Frank questions.

'All right, I meant Lenny Bruce.'

'Ohhh' they both sigh.

'Yeah, that som bitch and I fought over everything. He was always trying to steal stuff from me. He would say his property was bigger than it was. Even tried to say the outhouse was his.' He stated.

'You mean that one right there?' I say pointing out the back window. 'Yeah, that's it. Why you ask?'

'Well, I thought it was mine. '

" You mean I'm gonna have trouble with you, too! He yells. 'No, NO. I went out there the other day and was checking it out. I was

curious. I noticed a lock on the door….'

' Yeah, I have the key to it right here. He says as he pulls out a key ring that looks like it belongs to a janitor. He holds the key up in the air.' Best lock they ever made!'

I cringe and contemplate not telling him, but I do.' Frank, let me be frank with you. When I went to the shed the other day I didn't see a key for it and I broke it off.' 'You WHAT!'

'Oh, and the door fell off too.'[I was trying to figure out if I should run or go get a gun.] The initial look on Franks's face was of anger but then it changed to a little smirk.

' That bastard Potter broke that lock off once a week just to piss me off but never once admitted to doing it. I told you it's the best dam lock ever made. I'll go out later and fix it. It's nice to know I have an honest neighbor now. I don't recall the door ever falling off though.'

'I'll help you fix it later. By the way, I also borrowed your weed wacker.' 'Now you're pushing it! Only kidding, whatever I have is yours to use.' He says.

'And vice versa.' I chime in.

'I notice you have those rabbit ears on the T.V. Do you get any reception with that piece of shit.'

'Not much.'

'I have an antenna for the roof. At least you'll get ABC, NBC, and CBS on it. If you'd like I'll get it out for you.'

'Thanks that would be great

'You hear any footsteps in the house at night?' he asks.

'No, why do you ask?' I say 'No reason.'

'Frank! Molly says giving him a dirty look. 'Good crumb cake, he says, chomping on a big piece while changing the subject. Best in the state.'

'How long have you two been living in Summit.' I inquire

'Been here all our lives. Our families have been here since the 1800s. Molly and I went to school together since 1st grade. There was no such thing as kindergarten then. Molly went all the way to 12th grade and graduated. I had to stop in eighth grade so I could help my pappy on the farm. Corn is what we grew. Molly and I got hitched on her graduation day. Our anniversaries are in a couple of days. 65 years.

'63 years, Molly pipes in.'

'It feels like 65. Big party. The whole town showed up, mostly for the free sandwiches. I even caught that damned Potter sneaking some home in his pocket!' He says.

'Nonsense Frank! You did not!'

Molly butts in,

'Well, he had something bulging in his pockets.'

'Oh cut it out. You never liked him 'cause he had the sweets for me.'

'That's not it. I just never trusted the bastard.'

My turn to change the subject. "Anybody like more tea?' 'No thank you.' Molly says. Frank nods the same.

'Out of curiosity, what did happen to Mr. Potter anyway?

'Come on Molly, it's time we should be left. We'll leave that for another time. Do you ever hear any doors slamming at night?'

'No why?' I asked

'No reason, come on Molly, we've taken up enough of our new neighbor's time. I'll dig out that aerial for you. Thanks for having us.' He says.

'Thanks for stopping by. And you're right the best crumb cake I ever had. Here, take it home with you.'

'Okay thanks, Frank says. 'Frank Barton, you will do no such thing! We bought that for Patrick.' Molly chastises.

'O.K.' Frank sheepishly shrugs. 'That's all right he can have it.' I offer. 'There's no changing my mind. It's all yours.'

'Thank you once again.' I make a mental note to buy a crumb cake from Reinhoffs the next time I'm in Cobleskill. I walk them to the front door. Interesting morning and night come to think of it.

It was a little past noon and another stellar day outside so I figure since the Mets were going to be on the Sunday night game of the week, I was free to do a little yard work. One thing I don't have is a green thumb. I've tried to do everything right to start a lawn. I've turned the ground over, smoothed it out, taken all the weeds and rocks away, and planted the good quality seed. A beautiful lawn would appear in a couple of weeks. I would water it and nurture it but a month later it would start to fade away. Every time I try! Then just to burn my ass, the grass would grow heartily between the cracks in the sidewalk.

The lawn here looks like it's been established for quite some time. It's not sod looking, but it's green. In my world that's good enough for me. The lawn could use mowing so I put a lawn mower on my list. Most of the time you can find lawnmowers in garage sales or left out for the garbage man to take. While I'm not so handy mechanically, lawn mower engines are one of my fortes. As a kid, we would take old lawnmowers, fix them and make mini bikes. When I drove around on my mini bike, the wind blowing through my hair I always imagined being Peter Fonda riding with Jack Nicholson and Dennis Hopper in Easy Rider. I probably looked more like Artie Johnson on Laugh-In riding his tricycle.

I stride around the yard picking up dead branches and such. I look over the place and think while it's not a yard you would see in Better Homes and Gardens, and never will be as long as I own the joint, it's mine. I stumble, literally, upon an overgrown outdoor fire pit. I'll need to do some trimming to be able to use it but it will be worth the time. There's a little bit of firebug in me. I always loved playing with matches but one day it caught up with me. I was about 6 years old and living in Brooklyn. 6 years old in Brooklyn in those days meant you were on your own. My mom would send me to the store around the corner to buy bread and milk. She would give me a list of items, roll the money up inside the list and tell me to keep my hand closed till I gave the list and money to the grocery man, Mr. Butters. He would give me the items and send me back home, but I would always tell him my dad needed a book of matches, which I would put in my pocket for later. Today I don't think kids are allowed to go to a store alone today till they're 16. The good old days. I guess kidnappers weren't invented then [except for the Lindenburg kidnapper]. More likely married people stayed together and parents weren't kidnapping their kids from their spouses.

Well, this one hot summer day I decided to have some fun with my book of twenty matches. I would light up the paper I found and watch it burn to ashes. One piece I lit up started burning my hand so I threw it down. It landed on a small strip of burned-out grass in front of a house and ignited the grass [that's why I can't grow a lawn, the grass gods are punishing me for doing that! I wish I could figure out how I pissed off the putting gods because I can't make a putt to save my life.] I immediately started stomping it out and was lucky to put it out before it spread to the house. Someone was just coming to the front door and I boogied out of there and ran straight home. We lived on the third floor.

When I got in, I just stared nervously out the window waiting for someone to come and arrest me. My mom kept asking why I was hanging around the window and I said nothing. I was surprised she didn't notice that I smelled like a chimney. I learned a lesson that day, never burn your fingers.

After a couple of hours or so I called it a day. I went inside, had a bite to eat took a shower, and lay on my couch reading the Ute. It's been a while since I just sat down and relaxed and before long, I napping. I awake at 7:00 and get ready for the Jailhouse Rock Inn.

I walk to the bar and I'm surprised that the place is pretty empty. Mike is in his usual place but by his slurred greeting I could tell he wasn't long for here. A few other stragglers were around and out of the back room came the bartender for the night, Maryjane. We exchanged hello smiles and she served me up a Genny on tap. I didn't know what to say about last night when she started first.

'That was a lot of fun at the gallery last night.' She said

'Yeah, a great bunch of people I met and the band was super. I can't wait for the next one.' I said.

'Me, too.' she stated with a wink and a smile. 'Did you have any energy to do anything today''?'

'Yeah, I worked around the yard. Found out I had a fire pit buried under weeds in the backyard. I love a big barn fire with toasted marshmallows.' I say.

'Me too' but you'll have to make Smores for me.'

'I've never made them before but the first fire I get going I'll try.' 'Why don't you two get a room, already.' Mike pipes in playfully

sticking his finger down his throat like our conversation are making him nauseous.' I had enough of this crap, I'm out of here, he says as he stumbles his way to the door.' See ya tomorrow.'

We giggle like teenagers as he disappears past the window.

"Tomorrow a bunch of us are going to go to Katterskill Falls. It's the tallest waterfall in New York State, higher than Niagara Falls."Mary says. You want to join us?'

'Slowly I turn step by step.' Every time someone mentions Niagara Falls a sort of flashback occurs to an episode of The Three Stooges where that saying originated. They were the best but I still ain't crazy about Shemp. 'Sounds like fun. What time?

'We're meeting at the gallery around 11:00.'she said.

'Sounds good.' Would you mind putting on the Mets game? It's on ESPN. They're playing a little better, won three out of four.' I said

'Perez pitched great the other night, and Beltran went three for four with a homer and four rbi's.' Maryjane says.

Wow! What a gal!

The Mets game goes terrifically. John Maine tosses a beaut. The Mets win five nothing over the Marlins, another homer for Beltran. The Mets are now up four games over the Braves. It's almost the end of June now and the old saying is whoever is in first on the fourth of July will win the pennant

I finish my last beer and head home. I tip Maryjane and tell her I'll meet her tomorrow morning. It's a gorgeous night out. It's amazing how many more stars and galaxies you can see upstate rather than downstate. The only place downstate you can see such amazing stars is the Hayden Planetarium in Manhattan and the Vanderbilt Museum on Long Island. Outdoors, you're lucky if you can see the moon. I take my time walking home gazing at the stars and thinking about Maryjane. Maybe she is done with Brad.

Chapter 9
What Truly Matters

I head into the house and grab a lounge chair and a beer. I head out the back door and place the lounge chair on the grass. I stare at the sky wondering how many of these stars have a planet roaming around it just like the earth. Maybe there's someone in their backyard in some distant universe looking at the sky and wondering the same thing.

When we first moved from Brooklyn to Belmont it was like living in the sticks. I was seven years old back then; it was quite a change of life. Back then you were able to see the sky as I'm looking at it now. There were no street lights nor sidewalks no curbs. I fondly remember my dad on his lounge chair in the backyard staring at the sky every single night. I would go out and join him once in a while. He would point to the sky and show me the Big Dipper and other constellations. Then he would point out a star in the sky and tell me it was the satellite Sputnik, launched by the Russians. My dad didn't drink or do drugs but when he would point out a star in the sky and tell me to watch it move, I'd wonder. But sure enough, if you watched closely and for a long enough time the star was moving, it was Sputnik. Why isn't it that kids always think they're smarter than their parents?

I am awakened because I'm feeling cold. Then I realize I'm cold because I'm still outside. I dozed off staring at the stars. But one thing about being upstate is you never need an air conditioner at night. It could be 90° during the day but it will go down to 50 at night. I'm afraid to see what the winters will be like up here. I head back into the house to get into my bed and crawl under the covers. I never did find Sputnik.

The alarm went off what seemed like 1 minute after I went to bed, but it was already 10:00. I showered, grabbed a cup of tea, and was on my way to the gallery.

Another perfect day. I'm beginning to wonder if this place has the same weather as San Diego.

I jumped into my car and put the classic rock station on my radio. Seals and Crofts, Diamond Girl, is playing. It great song And I'm going to spend the day with my Diamond Girl.

Downstate when I got into my car in the morning the first thing I'd always put on was Howard Stern. Even though some people get tired of him telling us how great he is, he is great. Howard and his crew of Robin, Fred, Gary' Baba Boogie 'Boogieabate, and Artie Lange who took over for Jackie the Jakeman Martling. Artie's good but there's just no replacing Jackie. He had a million jokes and was always the fall guy. The reality of it is that Howard Stern could probably work with five monkeys and still have a great show. Shortly before moving up here, Howard went to broadcasting on satellite radio, and Sirius was the company. He reportedly received $500,000,000 for a five-year contract. I guess I chose the wrong business.

I pull up to the gallery and there are a couple of people already there. I see Mitch, Gary, Mike, and Maryjane. They're all hanging out in front of the gallery near a large UV as if that isn't redundant. It's a Cadillac Escalade. I felt like a midget when I walked by it. It was a nice-looking vehicle and had enough room inside for a small family of gypsies. It probably gets about 5 gallons to the mile, yes I mean it that way.

As I was making my way around the S. U. V. I notice someone in the driver's seat. Then I realized who it was, Brad. Was he here with Mary Jane or just along for the ride?

' Hey Patrick, glad you made it. It should be a lot of fun today,' said Mitch. 'Yeah, we packed up the cooler with plenty to eat and drink. It's a beautiful day to do some hiking, said Mary Jane.' I don't know if you've been formally introduced to my fiancé yet, Brad comes out here to meet Patrick.'

'Hi, I've seen you at the Rock Inn. Glad to meet you, I'm Brad, he says as he extends his hand.

'I'm Patrick I heard a lot about you. That's a fine fiancé you have there, I say. 'Thanks, I know I got lucky. He says.' Is everybody here?'

'Yes, that's everyone. Let's get on our way.' M J says.

'Okay, why doesn't everybody just jump into my car.' says Brad understating his vehicle.'

The six of us jumped into his SUV and there was still room for a few more if we needed. We make a u-turn and head west on rt. 23 on our way to Katterskill Falls, just west of Hunter Mountain, a very popular ski resort. The ride like all rides upstate is picturesque. The conversation is flowing nicely among everyone' Brad included. It seems that maybe he is an all-right guy. Then Brad reaches into his pocket and pulls out a big fat doob.

'Anyone want to partake in a little toking? He asks. 'Sure bring it on, says Mitch. Is it reg or what?'

'It's hydro Brad says, good shit.'

'Well, I guess if it's good shit we better not let it go to waste. I say. 'Yeah' fire that thing up. Gary shouts out.

The joint is passed around the car but Brad refuses because he's driving. The word hydro is a new term for weed that I was unfamiliar with, but by the excited reaction of the others, I'm assuming it must be GOOD SHIT!

'So, being that I've been out of the marijuana circle for so long what does hydro mean? I inquire because I would rather ask a stupid question than be stupid.

'Hydro, short for hydroponics is the way they grow much more potent weed than you got in the sixties. It's grown in warehouses without any soil. It's grown under special lighting and the plants are growing in nutrient mineral solutions. One hit of this is like five hits of reg, which means regular, the stuff you're used to. That's what we smoked the other night. I'm sure you'll enjoy this he says as he passes me the joint.

I take the joint and can still hear mom warning that this is probably the stuff that you're going to get addicted to and you'll be homeless before you know it. I look around the car and don't see anyone that's about to be homeless so I take a drag, still a little eerie. I pass it along waiting to start hallucinating and seeing tangerine trees and marmalade skies, thinking about a line from'' Lucy in the Sky with Diamonds. [John Lennon always said that song was not about LSD but about a drawing Jullian, his son drew, but I don't know.] At first, I'm just feeling normal but little by little a feeling starts to creep over me. A good feeling. The trees start looking even more beautiful and colorful. The streams on the side of the road are glistening as they roll along. I think I could get used to this hydro. The joint makes its way around and I take another poke.

A good way to start a day.

'Hey, Brad GOOD SHIT! I exclaim and everybody agrees then cracks up. 'Katterskill Falls here we come! Did anyone bring a barrel to go over the falls with?

'I have Cracker Barrel cheese' Mary says. 'I guess that will have to do. I said.

The ride to Katterskill is a laugh riot. It's like a school bus of kids going on a field trip. Even the jokes are from elementary school.

Gary starts "Knock knock"

"Who's there?" "Ach".

"Ach who?"

"God bless you!"

We all laugh as if Jerry Seinfeld just told one of his best jokes. Then a Neil Diamond song, Sweet Caroline, comes on and the knuckleheads that we are all start singing along 'Sweet Caroline good times never seemed so good, so good ....

We were near our destination and make a left off of 23A, the route we were on.

The sign says, Haines Falls.

'I thought we were going to Katterskill Falls' I ask

'We are, says Mary. I don't even know if there is a Haines Falls.'

We pull into a dirt road and park the SUV on a makeshift dirt parking lot, alongside a couple of other vehicles. Everyone gets out with a big shit-eating grin on their faces.

'My turn' says Brad as he takes out another joint and lights it up. 'Anyone else cares for some more?' Mitch and Gary take a few more hits but I don't because I'm already toasted.

I notice a trail going off to the right and I start to explore it.

The others join me and we're on our way. It's a beautiful walk among nature. The squirrels are scurrying around and we even see a deer through the trees. He is watching us closely as we make our way along the trail. I start getting anxious to see the falls and pick up my pace and get well ahead of the rest of them. I have a thing for waterfalls even though I haven't seen many in my lifetime. Niagara Falls [slowly I turn] is one of the most spectacular and not that far away but I've never been there, at least not that I recall. My mom and dad honeymooned there, as every married couple did back in the day, so maybe I was there.

The path is winding left and right and then without a sign or any kind of warning, I found myself at the edge of a cliff with a 175-foot drop. No fence to protect you just a long drop to the bottom of the falls and onto a rocky bottom. I panic because if I had taken one more step, I would have been dead. I want to back away from the edge but I am paralyzed with fear. My legs won't move. I feel like I'm going to faint and fall forward. Now I know some of this fear is probably brought on by the weed but I have a feeling if I were stone-cold sober, I would feel the same way. Then I fear that the others will come up behind me and by accident bump into me and knock me over. Then I think what if Brad knows about me and Maryjane the other night, even though it wasn't sex according to our ex-president, he may push me on purpose. All right that's the pot talking, or maybe not. Well, I'm not going to stay here any longer so I back up ever so slowly, an inch at a time until I'm safely away from the edge. The others still haven't arrived yet. I find myself a rock and sit there, my heart pounding like it's going to bust out of my chest. I make the sign of the cross, say a quick prayer to thank the Lord for getting me back to safety and let out a sigh. Just then my fellow hikers come down the trail smiling and having a good old time. MJ sees me and approaches.

'What happened to you?' she exclaims. 'You look like you saw a ghost.'

You're white as a sheet.'

I can barely get the words out. I'm shaking like a leaf. The others come over and wonder what is going on. I tell them my story and Mitch and Gary start cracking up. They're laughing so hard that they look like they're going to pee their pants. Brad comes over and can see the fear in my eyes. He says let's go take a walk up the path to clear my head. The other two clowns are going up to the edge of the falls where I had been and they're making believe they are falling and calling for help. Real funny.

Brad takes me for a walk and tells me to ignore those other assholes. He explains that 5 to 10 people fall off here every year. He tells how one lady fell to the bottom and lived. Then she sued the state for not having any warning signs. She lost her case because as you start on the path there is a sign that states enter at your own risk. I didn't even see that sign.

I'm starting to calm down a little. Although I don't recall ever having a fear of heights, I know I have one now. I do recall never being comfortable on a hotel balcony 20 stories up. I always felt that if I leaned on the balcony railing that it would give way and I would plunge to my death. This fear I always chalked up to Hollywood because it happened in so many movies that way, especially James Bond movies.

"You feeling any better, Brad asks showing real concern.

'Yeah, a little. I was still a little lightheaded but starting to get my sea legs back. "Let's go find the others."

We make our way down the 'PATH OF DEATH' toward the group. Mitch and Gary see us approaching and giggle, but with a little more control. We approach the site of my anxiety. For the first time, I get to see the beauty of it all. Without getting too close to the edge I can see the waterfall and the large surrounding valley that it empties into. I can't look for too long because my fear returns.

'Let's make our way to the bottom', Gary suggests. 'Sounds like a good idea, let's go says MJ.

"Do you feel up to it?" Brad asks me

'Sure, I'll give it the old college try.' I was saying this out loud but my mind was saying "NOOOOOOOO! I knew if I didn't at least try I would be branded the biggest pussy in Summit. So here I go.

The first part of the journey was to get to the other side of the falls. The others go across the stream leading to the falls, hopping on the rocks that were jutting out of the water. They were only about 20 feet from the edge of the falls. All I could think about was one of them slipping and getting washed over the falls. They make their way across without any problem and they egg me on to join them. Brad stayed behind me and encouraged me to try. I will give in to peer pressure with some things, but not when it comes to my life. If I'm going to die, it's going to be for something more exciting than crossing steam and tumbling to my death. I head upstream about another 100 yards and find a more suitable spot to cross. If I fall here, I will have plenty of time to save myself before going over the edge. I think back to the wisecrack I made about someone bringing a barrel to go over the falls and now I wish I was in a barrel so I could survive the crash. Brad has been tagging along with me. Sometimes first impressions are not true. He's been a help.

It's kind of fun, jumping from one rock to the other and making your way across. It's like chess. You have to calculate two moves [rocks] ahead. Maybe this will be fun after all. Brad crosses behind me and we join up with the others. We start hiking down trails through the woods. We come to a bend in the trail and I watch the first two grab a tree and swing around to the other side. When I get there 'High Anxiety', as Mel Brooks put it, returned. The tree they were swinging around was one foot from a drop-off of a hundred feet. On any other day I wouldn't have thought twice about it but today I couldn't shake the fear. Brad can tell what I'm thinking and tells me we can take another route to the bottom and I follow him.

'We'll meet you guys down below.' Brad tells the others and off they go. Follow me.'

He takes me deeper into the woods where we find another less adventurous decline to the bottom. It winds through the woods nowhere near the cliff.

'Don't feel bad we all have fears throughout life. Different kinds of fears.

Just the other day I feared I had lost Maryjane. I had a hard time at work, my dad was breaking my balls hard and I had to go away to see a client over the weekend. I wanted to go to the gallery and see the band play. I told my dad to send someone else but he wouldn't hear of it. Go do your job and forget your friends he told me. I was so pissed off. I went home to pack and Maryjane shows up at the door and I took it out on her. All she did was say how she was looking forward to seeing the band and that set me off. I told her about my trip and she said I should tell my dad that I couldn't make it. I flipped out. I told her she had no business telling me what to do. I said I never had this problem before I met her and that I had enough of her. I told her the engagement was off and told her to get out of my house, which she did but not before saying 'fuck you asshole.' She was right. The next day I sent her flowers and explained why I had been such an asshole. I called her later that day and we made up. She can be so understanding.

We were hiking along and he was asking about my life. I told him my story of losing my job and about other things in my life. We were hitting it off pretty well. We got to the bottom of the falls and we beat the others. When I turned to look at the falls my jaw dropped. What a wonderful sight! The water cascaded down the side of the mountain into a pool below. The people were bathing in the pool letting the falls crash down on their heads. It was almost worth the trouble. The falls seemed to have a calming effect on me. The fear seemed to be behind me and I could feel the makings of a fun day. It should also be a day of looking elsewhere to find another love. Maryjane is taken by a good man.

We spend the day hiking some more trails and basking in the sun below the falls. We feed our faces, drink some beer and smoke a Phillie before calling it a day. We hike back up the mountain on the same trail the others took coming down. Somehow climbing up isn't as bad as climbing down, even though it was steep and narrow. We get back to the SUV and I get a feeling of relief. I made it!

We pile into Brad's SUV and head back to the gallery. The boys are still letting me have it pretty well.

'Maybe we'll go swimming tomorrow. Patrick, don't forget your inflatable arm swimmies so you won't drown.' Gary jokes.

'And I hope you won't be afraid of those killer minnows.' Mitch pipes in. 'Some day, somehow, somewhere you guys are going to have an experience like that, and believe me I will be lurking somewhere behind you and I'll be the one laughing my ass off. I reply [What would happen if you laughed your ass off? How would you sit?]

"No swimming tomorrow, Patrick and I are going quadding." Brad comes to my rescue again. [This is news to me but I love quading]

Brad has two quads, which are four-wheel drive all-terrain vehicles. They are really fun to ride up and down the mountain trails.

'That's right, and I just might ride mine with no helmet. I joke feeding these guys a straight line.

'Whoa, that's scary' Gary says

'There's nothing to protect up there anyway. Mitch joins in. ' OH, is that why you never wear a jock strap? I come back.

'They haven't made one big enough for me. Mitch shoots back. 'Now you're talking about a helmet, right? Brad joins in

'Any time you want to have a contest to see who has the bigger one I'm ready. Mitch says.

'Let's go right now, but I'm only going to take out enough to win' I say.

Mary smirks.

The rest of the ride back is filled with more one-liners than a Henny Youngman convention. It seems like I found a good bunch of friends.

Chapter 10
Brad

The following morning I'm awakened by a call on my cell phone. It was my daughter Pamela.

'Good morning dad, how's your life as a hillbilly going.' She says.

'Well, gosh darn it, I just got in from milking the cows and feeding the pigs, I say in my best Gomer Pyle voice. How ya doing Sweetheart?'

'Good, I miss you. Haven't seen you in a couple of weeks.'

'I know darling. I'm trying to get settled in here. You'd love it up here. The people are great. There's a lot to do.'

'Yeah, if ya like milking cows I guess'

'No, you'll see. I'm going quadding today with a new friend, Brad. We'll be riding them thru the trails in the mountains. Now I know you'd like that.'

'Yeah, that sounds good.

I'll try that.' She says. 'I'll have you and your sisters up here soon.' I tell her 'Good. I spoke with grandma yesterday. She's coming up from Florida tomorrow. I hope you didn't forget her birthday is next weekend.' she said.

'How could I forget, it is on the 4th of July. She's a Yankee doodle dandy' "What?"

'Forget it, before your time. I'll be coming home on Friday.' I say

'A little Freudian slip, you'll be coming HOME?' She's such a wise ass. I don't know where she gets it from. Ha.

'You know what I meant. This is my home now until they run me out of town. How are your sisters doing?

'You know those two, probably fighting over a bag of Fritos right now.'

'Hey be nice they can't help it if they got their mother's genes.'

'Yeah, they got her jeans and they fit right into them.' 'You're bad! what are you doing today?"

" Nothing much, it's so boring. Maybe I'll go to the beach.' She wines. 'Well, you better bring a stick with you so you can beat off all the guys.' [she is very good-looking.]

'Oh, cut it out, dad. It feels like a year since my last date.' 'Good! Save yourself for Mr. Right.'

'Thanks. I'll be an old maid before I meet him.' 'Yeah, I know, you're all 23 years old.'

'24! You always forget.'

'Yeah, yeah, yeah. All right I'm getting a beep on my phone. Someone's trying to call me. I'll call you when I get on Friday. Love you.'

'Love you, too! See you Friday.'

I hit my call waiting. It's Brad. 'Yellow, I say. 'Patrick?

'Yeah, what's up.'

'What's up with yellow?

'You'll be stealing that from me, I know.'

'You ready for some four-wheeling?'

'I'm ready as I'll ever be. What's the plan? 'Meet me at my place and we'll go from there.'

'I'll be there in ten.' 'Sounds good. '

I make my way over to Brad's house. It was a beauty. He bought a large piece of property overlooking a nice size lake and had the house built. He cleared out enough trees so he could see the lake and the whole valley beyond it. He had about 30 acres overall. I pull up the driveway to the house. There's another car, a Mercedes Benz 560 SL already there. I wonder if that's Brad's, too. I walk up the stairs to the front door and ring the bell. A very distinguished man opens the door.

'Am I in the right place? Is this Brad's house.'

' Being that I paid for most of it, but yes this is where Brad lives.' 'Dad just let him in' Brad III says to Brad II.

'Step right in. I'm Brad Winston II. He extends his hand and we shake.

He tries to crush my hand but I hold my own.

'Patrick Hunnewell the 1ST I reply. By the look on his face, I can tell he doesn't enjoy my humor.

'Patrick, I see you met my dad. I have a couple of things to go over with him and then we'll go.'

'Going out to play. I assume you have everything ready for the Burgess case. He's one of our biggest clients. I hope I didn't make a mistake letting you handle this.' II bemoans.

'I'm all set. He'll be happy with the results. ' III replies.

'You still going through with the wedding to that old beer server?' ' Dad not now, not in front of my friend.'

'A built-in family to boot.' 'Dad! NOT NOW!'

Brads II and III finished their work and we were about to leave.

'I hear Patrick's a pretty good golfer, dad. You should take him out to the club. My dad won the club championship three years in a row.' 'Wow, you must be pretty good. What's your best round ever.' 'The next round I play because I don't get enough time to play. I shot a 69 when I was 24. I've been trying to beat it ever since. It's like a curse. What's your best?' ' 'Nothing close to that. I shot 76 a couple of times. I'm the world's worst putter.'

'Good, then maybe I will take some of your money. Be careful with those motorbikes. They're no toys. And wear helmets.'

'Ok, I'll see you at dinner tomorrow. Love you.'

'Love you, too! Nice meeting you Patrick. Be careful.' 'Thanks, nice meeting you. It looks like I'm going to have to work on my game to give you some competition.' I say 'You better. I take no prisoners.'

He left and we left.

We trailer the quads to the base of Mt. Jefferson. We unload them and park the SUV.

'These trails are maintained by the state, for mountain biking, and walking but mostly for snowmobiling. Some people frown upon quads saying that they destroy the paths but I've never seen or done that to the trails. I've heard that you can take this tra way to Canada. There are even gas stations along the way. The gas stations are by the big lakes for the boats. Wanna go to Canada today? Brad asks.

'Sure why not, I say. I'm pretty thirsty. I once drank Canada dry.'

'You drank all their Labatts.'

'And the Molsons, too!

'We really should plan to do that one day.' I

Speak

'What, drink Canada dry?'

'No wise-ass, quad to Canada.

'It will probably take more than a day, and do you have a passport? Since 9-11, the Mounties will probably hunt us down if we crossed the border through the mountains.' Brad says.

'Boy what those Canucks won't do to save their beer. So we will just stop before we go over the border.'

'What do you think there are lines on the ground like on a map separating the countries?'

'There's not? I just.

We mount the quads and place our helmets on. Brad tells me to follow him, and off we go. The quads have an automatic transmission, so you just press the gas lever on the right-hand side of the handlebars, and away we go. It takes a little while to get used to the gas feed. At first, I was almost popping wheelies, but I adjusted pretty quickly. I will probably do wheelies on purpose once I get the hang of it. Brad leads the way across an open field on our way to the mountain. This thing goes pretty fast, and you get bounced around like you're on the Cyclone at Coney Island.

The Cyclone was one of the first roller coasters in the world, and if you never heard of Coney Island you must have grown up in a cave. It was Disneyland before there was Disneyland. In the early

1900s, they built an amusement park in Brooklyn, N.Y. on Coney Island Beach. It had every kind of ride you can imagine. Besides the Cyclon,e they had the Tornado, and people would argue which roller coaster was scarier. Unlike today's roller coasters which are fast but smooth as a baby's ass, these coasters were made of wood and while you traveled around the rails you were bumped and rattled the whole way around. Chiropractors, if they were around then, were needed after every ride. Then you would take a ride on the Steeplechase ride, not your children's Merry-go-round. You would strap on to a mechanical horse and hold on for dear life as the horse made its way around a track at high speeds. You would never see this kind of ride today because of insurance purposes. After the steeplechase, it's on your way to the Parachute jump. This ride, which still stands on its original spot and has been designated a National Monument, would put you in a ski lift type of chair and lift you hundreds of feet in the air. Once at the top, if it didn't break down and leave you stuck up there which happened quite often, it would release you to freefall and a parachute would then open up and float you to the bottom. It was a great sight to see.

After having your stomach turned inside out it was time to head to the best part of the day, Nathans! The original Nathans was in Coney Island and is still there.

They had everything! Of course, they had their famous hot dogs and the best fries in the world. No Mcdonald's or Burger King comes close to these fries. They had the best corn on the cob, sandwiches, like corned beef and pastrami, and a sandwich that to this day I have never seen anywhere else a chow Mein sandwich. I know this sounds like crap but it was good. Much happy memory as a child was had at Coney Island!

We ride up and down some steep slopes and we end up on top of a mountain that once was a ski resort. The chair lift was still in place and the trails were accessible.

'Too bad they went out of business. This wasn't the greatest slope but it was cheap and there was never any waiting in line to get back to the top. I hear it's for sale. Got an extra 3 million lying around? Brad asked.

'Yeah, but I had my heart set on that custom Lamborghini. At the base of the mountain, it appears they had lodging too,' I say

'Still do. It's a resort used for people who have time to share. They're trying to fix it up.'

'Boy, what a beautiful view from here. You can see the whole town.'

'I'll have to take you up to the peak of Mount Utsayantha. From there you can see Hunter Mountain one way and Oneonta the other way. They also have a fire tower that use to have a fire ranger posted to see fires in the area. Then he could report them to the firehouses. Maybe next weekend well ride the quads up there.' He says.

'No, I can't go next weekend. I'm heading downstate. It's my moms' birthday, the 4th of July.' I tell him.

'Where downstate are you heading?'

'To the Island, where I used to live. I'm going to stay with my sister.'

'I've never been to Long Island before. I've only been to Manhattan once, and that was when I was little. My parents took me to see the Christmas tree in Rockefeller Center, but I don't remember much about it.

'I lived only a short ride from the city, but I didn't go there often.' I said

'Would you mind if I drove down with you? We can take the Caddy, and I'll get a motel.' He asked.

'That sounds great. My sister has a big house. I'm sure there's room for you, too!' ' I wouldn't want to impose. I'll just get a room.'

'Nonsense 'I'll talk to her when I get home.'

'Thanks. We'll have some fun.'

'And we'll go to the city one night and hit all the good bars. Let's race down this slope to the bottom. The last one down is a rotten egg.'

We jump on the quads and go speeding down the mountain like bats out of hell. Thank the Lord, we safely make it to the bottom, he beats me by the length of the quad. We ride for about another hour and call it a day.

'That was great, thanks again.' I say.

'Any time. We'll do it when we get back from downstate.' We pack up the quads and head home.

We planned on leaving on Saturday morning. I called my sister and she said Brad could stay, 'the more the merrier, was her answer.

My sister, Abigail Peabody, has been married to the same man, Henry, for 25 years. They have 5 children, all girls, ages 4 to 26. That's right, the math doesn't work. They had their first girl before they married. Henry was in the military, came home on leave, made a baby, and went overseas for a year. He's an architect for a big firm in Manhattan and makes big bucks. Their house was in Cold Spring Harbor, overlooking the L.I. Sound. The house had six bedrooms and only 3 kids still lived at home. My mom was going to stay there, also.

The week went by quickly. I searched the newspapers for a job but didn't find anything as good as the job I had right now unemployment. A nasty rainstorm on Wednesday almost blew my house away. It only lasted about 15 minutes and a beautiful blue sky, rainbow, and all followed. My next-door neighbor, Frank, told me if I didn't like the weather here, I can just wait 5 minutes and it will change. He was right. Another storm blew in over the mountains about an hour later, stronger than the first, followed this time by a double rainbow. Oh well!

Chapter 11
Happenings

Before I knew it I was heading for Friday happy hour at the Jailhouse Rock Inn. The place was already rocking when I got there. Maryjane was bartending and she looked fabulous. She had on a tight-fitting top that displayed her gorgeous breasts, and a pair of Daisy Dukes shorts.[Cut it out, she's engaged and her fiancés a great guy.]

I quickly pulled my tongue back into my head to cease the drooling. I wasn't in the door for 5 seconds and MJ already had my beer poured.

' Genny on tap, 1st ones on me. Heard you and Brad had a good time the other day. And you met his Dad, sorry about that.' She said.

' Yeah he comes on pretty strong, but I'm sure there's another side to him once you get to know him.' I reply.

' Don't hold your breath. I haven't seen it yet.' I'm sure she may never see it based on the way he spoke of her to Brad,

' Busy tonight, I see a lot of new faces around.'

' Yeah there was a big fight at the Watering Hole last night, cops came and everything. The crowd that usually goes there is here tonight,' Mike chimes in.

I'll talk to you later. I have to go fill up their glasses before there's another brawl.

MJ says as she heads to the other end of the bar.

' What was the fight all about? I ask.

' From what I hear, it started when they were watching Smackdown. One guy said Hulk Hogan in his prime would have killed The Undertaker. Another guy took exception to this bit of philosophy and slammed the guy over the head with a chair. Next thing you know guys were jumping off the bar top, slamming guys to the ground. All hell was breaking loose until the owner came out blasting a shotgun full of buckshot. A lot of guys that were there yesterday aren't sitting very comfortably today.' Mike loved to tell these kinds of stories.

' Boy, where'd you get all the details from? If I didn't know better I would say that you were there.' I tell him.

'I was the guy who said The Undertaker would have crushed the Hulkster, then I went to the back of the bar and watched the shit hit the fan. I got tired of watching all that fake bullshit on T.V. It was a classic!' he said with a shit-eating grin on his face.

There was a big muscle-bound guy back by the pool table having a good old time. He looked and sounded like Arnold Schwarzenegger, and he was grabbing all the girl's asses as they walked by him on the way to the lady's room. I don't know if it's because he is so big, but not one girl says a peep. I know if I ever grabbed a girl's ass, 1st she would crack me across the lip and then go get her big bruising boyfriend to finish me off. Ah, it's probably not as much fun as it looks anyway.

Well, he makes his way to the bar and orders vodka, a double, straight up. He throws it back like it was water and tells MJ to do it again. He seems to be having the times of his life. He grabs a guy's ass, and he doesn't say a word!

Across the bar I see Bill, the sergeant, yakking away with anyone whose ear he can chew. When the ass grabber walks by, the sergeant finds a new audience. They start chatting and I make my way over to them. I know this is going to be priceless. It turns out that his name is Arnold, not Schwartzenagger, but Weidman. The first thing serge says is about the ass-grabbing.

' Now I know it's not proper to grab a lady behind without her permission but what are you some kind of Queer boy grabbing a man's ass?' he says 'From behind, I thought it was a lady's ass I was grabbing. But it felt nice and firm, so maybe I am a queer boy as you say! Arnold replies.

' That's damned disgusting!!!

' Oh come on serge, I heard you were checking out all the asses on the young recruits while they were taking showers during boot camp.' Arnold said

' Who told you that bullshit, that's bullshit!!!'

[in the gayest voice possible from the back of the bar Michael says] I told him. And it wasn't just our asses big Bill was interested in you big brute. The place goes up in a roar and so does sergeant Bill's blood pressure. He takes off after Michael who is already out the door and down the block.

' YOU BETTER NOT COME BACK IN HERE YOU FRUIT OF THE LOOM SNIFFER. I'LL KICK YOUR GADDAMN ASS!!!

' You look kind of cute when you get angry,' says Arnold in his best broken English gay voice.

' Don't you mess with the serge, I don't care how big you are, you dumb Pollock. ' Serge screams. 'I'm not a Pollock, I'm from Austria you dumb German.'

' I'm a full-blooded American of five generations, not some illegal immigrant here to take our jobs and money.'

' And your women too, or in your case your men.' Serge had enough as the laughter in the place was reaching a peak. He was ready to throw a punch but Michael and I got in between to prevent any fisticuffs.

" Hit 'em' screams a voice from the front of the bar. 'Don't take that shit!' Of course, it was Mike trying to incite his second riot in two days. 'You don't have to take that from no dumb Pollock' This time cool heads prevail and Arnold puts out his hand to Serge.

" I'm only kidding with you, big guy. Come on I'll buy you a drink, Arnold says.

Serge was still hot under the collar, but he accepts a drink from Arnold.' I'll take a drink, but not one of those Commie drinks you're drinking. I'll have a good old American drink, Jack and Coke.'

' Jack and Coke coming up, says MJ.

Serge drinks his Jack and Coke in one gulp. Mary give me another and this time put some Jack in it. Serge didn't drink hard liquor very often, usually just beer.

' Coming up, heavy on the Jack, Mary says.

'That one on me, too. And give me one of my Commie drinks.'

Says Arnold. Mary delivers the drinks and Serge and Arnold bang glasses. 'To our American soldiers who save our asses from the bad guys of the world, Arnold toasts.

' And to the illegal immigrants who come here and buy us drinks! Sarge responds.

' Here, Here! But I am an American Citizen, since 1994. Arnold responds. ' Well, I'll be. Mary two more of these, on me this time.' Serge says.

The two sit down and start toasting the night away. I figure I'll come back in an hour and hear a real intellectual conversation. I check my watch. This is going to be fun.

' You're a real pip you know. ' I say to Mike. Who do you think you are, Michael Buffer.'

[In his best Michael Buffer voice] 'ladies and Gentleman LETS GET READY TO RUMBLE.'

' DO YOU REALIZE HE GETS PAID 50 THOUSAND DOLLARS EVERY TIME HE DOES THAT? I say.

' No way. Wow, how do I get that job?'

' Practice, man, practice.'

I put my money on the bar and yell to Mary,' What's a man got to do to get a beer around here?'

Mary comes over with a mug in her hand. 'You want good service around here, take care of your bartender, she says as she leans over and puts her cleavage right up to my nose.' They look so great and she smells so delicious I want to give her a Rubowski right here and now.

' Well, I always leave a good bartender a big tit, I mean tip. I'm turning all kinds of colors.

' Your mind is always in the gutter, Mike says. Do you want me to take him outside and beat him for you, Mary?'

' No, I'll beat him myself later.' She says.

' By the way, where's Brad tonight,' the troublemaker Mike asks. He's in his best element when he smells blood.

' He had some last-minute work to complete so he can go downstate with Patrick tomorrow.' She tells him.

' Nobody asked me if I want to go.' Mike bellyaches.

' You can come, there's room in the car. I say.

' Nobody asked me to go, either.' Mary says.

' I'm sorry, you can come too!

' I can't, I have to work the whole weekend. Maybe next time.'

' I can't go either, too many things to do around here, Mike says. 'Next time.'

' Then why are you guys breaking my balls?'

' Because they're there,' Mary says.

' You guys need to get a room.' Mike shakes his head.

I have a couple more Gennys and realize it's time to revisit Sarge and Large. I can hear them getting louder with the drink. I wander over for some free entertainment and I come in at the end of a conversation.

' Them niggers are all lazy asses. They think work is a four-letter word.' Arnold says.

'I trained with a bunch of good African Americans and I would welcome them in my foxhole any day.' Serge states.

' Oh you're one of them, are you, Then let's change the subject.' 'Good idea'

'You know what the strongest thing in the world is?' Arnold asks. 'King Kong is. I mean all those planes couldn't even bring him down' Sarge replies.

' No dummy, it's a vagina. Men give up kingdoms for them,' Arnold says. 'A nuclear bomb. It blows up everything.'

' Are you listening? I said a vagina. A VAGINA'

' A vagina? Serge says this so loud that some of the women stare at him and give him a dirty look.

' Men will do anything for one. Wouldn't you?

' Anything? I wouldn't do anything against my country for one.'

' Ah, all women are whores anyway. On the first date, they're all prim and proper, but on the second date they're eating dingleberries out of your asshole with a toothpick.' Arnold spews getting louder by the minute.

' Hey, that's not nice to call all women whores.'

' Look at my brother's wife. She looks like she was beaten with an ugly stick a hundred times. But even though my brother can't afford it, she goes to the beauty parlor once a week to get all done up. You can take a piece of shit, put whipped cream, sprinkles, and a cherry on top and it's still a piece of shit. That's what his wife is.'

' Enough with the bashing of women. There are plenty of good ones out there.' Serge yells at Arnold and the whole bar is starting to get annoyed.

' You know what all battered women have in common? Arnold asks with his bellowing voice.

[I don't think I want to hear this punch line.] ' They don't know when to shut up!'

I once read that if you put a hundred people in a room that there would come a point when everyone would stop talking at the same time and there would be silence. Well, it's happening right now. All eyes are fixed on Arnold and you can hear a pin drop.

' What? You all know I'm only kidding around. I love women. All of them. He reaches out to the girl in front of him and grabs her ass. She spins around and cracks Arnold right on his kisser. A stunning look comes over him as he takes a step back. First, one lady, then another started to clap. Before long the whole bar was cheering the actions of the lady.

' Fine, if you don't want us here we'll leave. Come on Serge let's go.'

' Why I wouldn't go with you if the President of the U.S.A ordered me.

Why don't you go on back to the Watering Hole so you can be with other jerks like yourself.' The crowd lets out another roar and gives Serge a standing ovation.

Arnold starts toward the door, stumbling all the way. As he exits the bar it elicits another roar from the crowd. I wonder if that leaves an opening at the bar for an ass grabber?

The crowd goes back to what they were doing, drinking and having fun. ' I saw you over there, what did you stir the pot for? Mike asks.

' Oh, I didn't know you had a patent on it. I didn't say a word. Just stood there and took it all in. Quite a character that Arnold is. ' I say

'Yeah, he'll probably kick a dog on the way home. Mike says.

The rest of the night goes along smoothly, except for Serge kneeling before the porcelain god. His bed will be spinning tonight.

The Mets win again, their 4th in a row and they are up 6 games on the Braves. That means they will be in 1st place on the 4th of July. Let's hope that the old baseball adage that 'In 1st on the 4th of July 1st at the end of the season holds.

I finish my beer, leave a nice tip and say my goodbyes, kissing Maryjane on the cheek.

' See you all when I get back.'

' Don't stay too long, MJ whispers to me.

' Don't worry, I'll have your fiancé back before you know it.'
' I was talking about you.'

[Get those thoughts out of your head right now.] 'As the real Arnold would say 'I'll be back.' I head out the door for the short stroll home. I don't know why, but Steven King comes to my mind. Maybe I better walk on the grass instead of the road.

I get home safely in a matter of minutes and start packing for the big trip home.[Another Freudian slip? I can hear my daughter's voice in my head] I pack way too much for the short trip. I'm looking forward to seeing my family. It should be a great weekend. I head to the bedroom, say a few prayers and head off to dreamland, ah, Maryjane! [Get that thought out of your head!!!]

Chapter 12
The Big Trip

The alarm goes off way too soon. I push the snooze button and it seems like a minute later it buzzes again. I get up and make myself a cup of tea. I take a quick shower. Brad should be here shortly.

I hear a car pull up in front of my house. It's Brad in his shiny SUV. ' You all set?' he asks.

' Raring to go. What did you spend the morning shining that bad boy up?' I ask.

' Brought it to the car wash. Gave it the deluxe job. They did a good job.' ' Yeah, they did. Let's get this show on the road.'

We head out for the long ride home [there I go again]. It takes about an hour to get to the N.Y. State Throughway. We get on the southbound side, Brad sets the cruise control to 80 and away we go. We hit the L.I. expressway at about 1 o'clock and of course, after cruising along for 150 miles, we come to a standstill. The large electronic board over the Expressway states TRAFFIC MOVING WELL TO EXIT 40. I guess the way the L.I.E. is getting worse by the day may be considered moving well.

' Man, where are all these people going?' Brad muses.

' Welcome to L.I. and the world's largest parking lot, the L.I.E. if you think this is bad you should see the rush hour.' I say.

' I did. The one with Jackie Chan. It was pretty good.' Brad quips.

' Wise ass. You wouldn't be cracking jokes if you had to drive in this every day. Some poor bastards have to drive into Manhattan every day. Some spend 5 hours a day traveling to and fro. Others choose to take the Long Island Rail Road. It takes just as long, but at least you can read or do some work on the train if you're lucky enough to get a seat. A monthly pass can run $400 +. You lose either way.

' Well, this may be a nice place to visit, but I don't think I'd want to live here.'

' It is a great place to live, minus the traffic.' ' Where are all the mountains.'

' Upstate. That's why you upstaters call us flatlanders. Just flat land here but we have the world's greatest beaches. And great fishing. You'll have to come and spend a week or more here sometime.'

' I had to pull teeth just to get these couple of days. Dad doesn't believe in vacations unless they are work-related.'

' Well, I guess you better find a client while you're here.'

Traffic starts easing up and we head to Cold Spring Harbor. There aren't many places on the Island, or in the world for that matter, as beautiful as it. We get off the L.I.E. at exit 41 and head north to my sister's house. The big party will be tomorrow and my whole family will attend. Today it will be just my mom and my sister's family. Just then my cell phone rings.

Cell phones. When they first started to become popular I hated them and swore you wouldn't catch me dead with one of them. I thought they were so rude. You'd be talking to someone and in the middle of a conversation, they would answer the cell phone and ignore you. I would see a table of 7 or 8 ladies at a restaurant and each of them would be on a cell phone talking to someone else, or maybe they are talking to each other. Now I have one and like Karl Malden used to say "You can't leave home without it.' Now I'm the one being rude to others.

' Yellow, to whom is it I am speaking.'

' Hi dad, are you home, yet?' it was Pamela.

' No. my home is in Summit, but we are very close to aunt Abigail's house.

' We? who's with you.'

' A new friend of mine from upstate. His name is Brad. He's a really good guy.'

'Are you going to be there all day? I miss you, I want to come to see you.' ' Yeah, we'll just be hanging around. Bring your bathing suit. Are your sisters coming tomorrow?'

' Yes, they're coming. Is everyone coming tomorrow?'

' Supposedly. Grandma will be glad to see you. What time are you coming?' ' I'm leaving in about half an hour.' ' I'll see you then, love you.'

'Love you, too.'

I close the cell phone and put it back in my pocket. We are only a few blocks away.

' Wow, this is a beautiful neighborhood. The homes are huge. How much do they go for?' Brad asks.

' You can probably get a handyman, fixer-upper for about a million and a half, of course without an ocean view. I say.

' I guess I better pass the bar exam if I want one of these. I'm taking the test in two weeks.'

' Have you ever taken it before?'

' Twice. Failed both times. My dad got the best lawyer in the firm to help me with this one. He was a professor at Yale before he started working at the firm last year. His students had the highest percentage of passing the bar in the country. 96 % passed. 89 % on the first try. I think my dad brought him on board just for my sake. My dad thinks I'm a dummy. It's just that when I was at school I would rather be playing sports than studying. This time I really bared down and I'll pass it with ease, but that still won't be enough for him.'

' I could never be a lawyer. I could never pass the bar, especially during happy hour.' I say as I try to add some levity to the subject.

We pull through the columns at the head of the driveway and make the long ride to the house. My two nieces are playing in the front yard when they spot the Escalade pulling in. They are not familiar with this vehicle, so there is no immediate reaction. Then they see me get out and start running over to me.

' Uncle Patrick,' they scream as I take both of them in my arms. They give me a big squeeze and a kiss. Bridget is 7 and Katie is 4 and they are as cute as buttons.

' Come and see my new Barbie doll,' Katie shrieks.

' No come and see my Hanna Montana dollhouse,' Bridget buts in.

They were so cute. 'Now let's take it slow. Uncle Patrick will have a lot of fun with you two but first I want you to meet my friend Brad.'

' He ain't gonna be stupid like your other friend, Katie snarls.'

' Katie, that's not a nice thing to say .' Bridget says.

' Patrick, you made it. I've been worried about you. All I keep dreaming about is the scene from " Deliverance" where they make Ned Beatty squeal like a pig.' My sister Abigail, another wise guy, jokes.

' And hi to you, too. I told you it is beautiful Upstate. It's not the back hills in Arkansas. I want you to meet my friend Brad, this is my wise-ass sister, Abigail. I say.

' Hi, nice to meet you, and thanks for letting me stay here. It's my first time on Long Island. Brad extends his hand.

' He's handsome and a big guy. He can't be from up in the sticks. He's not even wearing overalls.'

' Don't worry, Brad she'll stop this by Monday, I say. ' Don't count on it.' she tells him.

'I'm used to it. I haven't gotten a compliment from my own family in over thirty years, Brad says.

' Patrick, glad to see you. Did you bring your clubs? I got us a tee time for 11:00 Tuesday. Hi, I'm Henry, Patrick's brother-in-law. Welcome to our home.'

' I'm Brad, nice to meet you. What a gorgeous home you have.' ' Thanks, my wife picked it out.'

' She did a good job.'

' We brought the clubs. What course are we teeing it off on?' I say.

' Engineers. The greens are lightning-quick. They have the course in pristine shape.'

' Great, I'll shine my clubs up tomorrow.'

' No need. They will do it for you after they take them out of the car.'

' I forgot, I'm not used to that. The courses I play at take them out of your car put them in their car, and take off!

' There you are, mom says as she comes through the front door. How was the ride?'

' Good, how was the plane ride'

'All right, a little turbulence, they gave out peanuts and pretzels.' ' Boy, you must be full then.'

' I'm sure I could fit something else in.'

' Come on inside. Let's get you guys settled in. Henry suggests.

We head through the front door and the room is stunning. The spacious hallway runs right through to the rear of the house, where there is all glass and a view of the harbor and beyond that, The Long Island Sound.

'Wow,' Brad gasps. This is stunning.' I remember thinking the same thing the first time I saw the place. It must be nice to have money.

' If we're staying in the room I think we are, we'll have the same view, only with a deck to hang out on. The best spot in the world to sit and have a beer at night watching the sunset. Very romantic, but don't get any ideas, I don't go that way. Not that there's anything wrong with that,' I say to Brad.

'That's the room you are staying in. I know it's your favorite. I know you don't go that way, but are you sure my dreams about ' Deliverance' didn't happen, my sister says as she mouths the theme song from the movie. 'Da da da dant dan.' I can picture that weird-looking kid strumming his banjo on the porch, frightening.

We bring our bags into our room and start to settle in. I open the sliding glass door to the deck and step out to take in the beauty of it all. Brad follows me out.

' I love the smell of salt water. It's invigorating.' I say

' I could get acclimated to this very quickly. I love looking out my back door and seeing the mountains, but this is just as breathtaking. How's the fishing down there?' Brad asks.

' The best. When the blues and striped bass come in it's like a blood bath on the beach. You can't pull them in quickly enough. There may be a couple of runs while we're here.'

' That would be fun. Thanks again for letting me tag along with you.' ' No problem. Let's go get something to eat.'

My sister brought out a spread of cold cuts and salads, of course, they had to be Boars Head Brand. They have the best cold cuts in the world. Nobody can duplicate their bologna. I don't know nor do I want to know what they put in it but it's delicious.

And she even bought pastrami, not the dry round one but the thin fatty one. MMMM. I'll heat some up.

'Anybody want hot pastrami? I ask. 'What's that?' Asks Brad

' See, he is a hillbilly. My sister chimes in.

' I can't explain it. You'll just have to try it.' I tell him.

' Have it with heavy mustard on rye and you'll never be the same again, Henry suggests.

' O.k. I'll go with the hot pastrami, heavy mustard.' ' Guldens, not none of that yellow crap.' I say

' Guldens it is.' Brad boasts.

After his fourth sandwich, he is a big boy, he sits back with a shit-eating grin on his face. That's better than filet mignon. Think of all the pastrami sandwiches I've missed in my lifetime. Can you adopt me?' Brad sighs.

' Sure,' my sister says'\.

' Over my dead body,' Henry states.' I'll be damned if I'm going to work and leaving my wife home alone with a young stud.'

We all laugh hysterically because Henry never cracks a joke. It is a joke, right? He's not laughing like the rest of us.

' Brad's in love and engaged. Now that I think of it she is an older woman.'

' See, I knew it! No adoption!' Henry shouts, This time he is telling a joke and he laughs the loudest. Everybody's a comedian.

Now it's Brad's turn to put in his two cents. ' I wouldn't think of doing anything like that with someone in my good friend Patrick's family. I'm a pretty good gardener, and I'll take out the garbage.'

' Forget about it, Henry says in his best Brooklyn accent. He's a real barrel of laughs today.

' Oh, come on honey, just for a couple of years or so,' Abby pleads her case. Just then a voice comes from the front door. ' Anybody home?' It's Pamela, my daughter.

I get up and head to the front door and she meets me halfway and gives me a big hug.

' I thought you were never coming back from up there. I missed you.' Just then she glances over my shoulder and sees Brad. Who's that beautiful big stud muffin over there,' she asks me. Is that the friend you brought from upstate? Way to go, dad!

' Now hold on there. First of all, he's already taken, engaged to be married. And besides, he's too old for you! I tell her. She pushes me aside and beelines over to the stud muffin, yeah.

' Hi everyone, how are you all? Hi, my name is Pamela. And you are?' Brad starts to salivate like he just saw another pastrami sandwich.' I'm …ah, Brad, Patrick, er, your dad's friend. I didn't know, I mean he didn't tell me……

I come over with the fire hose to break these two dogs apart. 'Pamela, we were just eating lunch, can I make you a sandwich?' ' Try the pastrami it's delicious,' Brad croons.

' There's none left. Someone ate it all!' I say.

' There's plenty left, don't listen to your dad. Abby says

' I think you better give her something cold to drink to cool her off.' I say.

And Brad I think you might have forgotten something in your room." ' No, I don't think so. Brad says.

' I think you did. Let's go get it. I motion for Brad to follow me. ' Oh dad, Leave him alone.'

' Go have something to eat, we'll be right back.' Brad follows me back to the room.

' He's a real hunk, isn't he.' Abby says. ' I'll say. What's he like?'

' We only met him a short time ago but he is polite and he has a good sense of humor. And he's a HUNK!'

' And we're not adopting him, a hunk you say.' ' What do you mean Uncle Henry?

' Forget about it. You had to be here. Abby says. ' What's this about him being engaged?'

' Dad just said the girl he's engaged to be an older lady.' ' Good! Is he staying here? Pamela inquires.

' Yes.'

'Do you have an extra room for me?'

'Let's not get carried away now. He could be a real creep.' Henry says. ' My dad wouldn't hang around him if he were a creep.'

' What about Darren, ' Katie says. Out of the mouths of babes. ' Dad stopped hanging around that idiot.'

' He was a jerk!' Katie shouted.

' That's not nice, Katie, grandma says. ' But he is'

' It's still not nice.' Abby tells her. ' What's he do for a living?'

' I don't know, we haven't heard yet. He probably milks cows or runs the General store.' Abby says.

' I wouldn't care if he sheered sheep, he's the man I'm going to marry.' Pamela states.

' Pamela, I've never heard you talk like this before. What's gotten into you? Abby asks with a puzzled look on her face.

' Brads' gotten into me. Or he will soon, hopefully.'

' Now Pamela, that's no way for a virgin to speak!' Henry declares.

' Oh Uncle Henry, you're so sweet. It has been a long time since I've had a boyfriend, but not that long.'

' I'll hear none of this. If I were your dad I would put you over my knee right now. Henry spews out.

' Oh Henry [not the chocolate bar], you never put any of your children over your knee.' Abby states.

' Well, none of my children ever spoke that way in front of me.'

'What about the time Lorelei told you to go "F" yourself, using the whole word, and then went away with Sammy for three days BEFORE they were married? Abby says.

 'How old is he?'

'I don't remember that at all.' Henry says sheepishly. ' Convenient amnesia.'

' Come on you two. I wonder what are dads telling him in the room?' ' What did he say to you when you first came in?' Abby asked.

' Something about him being taken and being too old for me. He's not that old.'

' He doesn't look that old. You know your dad. You're his little precious angel.' Abby says.

' He still thinks I'm a virgin, too'

' I'll hear none of this! Of course, you are! Henry repeats.

Chapter 13
A Better Tomorrow

[Meanwhile, back in the bedroom]

' Listen Brad, I think you're a great guy, in the short time I know you, but you're too old for her and you're engaged to Maryjane. And besides that, my daughter is a virgin. I tell him.

'A VIRGIN? ' Brad says with a combination smile and the look of a child who found the keys to the candy store.'

' Brad, so help me. I know you're bigger than me but if you don't take that smirk off your face, I'll kick your 'effen'' ass right now.' I scream at him loud enough that it caused a stir downstares.

' Everything all right up there? Henry questions.

I poke my head out the door and yell that everything is fine.

' You know, Maryjane is the sweetest gal I ever met. I would never want to break her heart. I'm really not sure she's the one for me. I've been trying to convince myself and everyone I speak with that she's perfect for me, but something isn't right, not only with me, but with her ,too. Lately when I'm alone with her it seems her mind is a thousand miles away. I was going to tell you this on the ride down here, but I didn't want to say anything until I was sure.'

' And now you're sure?'

' More sure than ever .' he replies.

' I lied about Pamela being a virgin.'

' That doesn't change anything. I would treat your daughter with the greatest respect.'

' No sex till you're married kind of respect?' ' I just would like to get to know her.'

I weigh the situation. He is a good man, my daughter deserves a good man, he has a good job and a nice house, and that would open the door for me and Maryjane. ' Let's take this nice and easy. I will kick your ass if you break her heart.'

' I'll take it nice and slow. I don't even know if she likes me.'
' Oh, she does, I can tell.'

We head out of the room and make our way back to the kitchen. Pamela is eating a pastrami sandwich.

' Brad, good call on the pastrami sandwich. It's delicious.' Pamela says with a flirty little smile on her face.

' No problem, I'm an expert on pastrami. I've had at least 4 sandwiches of it in my life.'

My suddenly musical sister starts humming " Love is in the Air' by [?] I get " Deliverance", Brad gets 'Love is in the Air!" Come to think of it that's what the hillbilly was probably singing before he mounted Ned Beatty.

' What time are the Mets on? I ask Mom.

' 7:00, and they better those lousy Marlins tonight. They always lose to the last place teams.' She says.

' They beat 'em last night.' I say

' Yeah but they always have trouble with them.

My mom loves baseball, or I should say the Mets. She was a Brooklyn Dodger fan growing up so you can feel her pain. Every year the Dem' Bums would find a way to break her heart as well as the hearts of all Dodger fans. It was always the hated New York Yankees who would stick the knife in their chest. Year after year the Dodgers would get to the World Series only to have the Yankees walk away with the trophy. Then, when they finally manage to beat the Yankees for the World Series, they leave Brooklyn and take the team to Los Angeles. Brooklyn Dodger fans got so use to pain that they started expecting the worst, even waiting for it to happen because surely it would. My mom brought this same passion and pessimism with her when the New York Mets came along in 1962. Of course the 1962 New York Mets did little to dissuade these feelings.

Casey Stengels' New York Mets lost 120 games that year, which stands as a Major League record to this day. They lost in every conceivable way you can. The Amazin' Mets, as their manager nicknamed them, won the fans hearts, but broke them many times. Casey would keep the press amused with his wit and strange sayings. When asked by a sports writer why he chose Hobie Landrith, a catcher, as the first Met player ever chosen, he said "without a catcher there would be a lot of passed balls.' During that first season the Mets acquired" Marvelous" Marv Throneberry. He would become a fan favorite, not because he was a good player, but because he was a lovable buffoon. He dropped easy pop ups and would consistently throw to the wrong base. In one game, after making an error that allowed the Chicago Cubs to score 4 unearned runs, he came to bat the next inning with two runners on base. He ripped a shot to right center field and took off running around the bases till he came to a stop at third base. With the crowd cheering, the Cubs appealed to the umpire claiming Marv had missed first base. The umpired called him out. Casey stormed out of the dugout and started screaming at the umpire. With the argument heating up, the second base umpire wandered over and said to Casey, 'He missed second base, too. Such was the story of Marv and the Amazins.'

I remember watching opening day 2000 with my mom. They lost a tough game and my mom lamented, 'this year is over', on opening day! It reminded me of a fan, Karl Ehrhardt the sign man, held up a banner after an opening game loss that read 'WAIT TILL NEXT YEAR.' Mom was probably a bigger fan than I am because she would stick with the team through thick and thin. 20 games out of first place with 10 games to go, mom would cheer just as loud as if it were the world series. There would be no cussing coming from mom no matter what the situation, unlike me wwho curses the umpire if he calls the first pitch of the game a ball. ' Are you *#*@! Kidding me you stupid *###@#!' Mom not only doesn't cuss but, if she's reading a book and a cuss word appears, she skips over it. She won't even talk about that large cement thing holding back the water in Nevada, The Hoover Dam . My mom is a real saint and the best mom in the world.

After lunch we take a walk down to the beach. There's a long stairway you walk down to get you there. The house is high on a cliff, and you know how I feel about steep drop-offs. We climb our way down and just take in the scenery.

We spend the rest of the afternoon taking in the beautiful scenery and taking a dip in the pool. Brad comes out, with all his muscles, in a Speedo bathing suit, which just thrills my daughter. Not to be outdone, she comes out in a bikini that was made out of a piece of material the size of a handkerchief.[Why does anyone have a handkerchief anyway ? Why would you want to save your snot, then put the handkerchief in the washing machine and let the snot travel from it to one of your good shirts?] Well at least this bikini covers her behind, somewhat. I can see I will be spending the afternoon sucking in my gut, with Brad looking so buff.

Today is the kind of day when life just seems perfect. The weather is perfect, the scenery is gorgeous and I'm with the people I love. A little piece of heaven on earth. Mom is reading a book, my daughter is having a super time with Brad and my nieces are frolicking in the pool.

Tuesday morning and it's time to tee it up at the Engineers Club in Roslyn.. It is one of the oldest clubs in America, and it is very exclusive. The only problem is we lost one of our foursome, Brad! It seems he would rather go to the city with my daughter, so it will just be the three of us, me Henry and Henrys brother Harris, a nice guy and a good golfer. He is a 4 handicap.

We meet Harris at the course and go to the driving range to hit a bucket of balls. Henry and me are evenly matched, but he has the upper hand on his home course.[I can't wait to get these two upstate on that unpredictable Stamford course. I might even beat Harris up there.] Harris has a good swing, but he is deadly around the greens. We are just about finished warming up when the worst thing that can happen, happens. Darrell!

His father owns the firm Henry works for. He is the most obnoxious person you will ever meet, but put him on a golf course and the obnoxiousness increases tenfold.

' Henry how ya doing buddy. Long time no see. My dad treating you good? Ah, who cares. Playing golf today? Darrell asks.

' Yes, we are teeing off in two minutes.' Henry replies.

' Patrick, how the hell are you? Too bad your wife dumped you. I hear she was banging some big fat bastard behind your back. What a bitch! Well at least now there will be enough food around for you to eat. And how's that beautiful daughter of yours, Pamela. Man she's hot!

My inclination is to beat him to a pulp right here and now, but I don't want to screw up Henrys job. The funny thing, Darrell's father is such a great guy and he would probably give Henry a raise if I beat his son up. He knows what an asshole Darrell is.

' Darrell, it's been a long time. Find a job yet?' I snidely remark.

'Ha ha . I'm a scratch golfer now. I make more money playing golf in a day than you make humping milk crates in a month. How is that job anyway. Oh yeah I heard they canned your ass. Ha ha.' He says.

' Yeah, unfortunately my dad didn't own the business. But it was such a pleasure to see you again.' I quip.

' I only see three of you. You don't have a fourth? He asks.

' He's on his way, should be here in a mater of minutes.' I lie.
' Well if he doesn't show I'd be glad to fill in for him.'

' He called a little while ago and said he can't make it. Why don't you join us.' Henry asks as I cringe at the thought of spending the next four hours with this idiot.

' Thanks, let's let em' rip. What are we playing for?'

Darrell is a very good golfer, but he cheats on every shot. He would cheat if you were playing a penny a hole. My golf day is now officially ruined.

' We're just out here to have fun' no betting.' Henry states.

' Come on. Me and you against Harris and Patrick. Only a $50 Nassau, I know you're out of work . We'll even give you 3 a side. $10 dollar birdies, and greenies, and $50 dollar eagles.

A Nassau is a game broken down into three parts. The first nine holes is one match, the second nine holes is another match and the overall total is the third match. Each hole counts as one. If team A wins 5 holes on the front nine and team B wins four holes, then team A would win the front nine 1 up and win $50 dollars. If team B wins 6 holes and team A wins three holes on the back nine then team B would win the back nine by 3 holes and would also win the overall total 10 to 8,up 2 and win $50 dollars for the back nine and $50 dollars for the overall score and win an additional $50 dollars. Team B would then win $100 minus $50 lost on the front side for an overall win of $50. But if one team were to win all three bets, they would win $150. Add in $10 greenies, which a team wins for being the closest ball to the hole on a par three. The player must then sink the ball in two putts or less and win the money. Most courses have 4 par threes so that's another $40 dollars you can lose. The other monies that can be won or lost are the birdies and eagles. A birdie is shooting one stroke under par and an eagle is shooting two strokes under par, so on a bad day you can conceivably lose $200 dollars plus. That's a half a weeks I have to do nothing to make that much on unemployment. I know I can't afford this.

'Sure. Lets do it,' I blurt out stupidly playing right into his hands, but his arrogance annoys me so much I want to show him.

' That's a little steep maybe we should play a $10 Nassau.' My brother- in- law tries to negotiate on my behalf .

' Well, I guess if Patrick can't afford it than that's ok.

$50 Nassau it is! I state my conviction.

We make our way to the first hole. We flip a coin to see which team will tee off first. We win the toss and Harris tells me to start us off. The first hole is a par four with a slight dog leg left. I tee my ball and go through my pre-shot routine when Darrell interrupts.

"Good luck. I hope you don't shank your first shot of the day!"

He's already trying to get under my skin. I say nothing and rip one right down the middle.

"Whoa, that's the first time I've ever seen you hit a fairway." Darrell cracks.

Harris follows my beauty with one of his own. Darrell gets up and scorches one that pisses on my ball as it sails on by it. 300 hundred yards later it comes to a stop in the middle of the fairway.

"I missed that one a little." He says. What an asshole!

Henry hits a good one and we are off on the first of eighteen torturous holes. We win the first hole, lose the second and halve the next three. Harris is even par, Darrell and I are one over and Henry is three over.

Darrell bangs another one long and straight on the sixth hole. Henry hits his first bad drive into the ruff. Harris hits his usual ball, straight and true. I tee up my ball, address it and start my backswing. At the peak of my swing, Darrell, who was standing directly in my sight, starts walking. I lose my focus and top my drive. I'm lucky to get a hundred yards out of it. By the time I finish my swing, Darrell is half way to his ball. I want to throw my club at him, but this is an exclusive country club, so I hold my temper. I get to my ball and Darrell is at his ball, two hundred yards ahead of me. He's not supposed to be ahead the other players. I wave at him and tell him to watch out today.

"I'm standing in the middle of the fairway, the safest place to be with you hitting." He yells back.

I take out my three wood and take dead aim at Darrell. Lord, let me hit this shot good, even if it's the last good shot I hit, I say looking up to heaven. I take the club back and make the sweetest swing I ever made. The ball is bee-lining right at Darrell's as the ball whizzes by him. Henry and Harris giggle at the sight of Darrell scrambling.

Golfers in the next fairway, who know and also despise Darrell, start applauding my shot. "Hey asshole, maybe you won't get out in front of everyone now!" One of
them say.

"You'd better be quiet or I won't let you clean my clubs after the round." Darrell yells back.

"What are you talking about? You don't clean your clubs; you just steal a new set when yours get dirty!' Another one of the foursome says.

I'm walking down the fairway with the biggest smirk on my face. 'Thank you Lord," I say quietly but out loud, but I was only kidding about it being my last good shot of the day." He hears me again as I sink my wedge shot for a birdie.

Darrell shanks his wedge, flops a chip shot and three putts for a double bogey. We win the hole, with an extra ten dollars for the birdie.

I'm playing my best golf in spite of Darrell. We halve the next two holes and we are one up in the match, going to the ninth hole. I am one over par and Darell is three over. If we win or tie this hole we will have won the front and be up fifty dollars plus the ten for the birdie. I am teeing off first. The hole is a par three. I choose a five iron. I address the ball and start my backswing. Darrell had shifted over and was now directly behind the ball. At the top of my backswing, Darrell decides to do the Curly shuffle. I know this shouldn't bother me but I am distracted. I complete my swing and hit a duck hook way left of the green. Only the patience of Job keeps me from wrapping my club around his throat.

"Oh, too bad. You had a good front nine going." Darrell taunts.

I say nothing. The others hit their balls, each one hitting the green.

Darrell's ball lands two feet from the pin.

I hit a pretty good second shot, on the green about twenty feet away. I two putt for the bogey. Harris and Henry two putt for pars. Darrell one putts for a birdie. They win the hole and halve the front. With Darrell's birdie and greeny they win ten dollars on the front side. Darrell and I are tied at two over.

On the way over towards the tenth tee, I whisper in Darrell's ear, "I don't know what shot or what putt I'll do it on, but I will stick an M-80 up your ass on your downswing. You'd better be ready,'' and I walk away,

Darrell tees off first on the tenth hole. He starts his backswing, and just as he is about to take his downswing, he stops and looks over at me, expecting me to scream.

"Well?" he says.

I ignore him and look away. He then starts his swing again, appearing distracted and pulls the ball dead left, deep into the woods.

" I think you'd better hit a provisional ball. You may not find that" his partner Henry tells him.

"No problem. I know this course like the back of my hand. I'll find it."

The rest of us tee off and hit three good drives. I tee off last and after I hit my ball, Darrell goes sprinting toward the area his ball went in. He gets to the woods and after two seconds he finds "his ball" two feet into the woods with a perfect line to the green.

"I got it! It must have hit a tree!" he claims.

The three of us look at each other knowing it never could be where he found it. Harris just shrugs his shoulders. We end up halving a hole we should have won. The rest of the back nine goes the same way. He finds his ball "just" in bounds on another hole when we all saw the ball go ten feet out. The good thing is I'm in his head and he's waiting for me to scream on every shot.

We come to the eighteenth hole all square in the match, even though we should be up at least two holes. Darrell and I are "even" (I use this term loosely), five over for the day. Harris is two over and Henry is ten over. The eighteenth hole is a tough finishing hole. It's a long hole and the green is treacherous. Five putting it is not out of the question.

Darrell tees off first and he knows I'm running out of time to get him back. He rushes up to the tee and takes a quick swing to beat me to the punch. He hits a pretty good drive, just off the fairway left. (At least it's just off the fairway until he gets to it). The rest of us hit good tee shots down the fairway. Our second shots and the putting will decide this match. If we tie the hole, no money is won or lost. If either team wins the hole, they will win a hundred fifty dollars that I can't really afford now. Henry goes first and he hits a good shot to the edge of the green. I'm up next. Darrell is in close proximity to me. I know he has one last trick in his bag. I focus on the ball and try to drown out anything he does. I start my swing and sure enough he strikes again, this time dropping his whole bag. This time I ignore the clanking of clubs and hit a beauty; a high shot just left of the flag. It comes to a stop ten feet from the hole. Henry wants to go over and choke Darrell to death but is held back by Harris.

"Good shot. I'm sorry but I lost control of my bag," he says.

"I'm glad you did! The sound of the bag dropping made me jerk the ball left of where I was aiming. I probably would have hit it out of bounds if you didn't do that" I jest. "You want me to do the same thing for you?"

He knows its coming and now he approaches his ball cautiously. He takes his swing and barely hits the ball and sends a screaming liner down the fairway. It's the worst shot of the day, but they say it's not what the shot looks like but where it ends up. This piece of shit rolls all the way to the green, twenty feet from the pin. After cursing up a storm because of his miss, he now sees the unbelievable results.

"With the wind blowing I figured I would just run the ball up. Not bad."

He lies.

Harris hits his shot to about twenty feet left of the pin. It's now a putting contest. Henry is first and hits a good putt, a foot from the hole. We concede the next putt to him. He gets a par. Harris is next up and almost makes the putt, stopping an inch from the hole. He taps in for par. Now the match is up to me and Darrell. He putts first. He looks over to me and I give him a look that says now's the time. He hangs over the ball for an eternity, trying to offset my yell. He finally pulls the trigger and sends the ball toward the hole. The ball is on line but it's coming in hot. The ball hits the hole and spins out, about two and a half feet away.

"Aw, that was a perfect putt. How could it not go in," He walks over to the ball and picks it up.

"Whoa, what are you doing?" Harris asks.

"You gave Henry a putt from the same distance." He cries. "Henry's was a foot away, yours is three feet away."

He bends down and places a coin a foot and a half from the hole. Henry walks over to the coin and drops it back to where it belongs.

"It wasn't that far away. I almost made that putt."

I am up next. If I make the putt we win a hundred fifty clams, but clutch putting is not my forte. It's not my fifte or sixte either. I've been known to knock three foot putts twelve feet past the hole with the pressure on. I line up the putt and try to make a good put with my hands and knees shaking. Somehow, I make a good put, inside a foot. Henry concedes the putt.

"Don't give him that, he'll miss it." I lean over and tap the putt in. "Happy?" I say.

The whole ball of wax now depends on Darrell's putt. He makes it and the match is a wash. Miss it and we win. He knows this is my last shot at him. He steps away from the ball..

"Patrick is going to scream when I go to putt. He told me so. That wouldn't be fair." He cry babies.

Harris jumps in. I assure you he won't do that, right Patrick?"

I shake my head, no. Then I look over to Darrell and raise my eyebrows.

He gets behind his ball and checks for any break. He lines himself up and just as he is making his stroke, the fire alarm from the local fire department goes off, the siren to signal the time, twelve noon. He jerks his putt a foot wide of the hole. Game,set, match.

"I'll take my one fifty in big bills if you don't mind." I say grinning. "That's not fair. I should get a do over! He groans.

"Tough luck! I'm sure you would have made it. Now pay up!"
"I left my wallet in the locker room. I'll go get it."

"I saw you put it in your golf bag, bottom zipper." I say. He opens the bottom zipper and finds the wallet.

"Oh yeah, I forgot" Lying again.

He would have gone to the locker room and I wouldn't have seen him for years. He reaches into the wallet and pulls out the spoils. He goes to hand it to Harris, but I intercept.

"I'll take tat off your hands." I say as I grab the dough from his hand . "Probably the first time you've ever held this much money in your hands at one time! You probably don't have this much money in your savings account." He says.

"You're right, but I'm going to frame this and put it on my wall. It's the first time you actually paid a debt up. "Next time, maybe we won't play around noon."

"That's the only way you won. That's like cheating." "And of course, you would never cheat!" I say.

I grab my money and my clubs and head to the car, hoping I don't see Darrell anytime soon, like in my lifetime.

The ride back to Summit was mostly uneventful, except for me warning Brad not to use my daughter. If he wanted to stay with Pamela he'd better break it off with Maryjane. I said this to protect my daughter (but it wouldn't hurt to have Maryjane become available.)

We arrive in Summit around 5 o'clock', the middle of happy hour at the Rock. The place is hopping for midweek. I guess they are here to watch the games, Yanks at Baltimore and the Mets taking on the Dodgers, with Joe Torre as their manager. The Yanks got rid of him, sort of. They made him an offer he couldn't accept. Now he's out in La La land and probably better off . The Dodgers were in third place, 5 games under .500, but I bet he hasn't been called into the bosses office yet.

The place is pretty noisy but I still hear the unmistakable sound of Donald Nosticks' laugh/cough/choking in the rear pool room. We sit down at the bar and MJ wanders over. She brings with her our favorite libations. She seems happy to see us but not overly excited to see Brad. I kind of thought that after not seeing him for a couple of days that she would run around the bar and give him a big hug, but no. They say women have some sort of intuition, maybe they do. She asks about our time downstate and. we fill her with the details, well at least most of them. Brad said he would tell her when the time is right.

I take a big gulp of my Genny and scan around the bar and see that it's mostly the regulars, just like at Cheers. I head to the rear of the bar to go to the head . I pass through the pool room on the way and Donald Nostick motions me over.

"Hey, Patrick how you doin.'" He says as he grabs hold of me and kisses me on both cheeks. Not being up on mob symbolism, I'm hoping that this is a friendship kiss, not the kiss of death. He gurgles/laughs/coughs and says he would like to talk to me. I tell him sure, but I have to piss like a racehorse. More of the L/G/C.

"I'll be right back,' I reply. I walk briskly to the Mens room wondering whether I should take a leak or run like hell out the back door. What would he want with me.

Bump someone off? Rob a bank? Become a pimp? Maybe that could be fun. I would get a big giant hat and long overcoat and drive around in a purple Cadillac. Maybe I did something wrong and he did give me the' kiss of death'. I lift my hand and notice it's shaking. I reach down with my quivering hand to close my zipper and nearly sever my penis, which is hard to do in it's present state of shrinkage. All right, I tell myself, you're over reacting. He probably just wants to know how I marinate my steak. I walk hesitantly toward the Don.

' So what can I do for you my friend?' I inquire. ' Not here, lets go upstairs to my office.' He says.

Now I am scared. I hope he doesn't ask Lucky Louie[his muscle] to join us.

Lucky Louie was anything but lucky. He's been to prison 8 times, once for jaywalking [of course taking the jaywalking ticket from the police officer and crumpling it up and smooshing it in the officers face didn't help.] He wasn't the brightest bulb in the pack. In fact he would make Freido Corleon look like Einstein. Whenever he goes to the race track to bet the horses, he not only loses but so many of the horses he picks have died before reaching the finish line that Donald Nostick has forbidden him to bet on any of the same horses that he bets on. But Louie is as loyal as they come. Four of his prison sentences have been because he took the blame for something Don had done. He would do" anything" for Don.

We head upstairs, alone. He is gasping for air every step we take. My luck he'll have a heart attack and I'll have to break the news to Lucky Louie. Or maybe someone is waiting in the room. It's amazing how the mind can conger up all of these scenarios, mostly ones that you see in movies. If I were watching this same situation happening in a movie right now I would be saying no one is dumb enough to go upstairs alone with him. But here I go.

We get to the room. The door is shut. He unlocks the door and motions for me to enter. [Again the mind wanders and I picture someone behind the door about to hit me with the butt of a pistol. I think I watched too many Cagney movies. "Yeah, you're the dirty rat who killed my brother"].

I proceed into the room and so far my head isn't getting whacked.

" Have a seat. Sit down, sit down. I've been hearing a lot of nice things about you from people I trust. I've got an offer for you. I know that you're out of work so I got to thinking. I need someone I can trust to run the Jailhouse Rock Inn for me. You know, do the books, tend bar, hire and fire people, things like that. This place is my baby, my place to get away from business down state. I can't get up here as much as I'd like to so I would be very appreciative of any one who took care of my baby. I'll give you a thousand a week cash, off the books, and then you can keep collecting the unemployement checks. What do you think?"

" I'm honored that you would trust me with the business, but I have no experience in running a bar. Besides you have Maryjane. I think she knows the business better than me and would make a fine manager." I reply.

[a laugh/cough…but only a short one] " Maryjane is one of the people that told me to hire you! What are you schtucking her?' he raises his eyebrows Groucho Marxesque.

"Maryjane really told you that?" I asked.

"Yeah, she said she would love to work under you. And a bunch of others said you were the man for the job. So what do you think? " he asks.

" Wow, I don't know. This offer has taken me by surprise. I'll need a little time to think about it." I said.

" People don't normally make me wait for an answer, I am known for closing deals immediately, deals a lot more complicated than this. I'll make it fifteen hundred a week off the books. Try it for a while, if you don't like it, no problem. When can you start?" he demanded.

" You drive a hard bargain but I guess I'll give a chance. But I will have to stop my unemployment, cause that would be illegal." I say.

This time I thought he was really going to have a heart attack. The laughing/ choking/hacking was at its best. It's like it's the funniest thing he has ever heard. His face was turning purple. After a while he started to calm down and his face went back to its original color of beet red. " You crack me up. You collect your unemployment. No one will know any better. You're funny. He finishes.

"I'll need a couple of days to get some things together. How about if I start on Monday?" I ask.

" Great. Good to have you aboard!" What am I getting myself into?

We make our way downstairs to the bar. I go back to my seat next to Brad and down the rest of my Genny.

" Another,please! And give me a shot of Bacardi!" I state.

" A shot of rum? MJ asks quizzically. What are you a pirate?"

" Arghh! Want to touch my peg?" I ask. A groan from MJ and a laugh from the rest chimes in.

" With that small peg you have you would be walking on a slant." Mike ' You wouldn't say that if I shoved it up your ass!" I retort.

' What's with this hommo talk .WE don't want no queers in here. Sgt. Bill jests.

" Enough Bullshit. I want to introduce the new manager of the Jailhouse Rock Inn. Patrick is the man! You the Man!" Donald announces.

A mixture of cheers and groans fill the bar.

" Anybody Fs' with, him Fs' with me! Donald threatens.

" No problem Donald. As long as he doesn't try to stick anything up my ass, Mike shouts.

" You mess with him and you'll wish it were only a peg up your ass." Don replies.

The bar laughs a nervous laugh, wondering if I were a made man. They only knew me a short time. Now it's the crowd getting paranoid.

Maryjane throws me a knowing smile . "Welcome, now that you're my boss maybe I will touch your peg. I may even polish your peg." She offers.

"Are you trying to get a raise out of me? We can probably work something out." I say.

" Are you giving my money away already! At least you can wait till I'm not around." Don says.

" Your money is safe with me." I tell him. I think I'm starting to like this boss stuff

I don't stay long at the Rock. I start to think about the job I just accepted and want to be alone. I walk back home, grab a Genny from the fridge and go out to my car to listen to the Mets game. They are three games up on the Phillies. The game has already started and the Mets are up one to nothing over the Dodgers in the third inning.

It starts to sink in that I am going to start making good money again, even more than the milk company, all tax free, plus unemployment. Most people wouldn't bat an eye taking money off the books and still collecting unemployment but I feel guilty. I know to Don this is like stealing a candy bar from Hershey's warehouse, but I've always followed the law. The paranoia in me makes me feel like the F.B.I. is in the bushes across the street watching and charting my every move. They will tap my phone to intercept my call to the unemployment office and when the recording warns me I "must" be telling the truth or face prosecution to the fullest' they will wait for me to lie and break down my front door. I'm not too paranoid, am I. Like the F.B.I. has nothing better to do, with fighting terrorism and all, than catch some one stealing $405 from the government! Boy I don't know why I'm so paranoid.

I light up a joint to chase my beer down and turn my attention back to the ballgame. Both teams just seem to be going through the motions. It's the fifth inning and neither team has a hit. The Mets scored their run on a walk, a stolen base,a throwing error and a fielder's choice. Oliver Perez has eight strikeouts and is cruising along, but we all know he will reach 100 pitches and the wheels will fall off. Besides, Met pitchers don't pitch no hitters.

I start thinking about the job again. It was kind of nice not having to go to work. I know I can't afford to retire yet but it sure was nice getting a taste of it. But if you have to work, I guess working at a bar doesn't sound so bad.

I drink a couple of more beers, finish listening to the Mets lose 6-5 eat my 12 o'clock meal and go to bed planning an early stop at the Rock.

I wake up bright and early the next morning [10 o'clock]. That damned rooster and his cock-a-doodling is starting to drive me nuts. I wonder if they are an endangered species and would I go to jail if I had him wacked. Or maybe I could send over a couple of my neighbors cats to rough him up and quiet him down. Listen to me, I haven't even started working for the mob and I'm already thinking like them.

The Rock opens at around ten or eleven, whenever the bartender gets there. MJ is opening up today. I have never been there this early, so I figure I'll drop in and learn a little about the routine. I walk through the door around 11 o'clock and MJ is behind the bar straightening things up.

' What's a guy got to do to get a beer around here,' I loudly joke.

Mary looks up and sees me and goes back to what she's doing without acknowledging me. Her usual beautiful smiling face has been replaced with a frown.

" Something I said or did? Maryjane I wouldn't have taken this job if I knew it would bother you.' I say

She turned toward me and she didn't look happy.

"Oh, now you care about my feelings? After you stab me in the back?" she

groans.

' Maryjane, I told Don that he should give you the job, but he told me you said he

should give the job to me. If he didn't tell the truth I will tell him I changed my mind and you can have the job."

'Don't try to play stupid with me. You know I'm not talking about the job.' ' Really, I don't know."

'Does Brad and your daughter ring a bell?"

' Oh that. Maryjane, I swear I had nothing to do with it. I actually had an argument with Brad when I found out. I told him to leave my daughter alone. I don't want my daughter being played by Brad while he's with you."

" Sure. And what did he say?"

" That's between you and him. I imagine he has spoken to you, since you know about it. Did he say I arranged it or something? "

" No, he just told me he doesn't want to see me anymore."

" I'm sorry, but I didn't have anything to do with this, besides bringing Brad with me downstate and introducing him to my whole family, not just my daughter. It never occurred to me that this would happen.'

" You know me and Brad were on the outs, so this didn't shock me. I just thought maybe you helped it along. I'm sure you are really hate that me and Brad are done."

" I'd be lying if I said I was, but I would never hurt you in any way, even if it benefited me."

" I didn't think you would, but I only know you a short time. I want to see if you are what you seem."

"I am. You'll see. Is all forgiven?"

" All's forgiven. Did you really tell Don to put me in charge?" "Yes, and the offer still stands."

"Thanks, but no thanks. I don't like dealing with the bullshit and the paperwork." " Then it's settled. I'll do it. You're going to have to teach me the ropes."

" You don't know what to do with the ropes?"

" Wouldn't that be considered sexual harassment?"

" Ooh, I like the way you say that . You can harass me any way you'd like."

Now all I can think about is her ass. I got a feeling this job is going to be better than sticking a pin in my eye.

She shows me around the joint pointing out little things I'd need to know. She brings me up to my new office. The office is next to Dons office. It has a bed and a window, that's it, and by the looks of the bed, it seems like it's getting a lot of use. I have a feeling I'm taking away the room that's rented by the hour, if you know what I mean.

"Don said to tell you to make a list of what you need and he'll get it for you. Or as he put it, it will fall off a truck."

"For starters, I'll need a cleaning lady, a desk, computer, comfortable chair and a buxom secretary. "

" I'll see what I can do. But you can forget the buxom secretary."

" Aw, schucks. I always wanted one of them, named Candy or something like that."

" I'll be all the candy you'll ever need."

I look over at the bed and give it a thought, but not so soon. " I think maybe I'll keep the bed in here."

"Good idea." Oh that smile.

Chapter 14
To New Beginnings

I spend the next couple of days observing the Rock. Don has already sent his workers over to decorate my office. They've done a great job. New carpeting, a beautiful desk and leather chair with rollers on the bottom, and a new bed in the corner complete with sheets, pillows, and bedspread. There's a fresh coat of paint on the walls and curtains on the window. I think I could live here. I find out that MJ was behind the decorating.

I am gearing up for my first day on the job. Monday comes quickly and I am no longer unemployed, technically. I call for a meeting with all the employees of the Rock. The cook, two bartenders, not counting MJ and two waitresses fill the staff. I take them to my office one at a time to hear their likes and dislikes of the job and to add some input.

The cook, or chef as he prefers, is Phil Boyardee. He's originally from France, or so he claims. His French accent sounds more like Brooklynites. He tells me that he worked in a fine Italian restaurant, but Don informed me that he worked at Michelangelo's Pizzeria, owned by Don. He was flipping pies when Don brought him upstate, to keep him from giving every paycheck to bookies and hookers, and put him in charge of the Rock. He handles the kitchen well. The menu is your typical bar menu, burgers, wings, and so forth. The dinner menu adds steak and pork chops. Once a week he has a special pasta night. The patrons think it's great even though he just uses Aunt Millie's jar sauce and packaged meatballs.

" Hi Phil, have a seat. I've eaten here a few times, you do a good job. Is there anything I can help you with?" I inquire.

"No, I like working for Mr. Nostick. He takes care of me." He says this giving me a look that says just leave me alone.

" I just thought that you being a chef and all that you might want to expand the menu."

His eyes light up and he sits up straight in his chair. "That would be great. I have some ideas but do you think Mr. Nostick will let me?"

"Donald has put me in charge of the whole joint. What I say goes. I was thinking of adding pizza to the menu on Friday nights. Do you think you can handle that?"

" Yes sir! I will make the best pizza north of Manhattan." " Good, I think this is going to work out well."

" Me, too.'

Next up I bring in the two waitresses, Molly Purton and Tina Rae. Molly has been working the day shift at the Rock for thirty years. She is 62 years old but you wouldn't take her for a day under 80. The years haven't been kind to her face. Her wrinkles have wrinkles, but she's a real pip. They are spunky as they come. Tina on the other hand has only been here since the end of the school year. She graduated third in her class, out of ten. The local school went from kindergarten to twelfth grade. She had that upstate kind of pretty. By that I mean she was the prettiest girl in the school, but there are only 6 girls to compete against. Blonde straight hair, thin body except for a little pudge in the middle, due to her penchant for beer drinking.

Molly pipes up first. " I've seen you around here and I know you're a nice guy and everything, but there ain't nothin' you can teach me or show me I ain't seen before. I've been servin' burgers in here since you were in high school chasin' young pussy around tryin' to get your dick wet. And keep your hands to yourself 'cause my pussy is not up for grabs." [thank goodness because just the thought made my stomach turn.]

" No worry Molly, I'll try to control myself, though it won't be easy." " Maybe after work someday." She chimes in while batting her eyes. " No, a rules a rule and I will respect you." [Me and my big mouth.] " Tina, what can I do to make your day go by easier?"

" I'm just happy to be here working with you. I've also seen you around and I think you're handsome. And you can grab my pussy any time you want!" she blurts out shocking me as my face turns beet red.

" Now what kind of talk is that coming from a young lady like you? If I ever told your dad you said that he'd lock you in the closet and throw away the key." Molly retorts.

" You can bring up your pussy, why can't I bring up mine?" Tina asks.

" 'Cause your pussy is alive. Talkin' about my pussys' like talkin' about road kill.

I'm lucky it still pisses."

" All right ladies, enough talk about your anatomies. If there are ever any problems, I want you to know you can always talk to me. Thanks for coming in."

They left the room squabbling about vaginas. I've never been so conflicted in my sexual thoughts. One second I imagine a young pristine vagina and I feel the beginning of arousal and then 'BANG" the image of Molly's road kill. Boy, I may have some strange dreams tonight.

I bring in the bartenders, MJ, Martha, and Libby. Martha is _____ ending. She's on her second marriage. Her first husband _____ in a hunting accident and is just trying to make ends _____ azy no good bum of a 2nd husband lies on the couch _____ farting. She has a seven-year-old son from her 1st _____ protect him from his mean stepdad. She's thirty _____ te good-looking. Libby is also thirty years old and _____ od looking anywhere on the planet. 70 pounds _____ her teeth, all" 42" of them, point more ways than a _____ traffic cop. The saddest part of it is that as fat as she is, _____ ts and no ass. But according to MJ, she gets laid every night _____ ferent guys.

Men have no defense or shame when it comes to pussy. A pussy is the strongest thing in the world. Men give up kingdoms for it. But before I would put my penis anywhere near her I would have to drink Canada dry.

"Is there anything I can help you, ladies, with?" I say

' You could bring more customers in so we can make more tips." Libby says " I'm going to try my best. How can we liven up the joint?"

' Live bands always bring in good crowds." MJ says.

" And how bout a happy hour with drink specials? Maybe we can get the locals in here a little earlier.' Martha adds.

" I'll see what I can do. You girls just keep up the good work." Well, I'm not Donald Trump, but I'm going to try my best.

Things run pretty smoothly in my first week as boss.MJ and I haven't started dating yet. I figured I would give her some time between Brad and me. Brad on the other hand is spending more time downstate than up. Brad and Pamela are hitting it off pretty well.

Happy hour is a big success. Now we can get the locals drunker sooner in the day, and they still stay till closing. Pizza Friday is a smash. Phil does make the best pizza around. Most of the regulars have never tasted a real pizza before. They thought Dominos Pizza, sauce, and some unknown cheese on cardboard were real pizzas. Phil also adds baked ziti to the menu. This time he makes the sauce from scratch and it's not bad. After tasting his first batch I decided to add some spices to the sauce when Phil isn't around. I wouldn't want to insult a great French chef.

Donald shows up the following Friday and is ecstatic to see a large crowd. Word of pizza Friday is spreading quickly and we are getting people from surrounding towns to come and taste for themselves.

"Good crowd tonight Patrick. You are off to a good start. I see a lot of people eating pizza. Where are they getting it from?" Don asks

" Phil! We decide to have a "Pizza Friday. Here try a piece." I grab a slice of Mike's plate.

"Hey, whattaya think your doing." Mike protests.

" Aw, shut up and drink your beer." Don barks. " Pretty good! Almost as good as my place. I have to go pat Phil on the back. Hey, good call with the pizza"

"Thanks, but Phil is the man. "

I signal Martha over and tell her to replace Mike's pizza with two slices.

" Now your talking. And make them with pepperoni on top. And extra cheese." " Don't push your luck. By the way, I haven't seen your brother lately. What's

up?" I ask.

' The stupid bastard shot himself in the head with a nail gun. Pried it out with a claw hammer. Sick puppy."

" Is he all right?"

" Yeah, seems it touched a piece of his brain, I didn't think that was possible being that it can't be all that big. They're keeping him in the hospital for observation."

" Tell him I hope everything is all right. Bring him up a pizza, on me." " Thanks, but he'll be lucky to get a slice."

Donald returns from the kitchen happier than I've ever seen him." That Phil is all right. He even made baked ziti. Not bad. I knew I made a good move hiring you."

Business is booming. Friday and Saturday are two of the most profitable days the Rock has ever seen. People are asking us to make pizza every day, but for now, we'll make them crave it.

It was a great weekend.

After a couple of weeks, I am starting to adjust to the long hours. At the end of a slow Tuesday night, I go behind the bar to take the money from the till and do the night's receipts. Maryjane is cleaning up the bar as I squeeze through to get to the register. It's a tight fit and my groin rubs gently across her buttocks.

" Hey, watch it, big boy." She says. ' I'm always watching it." I reply.

" You could have fooled me. It seems like you have no interest in me. Ever since Brad broke up with me you seem to be avoiding me."

" Between taking over the Rock and wanting to give you some time to get over Brad I've been keeping my distance. I'm sorry I made you feel that way, but if you have any doubt about the way I feel, just look what my rubbing against your ass did to me." I step back and show her the pup tent in my pants.

' Did I do that?" she asks in her cutest little girly way.

" How would you like to come to my house and see my etchings?" I ask.

' Sounds interesting. What do you say we hurry up and close this joint up." MJ says.

"You got it!" I say as I hurry upstairs to do the books.

We lock up the Rock and start heading to my place. It's a beautiful night, the kind you don't get to appreciate downstate. There are a million stars in the sky, or billions and billions of stars as the late Carl Sagan use to say. Downstate you are lucky if you see a tenth as many stars, even on a clear night. I reach over and grab Maryjane's hand. She is beautiful right down to her hands. She squeezes my hand and gives me a sexy glance. My heart starts to melt and my legs feel like jello.

We walk through the front door, unlocked as usual. I keep the place pretty clean and I have a thing for always making my bed.

"The house is pretty clean, for a bachelor's pad. I was a little afraid to open the door." MJ says.

" You think this is clean, you should see the bedroom." " You're smooth, but if you insist let's see it.

We make our way to the bedroom and as soon as we open the door, clothes are flying all over the place. It must be some kind of Guinness record for the fastest time for two people to undress. We are both so excited that we orgasm simultaneously within the first minute of intercourse. After cooling down for a minute or so, we begin again, this time at a slower pace. After two hours and three more orgasms each, we lay in bed exhausted.

" I love you, Patrick," Maryjane whispers.

I don't believe this is happening so fast. Not only did I swear I'd never get married, but I swore I would never even have a girlfriend. " I love you too, Maryjane."

There is something to be said about living on your own. You come and go as you please without having to explain anything to anyone. You watch what you want on T.V., read if you want, and listen to music as loud as you feel. When you put your wallet and keys down they stay right where you put them [even though I still lose them somehow.] Then there is the other side of the coin. Living with someone you get along with, sharing your everyday experiences, good morning and goodnight kisses. You also have someone to blame when you can't find your wallet and keys. Sleeping is no longer just sleeping, just as last night went with MJ touching me and holding me all night long. We spooned with each other { spooning is when you are both lying on your side facing the same direction and your bodies fit together snugly, like two spoons in the utensil drawer.} it's nice to have someone around to share life with, good or bad.

We wake up around ten o'clock and I am grateful to find that MJ isn't one of those early birds that like to get up at five a.m. I would love to say she looks even more beautiful in the morning, but she doesn't. No one does. She is still pretty but her hair is all over the place and her make is smeared. She turns over and gives me that look and I melt, gnarly hair and all.

" Good morning" she whispers as she smiles.

' And good morning to you. " I say as I lean over to give her a peck on her lips.

The peck turns into a full-blown tongue-swapping, morning breath and all. The kiss wakes up junior from his rest and now he is at attention and ready to do battle once again for the good of mankind. We pick up where we left off last night, but when we complete the act, my boys are starting to hurt. They haven't had to work this much overtime since Pamela Anderson appeared in Playboy.

We lay in bed and I urge a cigarette, even though I no longer smoke. ' Do you remember what I said last night?" She asks. " I meant it."

' Yes, I remember what you said last night. " Oh yeah, baby do that again. Oh yeah right there, lick me, faster, more, put your huge penis inside me now, more, go, go, you're the best!!!" " You mean that?' I just.

" Yeah, that. I meant everything I said, except for the part about the, how did you put it, large penis?

' No, huge penis.'

' Yeah, that's the part I exaggerated, greatly. You are the best!" " Thanks, so are you. I remember what you said. I believe I said it, too" " You did, but did you mean it?"

" I do love you!" " I love you, too!"

Maryjane gets her things together and heads to her house. Since this was unplanned she had nothing to wear at my place. We kiss and I tell her I will see her tonight at the Rock.

Time is moving quickly. I have been in charge of the Rock for a month now. Business is booming and people are begging for pizza to be made every day. Mary sleeps at my place most every night now. It's just a matter of time before I will ask her to move in with me. Donald calls every other day and is thrilled that the place is doing so well. The money he makes at the Rock isn't even pocket change compared to what he makes at his other business." Somehow, though he feels a certain pleasure in making an honest buck.

He always felt that he could make it in the real business world, and this is proof. He starts to feel that maybe it's time to go legit.

"Patrick, how's my baby doing? Don asks.

"According to last year's books, we have tripled the intake."

" Wow! [then the coughing, laughing choking takes place.] I might make a franchise out of these and put you in charge of them all."

' Thanks, but you're giving me too much credit. It's everybody chipping in." " Ah, that's what you say. I know!

Donald Nonstick is a nice guy. You do for him and he takes care of you. I always judge a person on how they treat me, not what others say. I hear he is a mob boss, but I haven't seen any real proof. Maybe the locals are making it up.

"Are you coming up this weekend ?"

" Yeah, I should be coming in late Friday night sometime." ' Good! I'll have a slice waiting for you."

'Yeah, yeah. You kill me! A slice."

On Tuesday I announced in the bar that Wednesday will be a special night. Karaoke and pizza!

You would think I announced that I would be serving fillet mignon the way they reacted. People like pizza, and who doesn't like karaoke? Maryjane gives me that look because she knows I love to sing.

"I guess we're going to see you up there singing, big boy," MJ says.

'Well if someone twists my arm, maybe. I like that big boy thing." I reply. "You'll always be my big boy."

" That's right, you hear that guys.""BIG" boy." I yell to the crowd. " MJ already told us, pee wee." Mike giggles.

" All right, time for a dickout. Who wants to challenge me? I'm only going to take out enough to beat you. Anyone?'

The sarge puts in two cents from the back. My boys had a dickout in a bar near the base in North Carolina. Ten of them lay their dicks on the bar. While they're measuring to see who the winner is, a queer comes in and with a big smile on his face says "I didn't know they were going to have a buffet?"

The place roars in laughter. Too bad Don isn't here. I could hear him hacking now.

The rest of the night goes fine. Lots of laughter and imbibing. The only problem is the Mets lose for the fifth straight game. Their lead over the Phillies is down to one game. Their manager, Willie Randolph, says they'll take it one game at a time. No worry. If he says so.

MJ and I close up joint and head over to my place. We watch a little T.V. and then retire to bed. Unbelievably, no sex tonight. Just as well. My penis needs a break. But I'm sure if MJ so much as sighs at me it'll be ready for more.

Chapter 15
Donald

It's only four o'clock on a Wednesday and the Rock is rocking. Phil can't keep up with the pizza orders. Everyone is waiting to sing karaoke, but the DJ isn't coming till seven o'clock. That doesn't stop the crowd from singing along with the jukebox. It feels like a Friday night. I wonder if everyone's bosses aloud to them to take off early in honor of the first karaoke and pizza Wednesday.

"Where's the DJ? Mike asks

"The DJ will start around seven. What are you worried about, you can't sing a lick." I say.

"I do a great Bruce Springsteen- BORN IN THE USA. I WAS BORN IN THE USA." Mike sings/screams.

"Anybody can sing like Bruce just like anybody can sing like Dylan. That's not singing. Let's hear you sing like Steve Perry of Journey. Now that's singing." I reply and then let out my best/worst impression of The Boss EVERYBODY HAS A HUNGRY HEART.

"We'll see how good you are later Mr. bigshot.

It's around 5:30 and the place is packed. Almost everyone in the Rock has pizza sauce on some part of their body or clothes. Maryjane shoots me a glance of approval knowing that I've got the Rock jumping. Her tips have more than doubled since I took over and Phil is asking me for more help in the kitchen.

"I can't cook regular meals when I am making a hundred pizzas an hour." He screams to me over all the noise. You can tell he's flustered but at the same time proud of his success.

'We'll look into getting you help tomorrow. Do the best you can. I don't think anyone cares. They're just having a blast."

Phil's doing a great job but he looks like a ghost, covered in flour from flipping the pies.

The DJ shows up around six. It takes about an hour to bring in all the equipment and set it up. The DJ, Danny Flowers [he claims that's his given name] is a throwback to the seventies. He dresses and combs his hair like John Travolta in Saturday Night Fever. He's in his mid-fifties and either he has Ronald Reagan-like hair or he is using gallons of Grecian Formula. Jet black, as dark as I have ever seen. He places his loose-leaf folders, filled with all the songs he has in his catalog, around the bar so people can pick their songs. There is a scramble for the books. It's starting to look like a rugby scrum.

"All right everyone, calm down! We are going to keep Danny here as long as it takes for everyone to sing as many songs as you'd like. Keep this up and I'm going to make you take numbers like they do at the deli section of the supermarket. CALM DOWN! The scurry continues so I make my way over and grab a book and hand it over to Turk Roberts, a distinguished gentleman in his eighties.

" Turk is going first" I proclaim. "Pick out a song and start us off."

Turk looks through the book and hands a piece of paper to Danny with his selection. Tony Bennett's " I Left My Heart in San Francisco." Danny begins the song and the Rock quiets down as Turk waits for his queue.

You would swear Tony Bennett himself were in the room. Turk hits every note, perfectly. YOUR GOLDEN SUN WILL SHINE FOR ME. He belts out the finish of the song and the place goes berserk.

Turk Roberts is no stranger to singing live. He sang with the Tommy Dorsey Band and other big bands of the day. He was never a headliner, sort of like an understudy on Broadway. When Sinatra and Bennett were on tour, he would sing with the bands. He even had a small hit " Hold Me All Day and Night." He never married but he was quite the ladies' man, and still was. Just like his singing career, he was like an understudy to the women. He had no Eva Gardner in his black book, but he had the numbers of some beautiful dames, and groupies from the nights he would sing with the big bands. He had a good life and never had to work too hard. A friend he made during his years of singing offered him a job at Leeman Brothers' financial firm. His job was to show prospective clients around town to have a good time. He would take them to dinner, golfing, and watch the big bands play. He would take them backstage to meet Tommy Dorsey and some of the big-time singers, even The Chairman of the Board himself, Francis Sinatra.

Turk got to know all the biggies from working with the bands and sometimes they let him pal around with them. With the contacts he had, he quickly became a favorite with the firm, especially the bigwigs in the company. They all wanted to meet the celebrities. He worked into his seventies because it wasn't really working and retired upstate in a house on Bear Lake in Summit. He enjoys coming to hang around the Rock and tell us stories of the good old days, and we enjoy listening.

After Turk brought down the place, no one wanted to follow him. "What happened to all the big-shot singers," I ask.

"I'll go," Mike rises and heads toward the DJ. Here comes Bruce I guess. "BORN IN THE U.S.A. I WAS BORN IN THE U.S.A." Mike blares out. If it's possible he even sounds worse singing into a mike, accompanied by music.

He gets a nice ovation from the ever-increasing crowd. He also restores confidence in the rest of the aspiring singers. There now was a large line of people wanting to follow Mike. I wave toward MJ and call her to sing next. She waves me off, embarrassed. But the rowdy crowd urges her. MARYJANE, MARYJANE! She relents and makes her way to the mike. She picks out a Judy Collins "Send in the Clowns." She does a great job and gets a roar from the crowd.

The night goes on with everyone getting a chance. I sing my staple song "And When I Die" by Blood Sweat and Tears. I loved their lead singer, David-Clayton Thomas' voice. I sang this song terrifically and got high fives leaving the mike.

The night goes into the wee hours with fun for all. The crowd is starting to dwindle when MJ motions me over. She hands me the phone and tells me it's Donald. I pick up and in the most joyful voice give him a big hello.

"Hello! What's up." I ask.

"It's Don. I want you to know I won't be coming up this weekend. I don't know, if, or when I'll be there again. Something's come up that has to be taken care of. I just want you to know how much I appreciate you taking care of my baby. I always want it to be in your hands. O.K.?

"Sure Don, anything I can help with?

He forces out the slightest laugh and says no.

I haven't known Donald that long but I've never heard him sound so concerned.

Kind of put a bummer on the night. "What did Don want? MJ inquires.

' I wish I knew. I wish I knew."

The next couple of weeks goes by smoothly. Karaoke/pizza Wednesday is a big hit to go along with Pizza Friday. More and more women are making their way to the Rock, to sing and dance during karaoke. The guys are loving this. You have never seen a bigger pack of wolves. Hooting and howling, dancing with the gals. Unfortunately, they haven't had much experience dancing before. Their dancing style reminds me of a T.V. show, no not Dancing with the Stars, Seinfeld. They all dance like Elaine. The one thing is they are all having fun. And I never thought I would hear them talk about anything but sports and cars. Mike was chatting with Loraine, an upstate pretty brunette with all her teeth and a nice body. I happen in on a conversation.

"Did you see the Sex and the City movie? It was so good. Loraine asks.

"Yes I did [he said yes instead of yeah] I thought it was as good or better than the show. That Mr. Big, I think he's great." Mike replies.

"What! You watch Sex and the City?" I gasp [he didn't realize I was right behind him.]

"Why of course I do! How do you not like watching hot babes getting laid every week?" he says. Loraine walks away when she hears his review.

"You son of a bitch! Why don't you mind your own business? I was probably gonna get laid tonight. Bastard! Mike screams.

"Just thought it was odd, you watching a show like that. Mr.Big, what a hunk!" I kid.

"I didn't say hunk. Get the hell out of here. Mike mumbles.

Another night goes by and I and MJ clean the joint up. The only one left in the bar is Libby. She is the only casualty of the booming business, especially the influx of women. She looks lost, waiting for the last man standing in the bar, but there is none.

'We're closing Libby. You have to go now." MJ tells her. I feel so bad. Maybe I should call Mike. I owe him one.

No word from Donald, and it's been two weeks. Something weird is going on.

It's been a couple of months now and the Rock is starting to become more like a real job. Long hours and hard work are starting to catch up to me. The money is fabulous but I don't need a lot to be happy. The biggest problem of all is not having a place to hang my hat at the end of a hard day's work. I used to go to the Rock for my fun, but now even when I go there on my off time it still feels like I'm working. I like Don and appreciate the way he praises my work, even though I haven't heard from him in three weeks. I think I would rather drive a truck.

On Friday I decided to give the others a break and open the Rock myself. It's another beautiful day in the mountains and I'm humming on my walk to the Rock. As I turn the corner and head up the street to the bar I notice a bunch of black stretch limousines parked all around the Rock. Don must be back in town, and he must have brought some buddies. I make my way through the front door and there are about thirty goombas all over the place, dressed in dark suits and having a ball. It's eleven in the morning and they are partying like it's Nineteen Ninety-Nine, to plagiarize the artist formally known as Prince, or is he back to just being Prince, whatever. I look around the place and I don't spot Donald. I walk up to one of the suits and ask him if he knew where Donald is. He starts cracking up.

" Hey Jimmy, I got a guy here who wants to know where Nonstick is." The suit yells out giggling like a schoolgirl.

"You must be Patrick! Come over here. I hear you do a great job around here" Jimmy points to a stool next to him. Come, come, let me meet the manager of my place.

Jimmy "The Tux" Esposito is dressed in a tuxedo, cummerbund, and all. Patent leather shoes and his hair slicked back like Pat Reilly, the ex-Knick traitor basketball coach, now of the Miami Heat. Johnny always wears a tuxedo, some say he even showers in it, but they just don't say it to his face. He started wearing tuxedos after attending the senior prom at his high school. It wasn't his prom, because he quit school in sixth grade so he could work for his uncle Vinny, the bookie. It was his girlfriend and present wife, Gina Barone's prom. When told he would need a tux for prom he scoped around town and found the tuxedo he liked. That night around two in the morning, he broke into the place, Tuxes are Us, on Staten Island, and tried the tuxedo on. He admired himself in the mirror and liked what he saw. Instead of just taking that tux, he decided to take them all. Shoes, ties, shirts, the whole shebang. And while he was at it he broke into the safe and stole all the cash. Ever since it's been tuxedos every day.

Jimmy is second in command behind Donald. He's young, only 35 years old and he made his way up the chain of command the brutal way. When he had to "take care of someone" it wasn't just a matter of business to him, he enjoyed it. Baseball bats, screwdrivers, ice picks, whatever he found in the near vicinity he would use to complete the job. And he wasn't in any hurry to finish, either. He made the poor saps linger until he felt he got every last confession out of them. He learned a lot of things in the closing minutes of these jobs. Some that saved his life. Found out his brother, Dino, was about to betray him during one "job." He used a gun on his brother which might sound like he took mercy on him, but NOT. He shot him right up his asshole which does the job, but it is the most painful and lingering death there is. Of course, he wore his tuxedo.

'So I hear you turned this place around, making good profit and all. Hi, my name is Jimmy Esposito. Glad to meet you." He says as he extends his hand.

"Patrick Hunneywell, nice to meet you. Are you here with Mr. Nostick?" I ask. "Donald Nonstick, he was a good man. Poor guy got killed during a carjacking by some moolinyans. A couple of days ago. They buried him this morning." Jimmy told me while trying to look sad.

It didn't make it in the Daily Ute, the local paper, but it was a big story downstate. Donald Nonstick was shot and killed leaving his Brooklyn pizzeria, in broad daylight. Also getting killed was his trusted sidekick "Lucky" Louie Zito. Four henchmen, none African American, as Johnny insinuated, jumped out of a parked car and ambushed the two of them while they were headed to Donald's car. Forty rounds of ammo were pumped into them, but "Lucky" Louie was able to get off one round, shooting and killing one Frankie Frangellino, a street punk working for none other than Jimmy "The Tux" Esposito. Many people saw the killings, but there were no witnesses if you know what I mean. Everyone the police asked sounded like Colonel Schultz from Hogan's Heroes T.V. show "I know nothing." There's an unwritten law in Brooklyn that when there's a "hit" of a mobster it is none of their business. There was a power struggle between Donald and Jimmy. Not anymore.

I sat back and hunched over on my stool like I'd been punched in the gut. Even though I gave Donald the benefit of the doubt, I knew deep inside he was a mobster.

Maybe I hoped he wasn't, so I wouldn't feel like I wasn't aiding the mob.

"Hey, someone gets this man a drink. One of the suits pours a large glass of Seagrams VO and hands it to me. I down it and almost puke. I start coughing and choking which makes all the suits start to laugh.

" He sounds like Nonstick," one of them, Johnny Remo says. This adds another layer of laughter.

" It's not so fucking funny that Don is dead! This is no fucking celebration! Have some respect." I yell after composing myself. The room goes dead silent. Everyone is staring at me and glancing at Jimmy for a reaction. Jimmy stares at me and then speaks up.

'Patrick here is right! Most of us here are where we are because Donald helped us.

We are in his bar, drinking his booze and yucking it up like a bunch of assholes! Let's have some respect. A moment of silence in Don's memory. And you better keep quiet! Everyone zips their lips as we all sit in silence. After a while, Jimmy speaks up. He raises his drink.

"In memory of Donald Nonstick may he rest in peace. Saluda." Everybody raises their glasses and murmurs Saluda.

Jimmy whispers to me 'Let's go someplace quiet."

The thought of him whacking me with a queue stick comes to mind. "I have an office upstairs. We can talk there." I say.

We head up to my office and I open the door and let him in.

"Nice place you got here. I recognize the rug. We got a warehouse full of the shit if you know anyone who needs some." He says.

I can see he's not going to hide what he does for a living. He's proud of it, whereas Donald seemed to want to distance himself from it.

"I like the way you've been running the joint. Donald couldn't say enough good things about you."

' Yeah, I'd never run a business before. It was fun for a while, but I think it's time for me to move on."

" I respect you, it's your choice. Listen you have to understand that business is business. What happened, happened. I really would like you to continue to run the place. It would mean a lot to me. I would give you the full run of the place. Whatever you say goes. This was Donald's baby and he requested that if anything should happen to him that I make sure that you are in charge. It was one of the last things he

told me. You wouldn't want to go against a deceased man's last desire."
He asks.

I know he's telling the truth because Donald told me the same in what turned out to be our last conversation. " I would like to help you out, but my heart's not into it anymore," I say.

"Do me a favor, do it for a little while, and see. I don't forget when someone does me a favor. Tell you what! I'll double your salary. And that girlfriend of yours Donald told me about, Maryjane, I'll double her salary, too. Just for a while, then you can change your mind, no problem, scouts honor." He stood up and reached out his hand.

I knew I should open the window, jump, and run for my life. Instead, I reach out and shook his hand.

"Just for a while," I reply.

"Yeah, just for a while." He says with a weird smile.

Chapter 16
In Loving Memory

We make our way downstairs back to the bar. Surprisingly, the bar has pretty much cleared out. Only a few were left, Jimmy's driver Sammy Giavannoa and his right-hand man Vito D'Antonio.

"Where'd everyone go?" Jimmy asks.

"They lost their party mood. Your boy made them feel bad." Vito said.

"Too bad, but we'll all be back next Friday," Jimmy said. "All right let's get going, too. By the way, Patrick decided to stay. Meet a couple of my friends, Sammy and Vito."

They come over and hug me. "Good to have you aboard," Sammy says. "Thanks. I'll try not to scare business away next time."

Jimmy hugs me." Keep up the good work. See you next Friday."

They head for the limo and Sammy opens the door for Jimmy and Vito. Just before entering the limo, Vito gives me a scary look that says I'm lucky Jimmy was here.

Phil walks in the door just as the limo pulls away.

"Looks like we are starting to get some high-class clientele," Phil says.

"I think you better have a seat," I tell Phil the story Jimmy told me and he flips out. He runs out the door as if he could catch the limo. He looks down the road and shakes his fist screaming something in Italian.

"That bastard, he did it I, I know! I never trusted that slimeball. I used to tell Don to watch out for him. Now he got him." Phil agonized.

Phil buries his head into his hands and bursts into tears. Maryjane walks through the door with a big smile on her face just for me, but she can tell by the expression on my face that something's not right. Then she spots Phil crying uncontrollably.

"Patrick, what's happening? Tell me quickly!" her look is one of fear. "Maryjane, it's Donald. He's dead. I don't have all the details yet. A bunch of his

friends were here and told me he was murdered in a carjacking."

"Bull shit! I know that no good bastard Jimmy is behind this. I'm going to make a couple of calls, Phil sobs." I'll be right back."

Maryjane is now sobbing uncontrollably. I hold her close to me and try to comfort her.

"He was such a nice guy to me. He would always help me out if he heard I was behind on my bills. He treated me like a daughter. How could this have happened? When are they going to lay him out?"

"According to his friend, Jimmy, he's already been buried." "AND THEY DIDN'T LET US KNOW!! Mary angrily shouts.

"THEY DIDN'T LET US KNOW BECAUSE THEY KNOW I WOULD HAVE

KILLED HIM! Phil blurts out. "I just made a call and it was Jimmy's guys who got Don. Louie got one of them before he bought it."

"Louie's dead too!" I scream and start sobbing all over again. "He was the sweetest guy around. He wouldn't hurt a fly. [I'll let her believe that.] 'Maybe we should close the place down for the day." I suggest.

"No, we will stay open and have our farewell to him tonight," MJ says. "Good idea, we'll hold a real tribute to him tonight. Oh, If I ever see that greaseball around I'll show him!" Phil claims.

I don't mention that he will be here next Friday.

One by one the regulars enter the Rock to hear the bad news. I never realized how much Don had done for the people of the town. A little at a time I hear of his generosity to almost everyone. After hearing this I realize he probably could have won an election for the job of mayor, and that he would have loved to be mayor.

"My business would be gone if it weren't for Don. He helped me make my payments for my pickup, which I need for my business," Mike tells us. "He always told me to keep it to myself. He never wanted credit for it."

"I can't tell you how often he helped me out. The same thing, he said keep it quiet," chimes in Tina, tears flowing freely.

Everyone tells the same story about keeping it quiet. It seems Don gave a bundle of money to the locals. The praises given tonight are unbelievable. Maryjane found a picture of Donald sitting on his favorite bar stool, and she put it in a frame and placed it on that stool. Everybody was patting the frame like they were patting him on the head.

The night turns from somber to a celebration of Don's life. One by one they relay personal stories about Don. They all recall his laugh/cough/choking with fondness.

"Happy hour is on Don tonight. Free drinks and pizza." I yell. Phil gives me a dirty look knowing he'll be flipping pizzas for the whole happy hour. I tell him I will help. I'm sure Donald Nonstick would have been touched by the love shown here tonight.

The Rock wasn't itself during the next week. Pizza/ Karaoke Wednesday wasn't as loud and boisterous as the previous weeks. Turk got up and sang a tribute song to Don, My Way. Once again sang wonderfully. It brought tears to all.

I thought I could cheer MJ up a little by telling her that her salary was doubling, but it didn't do much more than put a brief smile on her face. She was taking this harder than I imagined, and so was the whole town. It's funny, not funny ha ha, but funny weird, that it takes for someone to die before people tell how much they loved them, and then it's too late. If Donald had known how much he was revered, he might have gone legit. Maybe he was going to and that's what caused his death.

I go on the internet to find stories of Don's demise. I try to decide which newspaper website to choose. The Long Island paper, Newsday, would have a vanilla, basic story about the murder. The New

York Post would probably have a photo on the front page with Donald's and Louie's bodies on the ground in pools of blood, with a headline that would read something like "DONS DONE AND LUCKY TOO! I decide to go on THE New York Daily News website. They won't leave any of the gore out, but won't sensationalize the story to the point of losing the facts.

It made the front page of the News, bloody and all. They just couldn't resist a good photo op. MOB BOSS GUNNED DOWN and on the bottom of the page Hit Outside his Pizzeria after Last Supper. Inside the story tells of a mob war that they fear might escalate. The word on the street was that Donald had become too soft. He was letting the other families move in on his territory and not striking back. His underlings were losing money and respect on the street. He wouldn't listen to the pleas from his men to do something about it. It was assumed that it was an inside job. They had a photo of Jimmy "The Tux" Esposito with a caption under it crediting him with being the new boss. They also had the obligatory pyramid of photos showing the new pecking order of the mob. Jimmy's photo was on top with Vito D, Antonio's photo just below, and assorted others down the line. I don't know what it is but you didn't have to be told they were mobsters. If there had been a hundred photos of people from all walks of life on this page, you would have been able to pick out the ten gangsters. No problem. I recognize a couple of the suits from the Rock. I guess I'll be seeing more of them soon enough.

They don't say who organized the hit, but a new name has been added near the top of the pyramid, Tommy "The Butcher" Perillo. He put the plan in order, but he had to have the O.K. from up above.

He received the nickname "The Butcher" because, well, he was a butcher, literally. Before taking to a life of crime he worked at his father's butcher shop. Not much else is known about him.

As per the norm, the F.B.I. staked out the funeral taking photos and license plate numbers. A great crowd came to the burial. All the other mob bosses came and could be seen shaking the hand of Jimmy "The Tux," respecting him as the new leader. It's been reported afterward that a truce had been made and the other families would pull out of his territory. Peace, but for how long.

I realize now that I am into something over my head. I'm not doing anything illegal, well maybe the unemployment thing and the off-the-books thing, but I didn't kill anyone. I start to plan my resignation speech for Jimmy. He doesn't need me to run the place. I'm sure he could get one of his goons to do the job. Yeah, it won't be a problem. Besides, he gave me a scouts honor, and that's nonrefundable.

I know I was never a Boy Scout, but I'm sure Jimmy was. Yeah, right.

Friday came around and the place was starting to liven up again. Happy hour was making the people happy again. So far there was no sign of Jimmy, and that's good. I still haven't mentioned to Phil about Jimmy being the owner now. I don't know what he'd do if Jimmy showed up. Maybe Jimmy was going to leave this joint alone and we can just go on like one big happy family.

The pizzas are flying out the door. The regulars are getting juiced up pretty well. The Mets game will be on soon. They are on a three-game winning streak and are two up on the Phillies. The Yankees are doing well, also. They lead the Boston Red Sox by three. Both teams are playing their Chicago counterparts, the Cubs and the White Sox.

The Rock is getting its feel back when through the door comes Jimmy and the suits.

"Wow! What a crowd! Drinks for everyone, on me!" Jimmy says making his grand entrance.

Most of the regulars don't know about Jimmy's alleged part in Don's death. They greet his offer with a roar.

"Patrick, set them up, whatever they want. And give me a Chivas on the rocks."

His suits follow in and no one pays them much attention. Jimmy comes over to me and tells me his boys are to drink for free, tonight and always.

A funny thing happens as the night progresses. The suits and the locals get along. The suits are amused by the way the locals talk and act and the locals are amused at the way the suits talk and act. Two different worlds colliding, and so far no animosity. Of course, Phil's so busy in the kitchen, that he has no idea Jimmy's here and what's going on.

Later on, a couple of guys dressed in jeans and tee shirts enter the Rock. Jeans and tee shirts are the fashion at the Rock, but there is something that sticks out about these two. The jeans are new and are pressed with a crease and the tee shirts are brand new. I guess the mind is working overtime again.

The place is abuzz and one of the suits, Anthony Fortunato, starts flirting with MJ. He blocks her path as she comes out from behind the bar and puts his arms around her. She pushes him away but he continues to fondle her.

"Come on baby, Antony wants to show you a good time." He says. "Beat it asshole, and get your paws off of me." MJ doesn't take shit from anyone.

'Oh, a feisty one. I like that. Me and you gonna hook up later." He says.

' Not in your lifetime. Why don't you go back to your corner and drool in your beer.' MJ spews.

The other suits have started paying attention to the conversation and getting a kick out of MJ.

"You tell 'em one shout. Tell him to go slap his pud." Now Anthony is starting to feel humiliated.

"No broad talks to me like that." He raises his hand to slap MJ in the face when I grab his hand from behind. He turns around and is ready to take a shot at me when Jimmy intervenes.

"Yo! Anthony! Cut it out, that's Patrick's lady." Jimmy sternly says. Anthony drops his hands immediately." Sorry, Patrick, I didn't know. My apologies."

"No problem. I was just protecting you. Maryjane has a mean right hand."

I say. The place cracks up as MJ shows Anthony her fist.

"You don't want some of this do you?" she jokes with Anthony. "Please no, I'll be a good boy." He says.

The crowd goes back to enjoying themselves. I wonder if the suits will ever show up on Pizza/Karaoke Wednesday. If they do, I better tell Danny he better has some Doo Wop music available. [no racial slur intended with the wop thing.] I just might have to do it on Friday one week. It would be worth it just to see Sammy, Anthony and Vito get up and sing "The Lion Sleeps Tonight [with the fishes]" a Tokens classic. Then I could see 'The Tux" get up and do a little Dean Martin, Chivas in hand. "Everybody Kills Some Bodies Sometimes." Ah, maybe not.

I feel somebody nudging up behind me on the way to the bar. She makes her way past me and calls out to MJ.

"Give me a Johnny Walker Black, and make it a double." She blurts out. Her name is Danielle O'Neill and she's a little bit of a thing. She was lucky if she reached five feet when she was younger and was of good posture. Now, with nature and scoliosis taking their toll, she's about four foot eight, seventy pounds, soaking wet. She visited the Rock every so often but wasn't much of a drinker. But don't think because she's a lightweight, she's a lightweight. She's as strong as an ox. I've seen her splitting wood for the fireplace. Paul Bunyon has nothing over her. She owns a Bed and Breakfast, a stone's throw from the Rock. A large house, circa the 1860s. She named it The Victorian House. Twenty-four rooms, eighteen bedrooms. two bathrooms. Two bathrooms! If they built this today, it would have twenty bathrooms. [do we shit more than they did in the nineteen century?]. Danielle, or Danny as everyone calls her, and her husband William, bought the place thirty years ago. They lived in Elmhurst, Queens and they were getting tired of the rat race. William was a long-shore man and worked in the Brooklyn Navy Yard. He saw the job taking a turn for the worse and took early retirement. They sold their house in Elmhurst and bought the Bed and Breakfast. It was in bad shape, but the two of them worked hard and made the repairs, and got the business off the ground.

They never made a lot of money, but they made enough to live comfortably, along with his pension. Plus they loved the slower pace of Summit. They were well-loved in the town. Two years ago, at the age of seventy, William had a massive heart attack, at the same age as his father, his fathers' brother and William's older brother had. On his seventieth birthday, Danny gave him a cake with Happy Birthday on it. Between Happy and Birthday he wrote on the icing with his finger "Last." He believed it was his last year and he never let it bother him. He enjoyed every day like it was his last. After he passed on Danny ran the place on her own[they never had children] but her heart wasn't in it. Last year she put the place up for sale. So far she had no takers.

MJ pours her the scotch and asks what the occasion is.

Just sold the Victorian! A man came by this morning with a lawyer and a suitcase filled with three hundred thousand dollars, cash, mostly hundreds, and buys it. Says he's buying it for his girlfriend Isabella. I say I could care less who it's for as long as you "show me the money" [Danny likes movies.] and the real kicker is he wants me to live there and will pay me to keep the place neat. I just gave the money to Harvey down at the bank. He put it in some CD or something and says I'll get five percent interest. Can you beat that? What a day! Hey, there's the guy who bought the place." She points at Jimmy "The Tux." Yoo Hoo, it's me. Thank you!" Jimmy gives her a wave and a nod.

I guess Jimmy is planning on coming up a lot more than I thought he would. There's a murmur as word of the sale makes its way around. Most are astounded that the place was paid for in cash. Not many, if any of the locals would ever have, or see that much cash at one time. Michael makes his way over to Danny.

"What does it look like, three hundred thousand dollars in one place?" ' Oh, it looked wonderful. When the gentlemen left, I took off all my clothes and rolled around on the bed on it. I swear I had an orgasm." She claims.

" I'm sure Harvey must have enjoyed counting that money!" Mike says.

All the buzz going around is making Jimmy look very uncomfortable. He motions to Vito that it's time to leave. Vito passes word around, and a couple of the suits groan. They want to keep going but they listen to the boss. They head out the door and head not to the limos, but to the Victorian. They are spending the weekend. At the table in the back, the two guys with the creased Calvin Kleins are scribbling something on a napkin. They leave shortly after Jimmy and his suits.

Danny was as happy as I'd seen her since William passed away, and everyone was happy for her. The place quieted down since Tux and his merry men had left, but there was still a good crowd. I was happy that Phil never emerged from the kitchen. When it's busy he's oblivious to the goings on in the bar. Again, I will stay mum on the subject, but sooner or later the shit will hit the fan.

MJ and I get ready to close the Rock, and once again Libby is without a man. I feel responsible and consider taking her to my office and throwing her a bang. Who am I kidding? If she were the last woman alive I wouldn't do her. Alright, if she were the last woman alive I'm sure my horniness would take over, but I would put two bags on her head, in case one falls off.

Chapter 17
The Tux

Saturday night the Tux and his suits come over for dinner, again, at the house. Tina sits them at the large table just to the left of the kitchen. The consensus for the meal is the one-pound burger. Everyone is placing bets, on who would finish first, who wouldn't finish theirs, and who would puke theirs up. The betting for the first to finish is closer than expected. "Big" Louie Panaci is getting all the early money. He is five foot ten, three hundred ninety pounds. He is so big, that I think only the crack of his ass is actually on the chair. His massive cheeks flop on both sides of the chair. His claim to fame is that he suffocated a guy, sitting on his face. This move became so popular that a wrestler in the WWE, Rakishi, a friend of "Big Louie" used the move in the ring, naming it "Stink Face." "Big Louie wouldn't miss a wrestling match. He loved the WWE. He would cheer the matches like they were real, and if you don't want a stink face, don't try to tell him they're fixed.

The contender is Johnny "The Lip" Scarpino. Five foot eight, one hundred forty pounds. He doesn't know real sign language, but during conversations, he uses his hands more than Leonard Bernstein did conduct Beethoven's Fifth. When he gets excited he looks like Bruce Lee taking on ten men at once.[of course, the ten men always come at him one at a time, while the other nine patiently wait their turn to get their asses whooped.]

The orders are placed with everyone ordering the burger platter except Sammy, who orders the spaghetti and meatballs. Phil didn't have time to make baked ziti, so it was Aunt Millie's sauce today.

The burgers start to arrive, and the contenders get the first two. Jimmy holds up his hand to start the race. There are over five grand bets.

"On your mark, get set, GO! Jimmy throws his arm down and the race is on. The locals come to watch. They have been listening to the whole conversation and made their little pool of bets. A whole twenty dollars was riding on the outcome, most of the money on "Big Louie."

"Big Louie gets the early lead, taking a bigger chunk off the massive one-pound burger than I could take off a White Castle burger. [Now I'm going to be craving a White Castle burger until I have one.] He has so much burger in his mouth that he has little room to chew. Johnny on the other hand looks like a squirrel, nibbling away. Three-quarters of the way through, Johnny takes his first lead. The last time I saw a crowd react like this was during a cock fight in Mexico. The crowd was sensing an upset. "Big Louie" peered over toward Johnny to see where he stood in the race. He saw Johnny ahead and made a desperate move. He placed the last quarter of his burger in his mouth and just swallowed, no chewing whatsoever. He opened his mouth to show the burger was gone, and Jimmy proclaimed him the winner. The only problem is Big Louie's victory is coming with a price. The burger is stuck in his esophagus and he's starting to turn blue. At first, no one notices. Then Mike sees him and alerts the others. Mike tries to give him the Heimlich maneuver but he can't wrap two arms around Big Louie's huge belly.

"Someone help! Vito jumps up to lend a hand. "I'll take the right side and you take the left. Put your fist right under his chest. When I say go, pull your fist into his belly. Ready, go! "Nothing on the first try. "Again, GO." Nothing. On the third try, the burger is airborne. Big Louies' gasping for air sends Mike and Vito flying. His color starts to return and everyone is looking relieved. Down the other side of the table, Johnny nibbles on the last part of his burger. He points to his empty dish.

"All gone. Oh, look, I see Big Louie's burger on the floor. I guess I win!

The Lip contests.

Jimmy walks over and sees Johnny has finished. He grabs his hand and holds it in the air.

"The winner and champion Johnny!"

Some of Big Louie's bettors grumble but to no effect. A bunch of Franklins starts changing hands in this room, while a bunch of Georgies changes hands with the locals. Big Louie is starting to recover and turns to thank Mike for his quick thinking.

"As long as I'm here, you will never pay for a drink again." He states. "What about me? What am I some horse shit or something?" Vito yells. "I'm sorry, I thank you, too. But the only reason you did it was that you bet on Johnny. Besides, you don't pay for your drinks anyway! Hey Mike, how about a one-pound burger and a beer?"

"No thanks, I lost my appetite, but I will take a beer," Mike says. "Maryjane, a beer for Mike and a round on me for everyone. I won the puking contest. Pay up!'

'That's right, He did! Pay up, everyone." Jimmy says. "But he had help, that shouldn't count. Anthony cries.

"Pay up! You could have stuck your finger down your throat if you wanted to win." Jimmy says.

Another groan and the money makes its way to Big Louie. He hands it to MJ

"Here use it till it's gone. Enjoy!"

A roar goes up from the locals. They like nothing more than a free drink. Most of the others lost their appetite watching Big Louie hurl his Burger, but some were just getting their food. Sammy Got a large plate of spaghetti and meatballs and it looked official.

"Man I'm starving." He states. He proceeds to shake the salt shaker over the meal. Twenty seconds later he hasn't stopped shaking. Then he turns to the pepper and proceeds to do the same. Likewise with the parmigiana cheese. You couldn't tell what kind of food he was eating, because you couldn't see it. He grabbed his fork and twirled the spaghetti on a spoon and placed it in his mouth. Taking no backseat to Big Louie, he choked up the pasta across the room. "What kind of shit is this. It tastes like watered-down catsup. Who made this crap!' he screams. Phil hears this from the kitchen. He comes barging out to see who's bitching about his food.

"Who the hell is bitching about my cooking?" Phil shouts as he comes barging out of the kitchen. "I'll show them catsup!"

Phil makes his way to the dining area and stops in his tracks when he sees Jimmy. He peers over to the table and spots a knife. He reaches over, grabs the knife, and lunges at Jimmy.

"You son of a bitch, you killed Donald!" he screams.

Vito intercepts the move. He grabs Phil's arm, the one with the knife in it, and twists it behind his back in one swift move. He pulls a revolver from his waistband and points it at Phil's head.

"No, don't do it! Let him go," shouts Jimmy. "If he lets me go, I'll kill you!" Phil screams.

Jimmy tries to calm the situation down, but Phil is hot.

"Why would I kill my best friend? Not only did I not do it, but when I find out who did, they will wish they were never born." [sounds a little like O.J. Simpson to me.] "Let him go. He'll be alright."

Phil starts to calm down a little and Vito slowly releases Phil's arm, minus the knife. Vito has a perplexed look on his face. He has never seen Jimmy be so easy on someone who just tried to kill him. That act was usually the kiss of death.

Little did Vito know that Phil had saved Jimmy's life. Jimmy loved the lasagna at Donald's pizzeria. He would come for it once a week, minimum. Phil was just a pizza flipper at the time.

Jimmy had recently been expanding his territory and infringing on the turf of the Bonamo Family. The head of the family was Eddie Perricone, and he put out a hit on Jimmy. He sent two of his "mechanics," the Arizza brothers, Guiseppe and Angelo to do the job. They weren't his best guys, but he figured they could handle Jimmy. They planned the hit at Michelangelo's Pizzaria, Donald's place.

Phil arrives for his weekly indulgence. He comes into the pizzeria and orders his lasagna and heads to the men's room. Shortly after the Arizza brothers enter through the front door. They head to the counter and asked Phil if he had seen Jimmy. They said they had an appointment with him. Phil sensed something was amiss. He told them Jimmy had just called and said he would be here in ten minutes.

"Come here and sit down and wait." He brings them to a table facing away from the bathroom. Can I get you a slice or something?"

"No thanks, we'll just wait. And don't tell him we're here yet" Angelo says.

'No problem."

Phil then heads to the men's room and intercepts Jimmy just in time. "Jimmy, there are two guys who just came in asking for you. They said they had an appointment with you."

"What did you tell them?"

" I told them you just called and said you would be here in ten minutes."

"Good!" he takes out his pistol and loads a bullet in the chamber.

" Jimmy, not here. We don't want this stuff happening in Donald's place." "You're right. Go back out to the counter. I'll call the pizzeria on my cell phone and tell you I changed my plans. I'm going to eat at Stella Lunas instead. I'll see what's going on there.

Phil went back to the counter and awaited the call. It came shortly after his arrival.

"Michelangelo's Pizzeria, what can I do for you? Jimmy hi, what's up?

Okay, then I'll see you tomorrow."

He walks over to the Arizza brothers, who overheard the conversation. "Jimmy just called. He changed his plans. He is going to Stella's instead.

You guys know where that is?"

"Yeah, did he say when he would be there?" Guiseppe asks. "He's on his way there as we speak."

The brothers get up and leave in a hurry, without even a goodbye. Phil retrieved Jimmy from the bathroom.

"Good work. I owe you one." Jimmy says.

Jimmy had heard that there might be a hit on him. He wasn't sure if this would be it, but he was taking no chances. He made his way to Stella's and peered into the window. His intuition was correct. He knew the reputation of the brothers. They were here to ice him. He could just avoid the situation, but he decided to meet it head-on. He headed into the alleyway on the side of the restaurant and ducked in the side door, which lead to the kitchen. He walked through the kitchen and peeked through the door leading to the dining tables. He spotted the brothers and approached from behind them. He reached the table and greeted the brothers.

"Hi guys, looking for me?"

Startled, they both reached for their guns. Before they could react, Jimmy shot them each once, right between the eyes. The place wasn't very crowded, and by the time anyone heard the shots and reacted, Jimmy was headed out through the back door. All anyone saw was the back of Jimmy's Tuxedo.

"Patrick, come here. Do you mind if I borrow Phil and your office for a little bit?" Jimmy asks.

"Sure. No problem." I say

"Phil, come with me," Jimmy says.

"You want me to come, boss?" Vito asks.

"No, no, just me and Phil. Come on Phil, Let's go."

Phil follows Jimmy up to the office, still steaming, but willing to hear Jimmy's side of the story. Jimmy opens the door and tells Phil to take a seat behind the desk.

"Phil, Donald was my best friend. He showed me the ropes and taught me everything I know. There's no way I would take him out. It seems there was a misunderstanding. Word on the street was I wanted Donald out of the way. A couple of street thugs were trying to impress me and get on my good side. They took it on their own to pull off the job. They even got Louie. He was like my brother, you know that!

Louie got one of 'em, the other three, let's just say they won't be able to make that mistake again.

They sleep with the fish. I took over the family because I was the choice of our families and the other families welcomed me. I don't know what else I can tell you. I hope you believe me."

"Jimmy, if you're telling me the truth, then I apologize. Donald treated me like a son, and I would avenge his death like a son would avenge his father's death. I just want you to know that." Phil says.

"I respect your deep feelings toward Donald, but I feel just as strongly as you do. What you did downstairs, you know, I can lose the respect of the men. The only reason you're still alive is that I owed you one for saving my life. When we get downstairs I want a sincere apology from you in front of the men."

"Okay, I'll do it. I am sorry, but I heard…."

" O.K, let's forget about it. But now we are even. If you try something like this again, I can't help you."

"Ok"

They make their way downstairs and Phil makes good on the apology. But inside he swears if he finds out Jimmy did it, he would kill him.

Chapter 18
The Normals

The Rock is doing great and would be doing better if Jimmy's guys would pay up, but they tip incredibly well. With MJ and me getting double our salaries, and the tips going through the roof, things are going great! With the locals, blessing their hearts, we were lucky if they left a dollar on the bar after serving them all night. The suits leave nothing less than a ten. Of course, they are drinking for free, but I'm sure they would tip the same if they were paying.

The town of Summit is experiencing a boom. The suits are enjoying it up here so much, they are starting to buy homes. They are shocked that you can buy a nice place for under a hundred grand. That amount in Brooklyn buys you a cardboard box, without the land. Jimmy starts off the frenzy. After purchasing the Victorian, he buys the house next door to the Rock. It was a beautiful house, a long time ago, and now needed repair. It had eight bedrooms and one bathroom and was on two acres. The asking price had been $75,000, but Loretta Tillis knew a sucker when she saw one. She's a keen realtor. When Jimmy came in to inquire about the place she told him it was $120,000. He bit. Bought it for cash, the same day. Immediately the price of property skyrocketed. The suits followed the leader and started buying up homes in the area. They loved the small town feel and felt it was a haven. Away from Brooklyn, they felt like they could walk around without constantly looking behind them. Each week brought more and more suits to the town.

Jimmy started renovating the place immediately. Truckloads of materials and workers were showing up daily. He changed the whole second floor into his master bedroom. There would only be three bedrooms at completion, but four full bathrooms. They finished the place in three weeks. And he left the exterior the way it was intended to be. Everyone was afraid he would brick the whole outside. They love bricks in Brooklyn.

I had asked Maryjane to move in with me and she agreed. It was a great time to have a house for sale, so since she was moving in with me she put her house up for sale. She thought she could get $65,000 for it, but Loretta told her to put it up for

$100,000. I told her to put it up for $150,000. She told me I was crazy, she would never get that much.

The next day a new suit shows up at the bar. Jackie Rizzo is a quirky guy who has a language all of his own. He runs the slum section of the city, East New York, a section no one else wanted. East New York He somehow not only makes it work but is raking in big bucks. The others say he makes it work because no one understood a word of what he says.

"Hi! I'm Jackie. And what should I call you?" he asks Maryjane. "My name is Maryjane, but you can call me MJ for short." She says.

'Can you give me a beer, MJ? It's been a rough week. A good friend of mine was killed in an accident on the L.I.E. He was driving his HOV and it flipped over. He was decaffeinated. It was horrible. They found his head ½ mile from the HOV. Ah, maybe it was better off that it happened this way. He had just found out he conducted HBO from a blood Transylvania. People woulda thunk he was a queer, so maybe it was better this way." Jackie stammered.

MJ looks at me and I shrug my shoulders. I think I know what he said. MJ places a beer in front of him.

"I'm sorry to hear about your friend," MJ says. "What friend?" Jackie asks.

"The one in the accident."

"Oh, that guy. I hardly knew him. Matter of fact, I think I just read that in the paper. I didn't know the guy. I'm looking to buy a house up here. You know anybody that's selling one?"

"I'm selling my house. Two bedrooms and in good shape. I'm asking…" "One hundred fifty grand" I jump in before MJ says differently.

"Hey, you're a pretty good ventricle, MJ. I didn't even see you move your lips and the words came out of that guy." Jackie says.

"Hi, I'm Patrick! I run this place and I'm MJ's boyfriend." I say.

'Oh yeah, I heard about you from Don and Jimmy. They got nice things to say about you. Sounds like a good price. I'll probably take it, but for one hundred forty, not a penny more!'

"MJ gasps and nearly faints. Her house has been on the market for a day and she got more than she ever thought.

"I'll…"

'Think about it.' I finish the sentence for her again.

"All right, one forty-five. That's my last offer, and this place better is nice."

"I'll [she hesitates and looks at me, and I nod my approval.] take it. When do you want to move in?" MJ says.

"Soon as possible. I'll have the money tomorrow." "It's a deal!" I say.

"Jeeze, I still can't see her lips move," Jackie says. I don't think he's kidding.

The town is abuzz, and everyone puts their house up for sale. The bulletin board in the rear of the bar was filled with pictures of houses at ridiculous prices. Before last week the last posting on the board was for a yard sale. The browning note was from two summers ago. Mike puts his one-room hunting cabin on the board for $1,000,000. Leave it to Mike, but who knows?

I'm in my office doing the books for the month when Jimmy walks in, duffle bag in hand.

"Hey, I see you're doing the books. How did we do last month?" he asks. "Looks like we cleared seven grand, best month ever!" I say.

"Sounds good, but that's not counting the money my boys owed." Jimmy states.

"I thought you said they drank for free?" I question.

'Free! Hell no! Those guys can afford it. Here I collected the money from them. Spread it around over the four weeks of the month." He says as he puts the duffle bag on the desk.

"This will surely be a record-breaking week!" I say as I reach for the bag. I open the bag and it is stuffed with stacks of bills, all denominations. I take out the bills one stack at a time and start counting and placing the figures on my calculator. Twenty-five minutes later I press the equals sign on the calculator and come up with forty thousand dollars.

"Wow, I don't think this is possible. I know they drank and ate a lot, but not this much." I say

"I asked each guy what he owed and this is what I got. Just mix it around.

No problem." Jimmy says.

I have never run a business before and my head was spinning. I've only been doing books for a couple of months. I had no idea how to match the numbers up.

"Listen, Jimmy, I don't know what to do," I state

"Don't worry. I have someone downstairs who used to own a deli. Maybe he can show you." He takes out his cell phone and dials a number. "I.E. come on up." He puts the cell back in his tux pocket. " Ira is coming up to give you a hand."

Ira Erwinski never ran a deli. He ran a large accounting firm in Manhattan.

It wasn't the largest firm in the number of clients he serviced, but he had some of the wealthiest clients. He was 'very' creative with numbers, and he found legitimate ways of saving them big bucks.

It seems Ira also thought he was an expert at picking college basketball games. He followed the NCAA like stockbrokers follow the Dow. And he was good, until March Madness 2005. He bet $25,000 on an opening-round game and lost. He doubled his bet on the next game and lost again. He figured he would have to win sooner or later and kept doubling and losing. The next bet he would have to put up 1.6 million dollars to cover it. He had this kind of money but not laying around in his draws. He asked Jimmy to front him which he did. And he lost. With the interest that Jimmy was charging, he would be paying for years. He decided to do Jimmies books pro bono. Now he was on call at Jimmy's behest.

He walks into the room carrying the cash register from the bar. He places it on my desk and I notice it isn't the cash register from the bar, but one exactly likes it.

He must have had a spare one lying around from his deli days I guess. Yeah right.

"Hi, I'm Ira, Ira Erwinski." He says with his hand extended. "Hi, I'm Patrick, Patrick Hunnewell.'I extend my paw.

"Jimmy tells me you can use some help with the bookkeeping. I can show you a couple of tricks to help you out." He plugs in the cash register and asks me for the monthly receipts. He starts punching away at the keys and, voila, a new receipt, only with higher prices, back-dated and all. Then he grabs a Jailhouse Rock menu from his back pocket and starts to change the prices with a pen.

"You will need to have new menus printed up with these prices on them," he says.

"Don't worry about the menus. I'll have them printed up. I know a guy.

He'll make them beautifully." Jimmy says.

I look at the menus and see the new prices Ira has inserted. The prices look like those of a top Manhattan restaurant. Hamburger platters; $15.95; Steak dinners;

$45.00; Bottled beer;$7.00.

"These local people could never afford these prices. The locals are our lifeblood. They will just go to Stamford and drink at the Cavern Tavern. This isn't fair to them." I say.

"Don't worry. These prices are not what you will charge. There will be everyday specials. They will pay the same prices they pay now.

We just need to show these prices, so they match with the receipts.' I.E. says.

"Patrick, you are doing a wonderful job here. You'll pick up all these little nuances. This is how all businesses operate." Jimmy says.

I ain't no brain surgeon, but I know when something isn't kosher. "I don't know, maybe I'm not cut out for this," I say.

"Nonsense, you are the perfect guy for the job. I wouldn't trust anybody with this but you. I'm so sure you're the only guy for the job that I'm going to double your salary again. We'll put the new part of your salary on the books. Then you can stop unemployment. How's that sound?" Jimmy says.

Over four grand a week. Over $200,000 grand a year. Wow! And some of it is legit. I don't like the feel of this, but somehow it feels great! I nod my approval. And Jimmy comes over and gives me a big bear hug.

"I knew I could count you in. Where are your parents and grandparents from.? He inquires.

"They were all born here in the United States, except for my mother's father. He came here from Sicily." I tell him.

"I knew it! I can spot a gumba from a mile away!" Jimmy says." Let's go downstairs and celebrate the best month ever at the Rock! You can do the rest of that stuff another time."

Away we go, down to the bar. I wonder what other rabbits Ira will pull from his bag of tricks.

Chapter 19
The Suits

It's Friday Night Happy hour/ Pizza Night and the customers are starting to filter in. We emerge from my office and I spot Mike checking out his ad on the bulletin board to see if he had any takers/suckers. He placed his phone number on the bottom of the ad in little strips so people could take the number with them. Of course, none were missing. The next time he looks there will be three or four missings, I'll see to that. He'll probably shit his pants. I might even call as a prospective buyer. Nah, I couldn't do that to him. He'd probably go out and buy all kinds of stuff thinking he was going to be rich.

I peer into the kitchen. Phil seems to have bought the explanation from Jimmy. He was smiling ear to ear and singing Italian songs while flipping the pies. Part of his happiness is stemming from his paycheck. Jimmy told me to give Phil a two hundred dollar-a-week raise. When I handed him his paycheck this morning he didn't say a word, wondering if it might be a clerical error. If there was, he was going to keep quiet and see if we'd find the mistake. Two hundred dollars is two hundred dollars after all. I noticed him place the check hurriedly into his rear pocket.

"Something's wrong? I asked. "NO, no," he replies.

"You didn't notice a little extra dough in your check?"

"I didn't notice." He says sheepishly as he takes the check out of his back pocket. "Oh, yeah, look at that. What's that for?"

"You got a two hundred-a-week raise!"

"Thanks a lot!" Now he seemed happier than when he thought it was just an error.

"You can thank Jimmy for that." "Yeah, I'll do that when I see him."

"Tomorrow night there's the annual Music Festival up on Mt. Ute," Sgt. Bill says to no one in particular, but to everyone just the same. "All the good local bands will be playing and it's free. And you can bring your booze and food."

Everyone seems psyched about it.

Johnny Scarpinto wonders what everyone is so excited about. "What's the big deal about this?" Do they got some good bands playing?"

"Yeah, The Country Cats will be there and Willie's Hootenanny Band. The guy plays a washboard better'n than anybody. And the guy in the Cats is the best Banjo player this side of the Mississippi." Serge replies with a smile ear to ear.

"Hootenanny, washboards, banjos, that ain't music. Electric guitars and drums, Led Zepplin now that's music." Johnny says.

"That crap isn't music either. Frank Sinatra, Dean Martin, Tony Bennett, now that's music." Jimmy says.

"You're so right, Turk chimes in." Everybody loves somebody sometime, he croons, beautifully.

"Here, here!" Jimmy yells. "Sing it, Turk."

"You have to be here on Wednesday if you want me to sing." "I'll give you fifty bucks to sing it now," Sammy says. "Make it a hundred and I'll do two."

"You're on. Jimmy says. "As long as the second song is My Way." "You got it!" The Turk sings acapella. The room gets so quiet you can hear a pin drop. Turk once again tears the joint down. He does the two songs and is coaxed to do another, this time for free. He sings Tony Bennett's I Wanna Be Around. Even Mr. Bennett would be proud of the job Turk did. Jimmy walks over to Turk and gives him a big hug, with tears welling in his eyes.

"It doesn't get any better than that. That's the best hundred I've spent in a long time." Jimmy says while handing a hundred dollar bill to Turk.

"No thanks," he says handing the bill back to Jimmy. "I was only kidding.

I enjoy singing, but thanks anyway."

"I'll take it! Mike yells. "And I'll sing all night if you'd like!" "We'll pay you a hundred to never sing again," I say.

"O.K., I'll take it."

"Now that "would be the best hundred ever spent," says Serge. "Well, if Turk doesn't want it, I'll put it on the bar. Drinks on Turk!" Jimmy says.

Another familiar roar goes up from the patrons. Mike lifts his Heineken [of course on the house he goes for the more expensive beer.] "To Turk, may he sing here every night!"

The crowd lifts its glasses and toasts Turk.

"Well I hope you guys enjoy your can clanking music tomorrow, 'cause we'll all be here." Johnny states and his suits agree. "Golly gee I hope you bumpkins enjoy the show," Johnny says in his best hillbilly accent, which isn't very good, but it gets a laugh from the suits.

" And I hope da boys gonna like stayin' here," Serge says with his best try at Brooklynese. The locals laugh as if Frank Caliendo had just done his John Madden impersonation.

Another good night of fun and laughs. MJ and I finish cleaning up and head for home. It's August, but upstate it's already starting to feel like September, late September. MJ puts a sweater on for the walk home. I tell her about my good news.

"Jimmy doubled my salary, again! He says I'm doing an unbelievable job.

The Rock made forty-eight thousand dollars last month!" I tell her.

"WHAT! This place never made more than six grand in a month. And Jimmy's guys don't even pay!" MJ proclaims puzzled and disbelievingly.

"Jimmy says we misunderstood, his guys will pay up in one lump sum at the end of every month. He handed me forty grand from them."

'FORTY GRAND! They didn't owe that much." "Hey that's what Jimmy said, so what can you do?"

'I don't know. Seems like an awful lot of money for the little ole' Rock." "He's having new menus printed up, too. Raising all the prices on it, but he says the locals will still pay the same."

"I don't like the feel of this, Patrick."

"Hey, between us we're making a fortune. Let's just see what happens." We get to the house and MJ remembers that her place might be sold tomorrow.

"Wow, we're gonna have a bucket of money. Before you showed up in my life I didn't have a pot to piss in, 'except what Brad would give me. I'm so happy I met you, even if we had nothing. She reached her arms around me and planted a wet kiss on my lips. Junior immediately went to attention and Mj felt its presence. She reached down and grabbed a hand full.

"I think we better take care of this condition you have." "That's what the doctor prescribed."

We make our way to the bedroom, but we can't wait that long. We roll down to the living room rug and the sparks start to fly. The lovemaking is so intense that I can't hold back. I beat Maryjane to the punch this time, lasting a 'whole' minute.

"You better have something left for me." She says. "I do!"

Meanwhile, back at the ranch, or more precisely, the New York Federal Bureau of Investigation, the head supervisor Larry Kramer, calls two of his rookies into his office. David Lloyd and Joey Nugent had only completed the academy six months ago. They were green and learning their way around. Larry sent them out on a wild goose chase. The F.B.I. got word that the new head of the Lucchio Crime family, Jimmy "The Tux" Esposito, and some of his cohorts were heading upstate New York to check on a local saloon Jimmy "inherited" from the late Donald Nonstick. The bar, The Jailhouse Rock Inn, was in a little town called Summit. The F.B.I. knew that the old head of the family, Donald, had been running a legitimate business in the small town, one of the few legitimate businesses he had. The F.B.I. had monitored Donald and the Rock and found no wrongdoings. Larry sent David and Joey to pursue Tony and his men knowing there wouldn't be much going on. It would be a good way for them to wet their feet. He was calling them into his office to get an update on their pursuit of the Tux.

"Gentleman, come in and have a seat. What are you guys wearing?" Larry

asks.

"We're sorry, sir. We know we are supposed to wear suits, but we were on our way back upstate when you called us in." David says.

"I don't mean why aren't you in suits, I mean what the heck are you wearing."

"Jean's sir," Joey says. "That's what everybody wears up there and we wanted to fit in."

'Jeans, yes, but not fancy jeans with a crease! You might have well just worn a turban. Before you head back up go and buy a couple of pairs of Wranglers or Levis. So what did you guys find out about Jimmy?"

They both take out their notepads, simultaneously. They flip through the pages and David speaks first.

"We first encountered Jimmy Esposito on Friday night, July 11th, 2008 at 5 pm….."

"All right cut the formal bullshit. Just tell me what you've observed." "Jimmy and his gang marched into the joint and joined the local patrons.

They seemed to fit in and they were buying drinks for the whole bar. The manager of the bar, let me see [as they both shuffle through their notes] here it is, Patrick Hunnewell, and Jimmy went to his office and when they came back he announced that Patrick would be staying on." David said.

"What do we know about this Patrick Hunnewell? Sounds like a porn stars name?"

"He just recently took the job, when Donald was around. From what we've found out, he didn't even know Donald till recently. We don't think he's connected. Would you like us to check a little deeper on him?" Joey says. "No, I see no reason."

" It appears Jimmy and his men are enjoying the environment up there. I heard Sammy Giavanna tell Vito D'Antonio that he likes being able to take a walk and not have to look behind him all day long. Sammy is Jimmy's driver and Vito seems like his right-hand man.

"Jimmy also purchased an eighteen-room bed and breakfast, The Victorian. The lady he bought it from, Daniel O'Neill, came into the Jailhouse Rock Inn and was rejoicing in selling the house for $300,000, cash. Jimmy's soldiers were staying at the place on weekend visits. Then Jimmy purchased the house next store to the J.R.I. and paid $120,000. He had workers in and out of the house, buzzing around like worker bees. They finished the job in three weeks. Some of the others have started buying homes in the area." David reports.

"Why do you think they're buying up the joint? Do you think they're up to no good?" Larry asks, testing their intuitiveness.

"As I said before, we have heard them speak of the peace and quiet up there and how much they enjoy the feeling of security, so I don't think they would want to mess that up. But you know those guys, give them time I'm sure they'll ruin that peace." Joey replies.

"Good work. Never take your eyes off them. Don't let them lull you to sleep." Larry warns. "Anything else to report?"

"Jimmy had a meeting in Patrick's office the other day. Went up there with a duffle bag. After a while, another guy from the bar went upstairs to join them. They were up there for a while. When they came back down they were celebrating the fact that Patrick would stay on and manage the place." Joey says.

"Did Jimmy have the duffle bag in hand when he returned? And did you find out who the guy was that joined him?" Larry asks.

David shuffles through his paperwork. "Here it is. His name is Ira

Erwinski."

"IRA ERWINSKI !? what is he doing up there? And with Jimmy?" "Who's Ira Erwinski? David inquires.

"Ira Erwinski, his friends call him I.E. for short. He's a big-shot accountant from Manhattan. His clientele is big-time players. What's the connection with Jimmy? Why would he be with such a slimeball?"

" Yes. They only charge a buck and a quarter for a mug of beer!" And they buy back every third one! Joey says.

"Good, you're doing a good job. Get back up there and keep me informed."

Time is moving on quickly. Winter is approaching. Summer ends a month earlier up here and winter begins a month earlier. It's early November and we've already had a snowstorm. It was a bright sunny day, about 20 degrees. All of a sudden, over the mountains the sky turned black. And I mean black. As the darkness approached, the wind started kicking up. Within minutes the sky was falling. Snowflakes the size of snowballs started pelting the ground. A blanket of snow covered the landscape within seconds. Within minutes there were three inches of accumulation. Ten minutes later there were five inches on the ground. Ten minutes later, bright sunshine. I can't believe what I am seeing. I spot my next-door neighbor, Frank, and ask him what the heck just happened. He says there's a saying up here. If you don't like the weather, wait five minutes and it will change.

The suits aren't coming up as often. They don't like the cold. They are, however, looking forward to hunting season. The third week in November is deer season. It attracts many people from all around every year. It's a three-week boost for the local economy. The Rock rents all the upstairs rooms, the only time of the year they put out the NO VACANCY sign. The Tux and the suits have been hearing about hunting all summer and are now psyched to try it. They all purchased shotguns [many already had the sawed-off variety] They bought all the gear and were ready to go. I think they liked the idea of shooting a gun and killing legally. They already had been shooting up the woods, illegally. Vito bought a house on forty acres of wooded property. During the late summer, they were going deep into the woods and shooting their Glocks and 44 Magnums into the trees. There were so many bullet holes in the trees; it looked like a paintball field.

Paintball is a great game. I remember playing war as a little kid and enjoying it. I and my friends would take our toy rifles and feign a war scene. Me, Jeff, Ron, and Julio would divide into two teams and stage an attack on an imaginary fort. Each team would get a turn defending the fort. We would make the sound of guns firing and the game was on. The only problem was that every time you would shoot Julio, he would say "You missed." You could come up right behind him and shoot him in the head and he would say, "You missed." I never got to play paintball with him, but if I did, I would have blasted him a thousand times. He would have looked like he had just got done painting his house.

Little kids these days don't play war. If a parent were to buy a child a toy gun, the neighbors would probably have social services called in. I'm so glad I didn't grow up in these times. Playdates!?? What the "F" is a play date. Time outs! Timeouts in my day were a crack across the butt from my dad. Then I learned not to do that again. All right, maybe not the first time, but I knew if I did wrong there were consequences to pay. Time outs. Phew! And would it be so bad to let your children jump on their bikes and ride to their ball games? Today both parents work and then spend the weekends chauffeuring the kids to soccer, karate, baseball… Oh well, what do I know?

The bad thing about playing paintball is that the damned thing hurt like a bastard when they hit you. I try to avoid getting hit as if they were real bullets. When playing, I try to imagine what it would be like if this were real, like Afghanistan. When I play that way it makes me realize what real heroes our soldiers are. While I'm getting a sting and some paint on me they are losing limbs or worse. My thanks to our servicemen for risking their lives so I can play games.

The Rock was a hopping place last two months. The Yankees and the Mets are both in the playoffs, in the first year of their respective new ballparks. There are more Yankee fans than Met fans, especially when the suits are here. There is excitement every night and both teams reach the World Series. The Mets sweep Atlanta in the first series. Chipper Jones goes hitless for the series. He named his daughter Shea because he hit so well at the Met's old ballpark, Shea Stadium. I guess he won't be naming his next child Citi, after the new ballpark. The Yankees beat the Cleveland Indians in the first round and beat there their main rival the Boston Red Sox in a tough seven-game series to advance to the World Series. The Mets sweep the Philadelphia Phillies to reach the Series. Jimmy Rollins only got on base once, on an intentional hit-by-pitch. Then in the World Series, the New York Mets sweep the New York Yankees and become the champions. Alex Rodriquez or A-Rod as he's known scorches the ball every game to wipe out his choking image but gets no help from the rest of the Yanks. {Hey, it's my book and that's what happened}

The Rock keeps breaking records with the gross intake every month.

Jimmy brings bags of money and adds them to the till. $50,000 in September and $52,000 in October. The best part of these days is when Jimmy reaches into the bag before counting it and grabs a handful of cash and gives it to me.

"Here's your bonus for the month for your great work," Jimmy tells me.

What a country. After the World Series ends the place had its first slowdown in a while. With the suits coming up less it's just the regular crowd coming in. even the creased jeans guys are coming less. They show up one day with regular jeans on and although they are brand new, at least they don't have a crease. The only thing is they have on cowboy boots which are as clean and shiny as soldier's dress boots. I went over to them to break the ice one day. Their names are David and Joey. They are stock brokers and have a small cabin in the woods. They come up here to get away from the rat race, they tell me. They are nice guys and jeans start fitting in with the locals and the suits. Neither of them likes sports, but they don't miss a game. They eat more than they drink, but got hammered on Karaoke night and started singing Kid Rock songs, and they were not too bad. When they were done they yelled into the mike; "Drinks for everyone on the house." They paid for it with a credit card. "This round is on our boss," David tells me.

And the Rock goes on.

Chapter 20
The Hunts

Hunting season is about to begin. They now start it on a Saturday instead of Monday to make it more convenient for the hunters. The Rock gets mostly the same hunters year in and year out. Some stay upstairs in one-room "suites." There are five of these rooms and they all share one bathroom, with a shower. Each room has two bunk beds, so it accommodates four hunters, at a whopping price of fifty dollars a night. The "Honeymoon Suite" has two rooms and a bathroom, with a heart-shaped Jacuzzi. It goes for a hundred a night and sleeps six. It's usually the last room rented. Hunters are not looking for luxury. They like blood and guts. They don't care about heat or any conveniences. They are here to be real men, cavemen. They slosh their beers down till they go to sleep, wake up at ungodly hours to go sit, freezing in a tree, hoping to catch a glimpse of a deer at least once in their week-long stay. Many a year they never see any. When they get lucky enough to shoot at one, they feel the week was a success. If they hit the deer and kill it, they get to gut it, then drag the 120-160 pound deer a couple of miles back to the camp. They hang the deer from a tree and when it comes time to go home they drop it off at a local butcher. He cuts it up into roasts, chops meat, sausage, or whatever way you would like, for about $80. You end up with about 80 pounds of meat that nobody likes. They say if you marinate it for a hundred days in beef gravy, it won't taste terrible. There are a lot of things I don't "get" in this world. Then here's a part of me that wonders what I'm missing. It's like I said about Bruce Springsteen. Everybody loves him, but I don't get it.

Although I'm new here I am informed by Mike that there are a couple of hunters that are third-generation guests at the Rock. Jack Gibbs and his brother, James, have been staying at the Rock for thirty years. Their dad, Jack Sr., has been staying at the Rock since he was a teenager. He has since passed on to the great hunting grounds in the sky. For the last few years, Jack has been bringing his sons to continue the tradition. Brent and his brother Pace enjoy hunting and spending time with their dad.

Most people that come up enjoy hunting, but then you have the ones that go hunting to get away from the wife and family. Their sole purpose up here is to get drunk and have a good time. Some of them never take their guns out of the case. Some will go out at noon for a ten-minute walk in the woods with their guns just so they aren't lying to their wives about hunting. Jack's brother, James is one of these.

James is a weight lifter and is built like a brick shit house. His muscles have muscles. He comes hunting every year and enjoys getting away from his nagging wife and five daughters. The bitch can't even have a boy, he complains to everyone. She tells him it's his disgusting sperm that determines boys and girls. She says maybe if he knew how to fuck right he might have a son. If only he could bring her hunting just once. Then he could be hunting the bitch. He says when the bitch team gets together; his wife wears the "C" on her jersey. Captain bitch they should call her.

James is one of the nicest guys around. He would give you the shirt off his back and stays that way until he drinks six and a half beers. At six and five-eighths of a beer, he wants a fight, with anyone, for any reason. If you weren't counting his beers, you can tell by the sound of his voice. He immediately starts to slur. A fight is not far behind. As big as he is, his record when fighting drunk is 1-107.

It's the Friday before the opening season and the Rock is packed. The suits are here but dressed in their newly purchased hunting gear. Their gear is bright orange. They couldn't understand why you would wear orange to hunt. They figured the deer would see them from miles away, but the locals explain that deer are color blind. They smell your way before they see you, they are told. Plus with the orange gear, you won't mistake a hunter for a deer. Some of the suits say, "There goes that idea."

There are some new faces in the crowd this year; I'm told mixed in with the yearly regulars. One guy named Larry was a late addition. He called for a room just last week. I told him we were booked up. He left his number and said to call him if there were a cancellation. I told him I would do that but he shouldn't hold his breath. Nobody ever cancels, especially this late. The next day I got a cancellation, unbelievably. I called Larry and he took the room.

The lodgers at the Rock have become friendly through the years. They all seem happy to see each other and catch up on the past year's happenings. There's big Bill Hunter, aptly named for this sport. At six-ten-two-eighty, he towers over the bar. He has a full beard and looks like Grizzly Addams. He is as gentle as a teddy bear. He has been lodging at the Rock for ten years and knows the Gibbs well. He also got stuck with the bridal suite, that he shares with his brothers Steven, and Kevin, the runt of the litter. Steven is six-eight, three-fifty. Kevin is five-ten, one-seventy. They say if you had to pick a fight with one of the brothers, don't pick Kevin. He's been known to take out guys twice his size. His brothers never mess with him.

"So how the hell have you been? Jack asks Bill.

"Great, even got laid twice this year. Of course, zero times with my wife.'

Bill jokes.

"Well I banged my wife just once this year, and the bitch just had another girl. What do I have to do to have a boy!?" James says.

"To have a boy, you have to bang your wife on all fours." Mike joins in.

"I remember that time you had a female on all fours. Her mother was there watching." I chime in.

"What did the mother say?" Johnny "The Lip," asks. "BAAH! BAAH! I say. The place cracks up.

'Hey, don't knock it till you tried it." Mike retorts. The place cracks up again.

"Can you screw a sheep?" The Lip asks.

"Hell yeah, the best I ever had! And they never say NAAH." Mike says. "Old man Potter married his sheep. Slept with her in bed every night. Too bad about what happened to him." Sergeant Bill adds.

"Are you guys shittin' me? Married a sheep? Is that legal up here? That's worse than marrying a man." Lip says.

'I'd rather have my son bring home a sheep than be a homo", Jimmy interjects.

'Not that there's anything wrong with that," David says with his best Jerry Seinfeld impression. Again laughter breaks out.

The frivolities continue as a good time is being had by all. The suits are so excited about hunting. They are acting like kids on Christmas Eve, awaiting Santa.

Jimmy isn't going to partake in the hunting. Seems they don't make hunting gear in tuxedos. Besides, what's the thrill of killing a deer? They won't even plead for their lives, and they haven't stolen any money from him. The boys are banging them back pretty well.

"Pretty crowded in here tonight," Jack comments to me. "You're new here. Hi, I'm Jack and this is my brother James and my sons Brent and Pace."

"Hi, I'm Patrick, glad to meet you. Where are you guys from?" "The Island," Jack says.

"Me, too! I'm from N. Babylon." I say "We're from Huntington." "Practically neighbors," I say.

"Neighbors! Hell, that's on the other side of the island, asshole." James slurs.

"I was speaking figuratively." "Are you calling me stupid?"

"James, enough. Look, I'm sorry. He's had too many." Jack says. "I'll tell you when I had too many. And how come there are so many grease balls in here? I haven't seen so many greasy heads since I went to Little Italy." James says loudly but barely intelligibly.

"What did you just say?" the Lip wanders over to James.

"What's a matter, too much grease in your ears, you guinea bastard!"

163

The lip reaches back and pops James right in the mouth.[Gutsy little bastard. He doesn't know James sucks at fighting when he's drunk. And James is twice his size.]

Jack quickly jumped between his brother and Johnny to calm things down, but Johnny was hot and he threw a roundhouse at Jack, which Jack ducked. Johnny then was about to throw another when Jack popped him right on the nose and sent the Lip to the ground. I leapfrogged over the bar and got between Jack and Johnny and tied to calm things down.

"Enough, stop this shit right now! I yell, but the place is ready to explode into a brawl. Then from the rear of the bar comes a voice, stern, but not as loud.

"Stop this, right now. The crowd hesitates but then seems ready to go back to business. Then comes the voice again, a little louder this time. "I said stop this RIGHT NOW! It's the voice of Jimmy and the place backs down, all except Johnny, who is finally getting up from the shot in the nose.

"I'LL KILL YOU, BASTARDS! I'LL KILL THE BOTH OF YOU. He tries to make his way to Jack, but the other suits are holding him back. "LET ME GO, I'LL KILL THESE BASTARDS! He can't free himself. Jimmy yells from the back again, this time making his way toward Johnny. "Johnny, shut it down."

Johnny starts to calm down but throws in his last verbal jab. "You two better watch your backs!"

"Johnny, what did I say?" Jimmy repeats.

Johnny then retreats to the rear of the bar, steam coming from his ears.

I turn toward Jack and ask him to take his brother and go to the room along with his boys. He responds positively. Then Jimmy gets in his words of wisdom.

"We don't like troublemakers in here. This is a place to come and enjoy. If this happens again, you are going to have to leave. And I know you were defending yourself, but don't ever so much as lay a glove on any of my men again, or I won't hold them back.

Jack nodded and turned toward his brother and gave him a stern look. "This is the absolute last time I defend you. Next time I'm walking out the door and I'll come back and scrape you off the floor.

James' record drops to 1-108. They head upstairs to the room. Johnny watches intently as they pass him.

Peace has been restored but was to be an early night just got earlier. The fight seems to have taken the parting spirit out of the place. I approach Jimmy and thank him for getting the place under control.

"Good job Jimmy. That could have gotten ugly."

"Yeah, I know. That was very brave of you to jump right in the middle of that mess." Jimmy says as he puts his arm around my shoulder. "You know those guys?"

"The locals say they have been coming here forever. I'm told they are great people, but the brother James doesn't hold his liquor very well."

"In the future, keep an eye on him. Don't serve him more than a few."

"Okay. What can you do? Shit happens." "It sure does."

The bar is emptying at a pretty fast pace, but as they are leaving, the excitement of opening day starts to creep in.

Jackie Rizzo can't wait. "I'm gonna shoot me a bigass moose tomorrow!" He claims.

"We ain't hunting moose, we're hunting deer." Big Louie yells to him. "That's what I said, moose." Louie waves him off, giving up.

Johnny asks Mike, "What else can you hunt for out there?"

"Just deer or doe, if you have a license for doe. And if you see one, you can shoot a henway." Mike says.

"Big Louie asks, "What's a henway? {drum roll please}

"About four pounds." Mike gets the last laugh of the night from the crowd, or should I say guffaw.

MJ and I close the Jailhouse Rock at about midnight. We will both return around ten to get ready for the hungry hunters, on their lunch breaks.

Four thirty in the morning the hunters staying at the Rock are gearing up for the big hunt. There is a blanket of snow on the ground, which I'm told makes for better hunting. The deer blend in so well with the background that they are tough to spot, but against the white snow they stand out more. Jack has been hunting in the same spot in the woods since he first started coming here. He stands in a tree and knows the surrounding area like the back of his hand. He will bring his sons to their spot and then set himself up. James usually at least gives it a try on the first day. He may even spend the whole morning, but he doubts it. The other hunters at the Rock are gearing up as well. There is excitement in the air as they make their way to their pickups. The Rock is empty, except for the last person to rent a room, Larry, Larry Kramer. F.B.I. Larry.

Larry waits till the place is empty and makes his way to my office. The door is locked and Larry laughs as he picks the lock with his expert tools. He thinks to himself that he could pick this lock with a key from the top of an old can of Spam. He enters the room and surveys the premises. He notices a cash register, identical to the one in the bar. He sees a garbage pail full of receipts. In the corner of the room, he notices a safe. He makes his way to the safe and starts turning the dial. He has it open in ten seconds. He reaches inside and retrieves two large books. He places them on the desk and starts examining them, clicking photos as he goes along. He reaches into the garbage pail and takes a handful of receipts and places them in a folder he brought along. He then goes over to the cash register and punches in a few indiscriminate numbers and places those receipts in his folder. He then scopes the place out determining his next move. He's got what he needed. He tidies the place up and heads back to his room. Like stealing candy from a baby.

Meanwhile, the suits are gathering up at the Victorian, putting on unfamiliar garb. Ear muffs, hats, gloves, long johns, and orange outfits. There is excitement in the air as they finish their morning coffee.

"Let's go kill some gazelles," Rizzo says.

"Deer, it's fucking deer," Big Louie pleads. "Yeah like I said, let's go get the som bitches."

It's a cold day, 22 degrees with a wind chill factor that makes it feel like ten degrees. For the regular hunters, this is par for the course, but for the suits, this is torture. Big Louie, even with all his fat to insulate him, can only last two hours. He shows up back at the Victorian shivering like a heroin addict needing a fix. The funny thing is he not only saw a deer but took a shot at one. The deer was 200 yards away and he had no chance of hitting it, but he still took a shot. The impact of the shotgun knocked him to the ground. He was twisting around like a turtle on its back. He got up full of snow and that's when he headed back. He left behind a perfect Snow Angel, albeit a large one.

"FFFFFFuckkk hhhhhunting" he said, shaking violently. "Why can't they have hunting season in the summer? What's next, ffffuckin' ice fishing? I'll get my food in Gristedes."

"And it looks like you haven't passed one up in a while," Jimmy says while making hot chocolate for Louie. "Don't feel bad, here come the others."

More than half of the suits had called it quits before lunchtime. Some can't even move their fingers. One of the suits, Paul Marino, is sticking his hands so far into the fireplace that he's going to burn his hands.

"Whose idea was this? This shit is for the Eskimos! From now on my only sport is shooting pool." Paul says.

"Come on, let's get over to the Rock for lunch. It's almost noon and the rest of the guys will be there soon." Jimmy says.

"I ain't going out again till it's summertime," Louie says. "Not even for food?" Jimmy asks.

"Well, only for food."

"Bundle up and let's go. A one-pound burger should make things better." Jimmy says.

"Hell, I think I might need two!"

They make their way to the Rock. The place is starting to fill up with the real hunters."

"It's almost balmy out there," Bill Hunter chimes in, noticing the freezing look on the suits.

"It got so hot out there I had to get down to my tee shirt." Bill's brother Steven joins in. The suits look at them like they're nuts.

"So, who bagged a deer? Does anyone even see one?" Jack asks. "Yeah, I took a shot at one, just missed." Louie proudly orates. "Really, how close did you get?" Mike asks.

"He was about two football fields away." He answers with a wide smile. The locals laugh at him, but at least he saw one.

"What's so funny? He asks

"Nothing at all. You're the only one that saw one. Let them laugh. They're all just jealous." Mike says.

"That's right. I earned my lunch. Patrick, order me two one-pound burger platters! Extra pickle, extra catsup. I want it so rare that it moos when I bite in." He says. "That sounds good. I'll take one too, only just a one-quarter pounder." Jack orders. Now everyone wants a burger platter.

Sitting on the corner of the bar are a young couple that has been coming to the Rock for the last three years. Zach and Dawn are a perfectly matched couple.

Dawn, five foot eight, one hundred ten pounds, looks more like a model than a hunter, but don't let that fool you. She is the only woman that shows up to hunt, and the male hunters don't give her any shit. The first year she showed up with Zach, who has been hunting these parts for years, the hunters rode Zach real hard. Pussy whipped was the nicest thing they said. The ribbing only lasted till lunchtime the first day, when Dawn bagged a ten-pointer, 150lbs. She gutted it and dragged it to the road herself. It was the biggest and only deer shot by the hunters at the Rock. End of ribbing.

After the lunch break was over the real hunters went out for an afternoon of stalking. Most of the suits were settling in for the long haul. Johnny got up and grabbed his gear and headed for the door.

"Where are you going?" Louie asks

"I'm not done in the woods yet. I ain't afraid of a little cold." Johnny says. "Yeah you big pussies, grow some balls," Vito says. A few more suits grab

their gear for the afternoon hunt. The rest look very comfortable and remain.

The hunters scatter, some to the right, some to the left and away they go. "What about you, Mike, no hunting this afternoon? Vito asks.

"Nah, I'm done for the day. I got my quota this morning." He replies. "How come you didn't tell anyone? Seems like you're the best hunter in here." Vito says.

"He didn't say anything because he doesn't HUNT! The serge says as he's heading out for the afternoon hunt.

"What'd ya mean? Vito inquires.

"What that bastard does is he hangs deer food from the tree behind his house all year long. When hunting season comes around, he sits in his warm kitchen, waits for a deer to come to the feeder, opens his window enough to fit the barrel of the shotgun through, and blasts little Bambi! Serge protests.

Big Louie stands and applauds ingenuity of Mike. "Add a bowl of pasta to that situation and I'll start hunting again."

"Add a bowl of pasta to any situation and you're in." Jimmy laughs.

Serge heads out the door, turns to Mike and says, "I'm going to do some real hunting," and slams the door shut.

Mike waits till he's a safe distance away and says, "Go freeze your ass off asshole!" The guys crack up.

"I think he heard you and he's coming back," I announce urgently.

Mike's head snaps around to look at the door so quickly that he almost gets whiplash. He sees Serge in the distance heading toward the woods. He looks back at me. "Asshole!"

Another laugh from the boys.

I've been told that the hunters don't stay out past dusk. Between four and five o'clock they call it a day and head back for happy hour at the Rock. Sure enough 4:01 they start walking through the door. As per usual, Mike is there to "greet" them back.

"Skunked again?" is his usual greeting. Most of the time he's right. "Shove it up your ass!" one of the freezing locals, Richard Weed says.

"Why don't stick your gun out the window and shoot your mom."

'I think I'd rather stick my cock out the window and have your mom suck it!" Mike retorts. A big laugh rolls through the bar as Richard searches for a reply. He's no match for Mike.

"Oh yeah! You're a mother." Is his unwitting reply. Mike cracks up and gives him a stupid reply.

"Oh yeah! Your mother." That's it.

As the others arrive, Mike continues his greeting, but the others know better and ignore him.

The hunters start warming up as darkness creeps in. most of the hunters are back from hunting. Both Zach and Dawn bagged a deer, the only success stories, besides Mike's, of the day. Surprisingly, the suits lasted out the afternoon hunt and didn't look as bad as lunchtime. Johnny the "Lip" came in with his chest pushed out [what little chest there is] and plopped down on a bar stool.

"Give me a Johnny Walker Black, straight up. Make that a double!" He tells MJ.

"You must have something to celebrate," Jimmy says. "You usually only order that after a big day."

"It was a big day! I don't let the weather or no one get the best of me. I do what I have to do. If that means freezing my ass off, then so be it!" He responds.

"You got a deer?" Big Louie asks. "Nah, I go for a big game."

"You shot a bear? Louie asks.

'Why would I shoot a bear? He never did anything to me." Louie gets a puzzled look on his face and drops the subject.

Fish stories, or should I say deer stories are flying around the room. Zach says he hit his deer, a six-pointer, right in the heart. "It took three steps and down it went." He proudly states.

Dawn tells how she hit an eight-pointer in the heart, also. It took no steps.

Zach's shoulders slump.

"It wasn't three steps; it kind of just stumbled down." "Yeah, mine too," Dawn says with a knowing grin.

It's pitch black out now and the place is coming alive. A few beers and shots no doubt are helping the atmosphere. On the corner of the bar sitting on a stool with a coke in hand is James Gibbs. He spots his nephews across the bar and calls them over.

"How'd you guys do today?" he asks. Brent and Pace shrug their shoulders. '

"Didn't see a thing, not even a squirrel," Brent replies. "Me either. Says Pace.

"How about your dad?" James asks.

"I don't know, I haven't seen him yet," Brett replies. "Me neither." Pace says.

"He must be up in the room. I'm going up there anyway. I'll see what he's doing." James pushes himself away from the bar and heads upstairs.

The place is jumping now with all the hungry and thirsty patrons. MJ and I are serving drinks nonstop, although I manage to grind on MJ's ass every time I squeeze by her. Now and then I just grab a handful, discreetly. Sometimes I get a smile and other times she gives me a "don't you dare" look. I go for it anyway.

James comes back from the room with a concerned look on his face. "He's not up there." He tells his nephews. "Patrick or Mj, did you see Jack

come back from hunting?"

"No, I haven't, you MJ?" I say

"No, not since lunch," MJ responds.

Jack has been hunting these parts forever and knows his area like the back of his hand. He is also a very cautious hunter and would never stay in the woods past dark. James starts to get more concerned.

"Has anybody seen my brother, Jack, since lunch?" he asks the whole bar. Most of the patrons turn toward James and shake their heads negatively. Johnny the lip is telling stories to the suits and they are all laughing. James walks over to his table with anger in his eyes.

"Can't you here, I asked if has anyone seen my brother?" he snorts. "Who gives a fuck about you or your brother. Get the fuck out of my face." He states.

"I swear if you had anything to do with this I'll skin you alive." James Johnny gets up from his seat and is ready to go at it. Jimmy shoots look over to the "Lip"

"Johnny, not now!" He walks over to them and separates them. I assure you Johnny had nothing to do with your brother, right Johnny? He looks Johnny in the eyes to get a read on him.

"Fuck that bastard! Who cares! I hope he's freezing his ass off!" Johnny says.

James tries to get at Johnny and is held back by Jimmy and others.

"I know my brother! He has never and would never stay out this late.

Something's wrong. I'm going to his post and find out what's wrong."

"Come on everyone. Let's give James a hand." Mike yells to the crowd. The crowd responds as everyone grabs their coats and gloves.

"We're going to need flashlights. Anybody who has one, grab them." Mike says.

"I have a couple in my office. I'll go get them." I say and head upstairs. Brent and pace are looking very scared.

"He's alright, don't worry," Mj tells them.

Everybody, even the suits are gearing up to help out. The jeans guys, now with their new cohort, Larry, are gearing up while looking very serious. Jimmy grabs Johnny in the corner and seems very angry.

"Where is his post? Serge asks.

"It's down on old man Prazzes's farm. I know exactly where it is." James says.

"When I was packing it in I heard a couple of shots coming from that area, around four thirty or so," Serge says.

"All right everyone let's go!" Mike says.

The crowd makes their way to the door. Everyone jumps into their pickup trucks and follows James to Prazzes Farm.

It's only a short ride and they empty the vehicles to start the search. James leads the way. They form a horizontal line twenty-five people wide. "His post is about a half mile in," James says.

They follow James' lead and start the search. Snow is falling and it may cover any footprints made by Jack. So far no sign of life as they near his post. James is the first to reach the site. It's empty and no sign of Jack. They start tracking beyond the post and James discovers a disturbing sight 20 yards from the post. It's a pool of blood.

"Over here!" he screams.

They all come to the area and see blood. The boys, Brent and Lacy shudder at the thought.

"Look, footprints leading deeper into the woods!" Mike yells.

They make their way over toward Mike. What they see is not only footprints leading deeper into the woods, but a trail of blood following the prints.

"Why would he go deeper into the woods if he were wounded?" Mike asks James.

"He wouldn't unless he was disoriented. Let's spread out and follow the tracks. We'll find him, hopefully on time." James broods.

They follow the blood and prints deeper and deeper into the woods, but still no sign. Then Larry sees something on top of a hill. He yells out Jack's name.

Everyone joins in. They hear a faint voice come from the area. James runs as fast as he can, and when he gets there he sees his brother lying on his side, covered with blood. Then he notices lying on the ground next to Jack the largest deer he has ever seen. Jack stops gutting the deer and turns toward his brother.

"Why is everyone out here?" he asks. Now James is as mad as he is relieved.

"Do you realize how late it is? We thought you were dead. You never stay in the woods this late!"

His kids come over and hug their dad, blood and all.

"Do you see the size of this beast? I think it might be a record kill. I shot him just when it started to get dark. I had to follow him or I would never have found him."

All the others marvel at the size of the deer, which was more like a moose than a deer. It indeed was a state record. Three hundred fifty pounds and a sixteen-point rack. This one is going to cost him some cash to mount it.

'You scared the hell out of us. You're lucky that the deer was this big. If you made us leave our beers for a little doe, we'd be kicking your ass right about now." Mike says. "Hurry up and finish gutting him so we can help you carry him to the truck." Mike places his hand behind his ear and asks, "Do you hear that? That's my beer calling me, and he wants me there quick so let's get going." Everyone starts to head back to the trucks.

"Listen, everyone, let's stick together, you can very easily get lost in here, and we're not coming back out here again!" Serge says.

They take turns dragging the deer out of the woods. Everyone is relieved, but they realize this could have been a lot worse. Why were they so sure that Johnny Scarpinto would kill somebody?

They have the deer into Jack's pickup and head back to the Rock.

Everyone is freezing their asses off. Jack thanks everyone for their concern.

"My family has been coming here as long as I can remember, and one of the reasons we chose to keep coming back to the majestic Jailhouse Rock Inn is because of the wonderful people of this town. Even though we only come here a few weeks a year, you've always treated us like we were family, and for that we thank you. There isn't a better town in the world. I'm going to show my appreciation to you the way I know you would like it best. DRINKS FOR EVERYONE, ON ME!" Jack says.

The whooping and howling start as expected. And of course, Mike orders the most expensive drink.

"Everybody, raise your glass to the Great White Hunter, Jack! May he shoot many more deer and buy many more rounds!" Mike says.

The only one not raising his glass is Johnny "The Lip."

After closing the Rock for the night, Maryjane and I head home in our car. "When all of you left to go find Jack, only Jimmy and Johnny stayed behind. Jimmy was scolding Johnny. He said that this place was like Camp David, the President's getaway. He told him that they come here to forget about downstate, to relax and enjoy it. He then told him he wanted no blood on any of their hands up here. Johnny was getting irritated and saying he had been disrespected in front of the men. Jimmy gave him a stare that made me shudder from across the room. He told him no more, that's the end, and walked away. What do you think he meant by all of that?" MJ asks.

"MJ, you don't mess with these guys. You see what they did to Donald.

They are not to be trusted. Let's keep our distance from them and keep our noses clean." I say.

"Patrick, we work for them. We are running the Rock for them. I think we are already in too deep." MJ says.

"But the Rock is a legitimate business. We're just holding down the fort." "I don't know, but if you say so."

"Don't worry; we'll be alright. Man, all this talk is making me horny!" "Is there anything that doesn't make you horny?"

"Libby." [As long as there is one other woman left on the planet.] "You'd do a snake if I held it."

"You'd do that for me?"

"Let's just get inside and get to bed. I am kind of a little horny. I could go for a little kissing and licking in my southern region. You up for that?"

I reach into my trousers and pull out Mr. Penis, fully loaded. "Does that answer your question?"

MJ pulls into the driveway and leans over and gives me the best BJ I ever had. After a very happy ending, she looks up at me and says, "My turn." I repay my debt right then and there. After a stiff neck and bumps on my head from the steering wheel, I file in my brain that this is not a good place to give oral sex, although, by the foggy windows and MJ's panting and screaming, she didn't seem to think it was such a bad place. MJ is one of a kind and I plan on keeping her around forever!

The rest of the hunting season goes on without any hitches.

Chapter 21
The Passing

Hunting season lasts only a few weeks and the bulk of hunters from downstate come during the first week. After that, there is only a smattering of hunters, mostly the locals. The locals eat deer meat, and venison, it's called, to make it sound better like fish soup is called bouillabaisse because no one would eat fish soup. The locals swear they like it too. One of the hunters shot a deer and asked me if I wanted it. I went to Phil to see if we should put it on the menu. He said yes and he made a venison roast and venison chili. It wasn't ordered by anyone. Phil and I tried it and it sucked. So much for anyone liking it.

It's the end of the month and Jimmy shows up with the big bag of cash. Once again my favorite part is when he reaches inside the bag and hands me my portion of the loot. He forks over about eleven hundred. The take for the bar is forty-five g's this month and the suits were only here one week, but he tells me that's what they owed.

MJ tells me business will start to taper off as the weather starts to get colder. She says most of the regulars will still come, but no more down staters till about May. There are many snowmobile trails and ski lodges nearby, but they aren't used as much anymore.

I am not a fan of the cold. Cold hurts. I'd rather be hot. No matter how hot you get, it never hurts. Cold hurts hands, feet, toes, and noses. And then there's snow.

Snow is beautiful when it's falling, but after that, it's a pain in the neck. I always envisioned retiring to a warm climate. I figured if I ever left the Island I would move to Carolina or Florida. How I ended up here is beyond me. Must have been those drugs I took back in the sixties.

It's the middle of December, and MJ was right. Business sucks. The good thing is that everyone seems to have the Christmas spirit. MJ has decorated the place beautifully. Wreaths and balls hanging everywhere. Garland strung over the whole joint. And the signs say Merry Christmas! No "Happy Holidays" here.

Business is so slow that I decided to go back downstate for Christmas Eve and Christmas Day. MJ says she wants to spend Christmas with her children and family, so we part different ways for the holidays. I will miss her but it's only a couple of days. I make sure I get plenty of sex before I leave.

I drive downstate with Brad. Seems my daughter and him are doing well. They are deciding which one of them will make the move. Brad loves the Island, but his job is up here. Pamela has no problem moving upstate, but she hopes they can stay on the Island. Brad is bugging his dad to let him work from the Island. His dad seems to be weakening.

It's great to see the family. I am still like a little kid when it comes to Christmas. It brings such joy to everyone, especially the little ones. When I see the look in their eyes when they see Santa Clause, it brings back childhood memories. My family always celebrated Christmas Eve the same way. One of the grownups would sneak away and dress up in a Santa suit. He would come to an HO-HO-HOing into the house, jingling his bells. He'd hand out presents to the children, and pandemonium would ensue. Gift wrapping flying everywhere; kids jumping for joy with their new toys. Then Santa would leave and more presents were handed out. And another Christmas is gone. Wait till next year.

Well, it was much the same this year. But something was missing, Maryjane. In such a short time I've fallen hard for her. I can't wait to get back in the car heading back "home." The day after Christmas I head back.

I get back to the house and MJ is inside waiting for me. To my joy, she missed me as much as I missed her. She greets me at the door with a great big hug. Tears are rolling down her cheeks.

"Let's not be apart anymore. It was the longest three days of my life. I had fun with my family, but felt empty without you here." MJ cries.

"I felt the same way. From now on it's me and you." I say.

Of course, all of this hugging turns into sex. And what a session it was. It was the best Christmas present ever. Pandemonium ensued and clothes were flying everywhere.

Welcome home!

Back to work again. The boss shows up on Saturday with his bag of goodies. He hands me my bonus for the month, $1,200.

"I don't think I deserve a bonus this month. This is the worst month since I took over." I say.

"Nonsense!" He says handing over the bag of cash. "It happens to be the best month!"

I open the bag and it's filled to the brim. 80 g's worth.

"Your guys don't owe that much. They weren't even here." I say. "They owed it from other months, and some that didn't pay last month paid double this month. Now, do you get it?" He says, grabbing the bag from me, reaching in, and handing me another four grand. "Here's the rest of your bonus."

"Thanks, but I don't get it."

"Don't worry, Ira is coming next week to file the year-end tax for the Rock. I'll have him do the income tax for you and MJ. He's good. For now, just do what he showed you to do."

"I'll be writing receipts for two days, with this much cash." "That's why you get paid the big bucks."

He leaves the office and I begin writing, just like Ira said. What did I get myself into?

New Year's Eve is tomorrow night, but according to MJ, the locals stay home. They call it amateur night. They don't feel safe on the roads with all the amateur drunks driving and with the extra police out putting up roadblocks, so as MJ predicts the year ends quietly for the Jailhouse Rock Inn. Although I'm sure that once Jimmy gets done we will have made ten grand for the night.

Ira Erwinski shows up bright and early on Monday morning. He's carrying a large briefcase, or should I say suitcase, and proceeds to the office. He opens the case and starts placing papers, computer calculators, and whatnot on the desk.

"Give me all the paperwork for the Rock and then you can go do whatever you want. It'll be a while. Jimmy asked me to do the income tax for you and Maryjane. Get that paperwork to me and I'll do it for you." He says.

I open the safe and give him both books, and I give him the W 2's for me and MJ.

"That'll do. I call you when I'm done."

I close the door and head back to the bar. "That's that Ira guy. Why's he here?" MJ asks.

"He's here to do the year-end tax for the Rock and he's going to do our taxes for us."

"I usually do my own. Why didn't you ask me first?" MJ asks. "He didn't start yet. I can go get them."

I turn to head upstairs.

"Hold on. Why did you want him to do our taxes?"

"First of all, he's a professional. Secondly, we both made more this year than at any time in our lives. We could use his help." "O.K. but next time, ask me first."

"Whoa, I've never seen you be so firm with me before. I like it, it kind of turns me on." I remark.

She just shakes her head and tries to suppress a smirk.

About four hours later he calls for us to come up.

"Patrick, I need you to sign everywhere I placed an x on these forms." He spreads out the papers and I start signing. As I'm signing I notice that the Rock has paid substantial taxes. I hope he's done a better job with MJs and mine. I finish signing and hand him back the papers. "Now you have to sign your tax forms. He hands them to MJ and me. MJ and I look at the forms and see the bottom-line figures. We are getting back almost a hundred percent of the taxes we paid. Ira sees the looks on our faces.

"Not too bad, and it's all legit. It's amazing how many people pay too much." He says.

"Thanks, how much do we owe you?" He laughs. "It's on me and Jimmy."

He starts packing his things and heads out the door.

"You did a good job! I have CPs that have six years of college on my staff that don't pick things up as you did, Patrick. Call me when you need me. See ya."

He labors down the stairs with his case and disappears out the front door. The following Monday, Mj and I are hunkered down on the couch. It's five degrees outside, with a wind chill factor that makes it feel like five below. I peer out the window and see our mailman, Ed Peters, placing the mail in our box. Ed is also the garbage man and the water meter reader. He was also from L.I. but moved his family up here ten years ago. He couldn't take the traffic and the mobs at the mall.

I get out from under the blanket and make my way to the door. I wave to Ed. "Cold enough for you?"

I notice he has no hat or gloves on.

"I don't feel cold till it hits at least minus twenty!" he claims.

I barely have my head hanging out the door and I feel like my ears are getting frostbite. "At minus twenty even my penis won't work," I say.

"I doubt it," MJ says from under the covers.

"Hold on you big sissy, I'll bring the mail in for you," Ed says getting out of his mail/garbage/water meter truck. He hands me the mail while I barely open the door wide enough for him to give it to me.

"Join me and Mj for a coffee or soup or something?" I ask.

"Naw, I got to pick up garbage when I'm done. I'll take a rain check on that." Ed teases.

"You mean an ice check!" I say.

"Aw, hurry and close the door so your little toesy-woseys won't get cold."

"Thanks for bringing it up. This will reflect in next year's Christmas tip." "Wow, thanks. You mean I'll get more than the two dollars I got this year?"

"That was a two-dollar bill? I could have sworn it was a twenty."[it was] 'That's right, I was thinking about the other cheapskate on the route Stevie."

'All right, wise ass. See you tomorrow. Keep warm.'

I close the door and run back to the blanket, mail-in shivering hand. I snuggle with Mj, but she pushes me away as I try to place them on her ass. "Keep your hands off me, they're freezing." She says. "That's precisely why I'm putting them there!"

I remain wrapped in the covers and start to thaw out. I start flipping through the mail, ninety percent of which is pure garbage. Six credit card offers, three charities looking for cash, an ad to buy an air conditioner and to my chagrin, two letters addressed to Mj and me, with return addresses from the I.R.S. I knew Ira got us too much money back. These are probably to tell us we're going to be audited. What did I get Mj into? She wanted to do her own. Oh boy. MJ sees the look on my face.

"What's the matter, bad news?" she inquires.

I hand over her letter, and by the look on her face, she is thinking what I'm thinking.

"First of all, are we getting audited? And how could they get it back in one I hadn't even given that a thought, but it scares me even more."

"Well, who's going to open theirs first?" I ask.

"You! This was your big idea, Mr. my ship has come in, Ralph Kramden."

She's right. This is another fine mess I've gotten us into. I slowly open my envelope. I reach inside and to my joy and relief, I find a check, in the full amount Ira had figured. MJ quickly opens hers and finds the same result. We both breathe a sigh of relief.

"Wow, that was scary, but look at these checks! Nice!" I say.

"Yeah, let's go put them in the bank! I think I'll do some shopping. This is exciting!" MJ says

"Yeah, it is. Are you thinking what I'm thinking?" I ask. "You sure it's not twenty below out?"

"No, but I'll show you how you can make twenty, below."

"With this check in my hand, twenty's not enough! The price has gone up!"

"It's a deal. But when you're done, that's it. None for you!"

"That's not fair! All right, I guess it's for free." She says as she disappears under the covers.

I run out and start the car. Car batteries hate the cold as much as I do. No matter how new the battery is, it takes time to crank the engine over. Every time in this weather I hold my breath when I turn the key. At first, you get that slow cranking sound, raow, raow. Then you hope the engine engages before hearing the dreaded sound, clickclikckclickclick. Today is a good day. The engine cooperates with the battery and turns over. I quickly run back to the house to warm up.

MJ is bundling up with her furry hat, scarf, and giant gloves. I have two pairs of Long Johns on. Try doing that. I'm walking like the Tin Man. When the car is warm enough, we run from the house to get in. It's not that warm, but it's better than being outside. We head to the bank to cash our income tax checks. On the way over, coincidentally, we hear the Beatles' tune, "Tax Man." It's a song George Harrison wrote about his displeasure with the high tax rate in England. They should have met Ira Erwinski, but then we would have had one less great Beatles song. We pull in front of the bank and of course run in. We are greeted at the door by Harvey.

"Hurry in," he says as he holds the door for us. "It's sure a cold one today!

Grab a cup of java, and get warm. How can I help you today? How's old Jeb's place doing, that poor guy."

"Thanks, but can I get an electric blanket if I deposit this check in your bank." I kid.

Harvey looks at the check and raises his eyebrows.

"Nice check, maybe we do have an electric blanket lying around somewhere. I hope I'm not being too intrusive, but is this your income tax check?" "Yes, Maryjane and I got them in the mail this morning."

"I don't believe I've ever seen one so soon. The Jailhouse Rock Inn must be doing awful well," he says seeing the large refund Mj and I receive. "Do you need any help over there? I make a mean "Old Fashion!"

"Then who would supply the good people of this town with all this wonderful money you loan out?" I say.

We get our coffee, cash our checks and run to the car.

A few days go by and we head to the Rock to get ready for the lunch crowd. MJ goes to work behind the bar and I go up to the office to take care of some paperwork. After a short time, there's a knock on the door.

Chapter 22
Larry

"Who's there?" I ask

"It's Larry Kramer. Got a minute?"

"Sure Larry, come on in. What can I do for you?"

Larry enters the office with a notebook under his arm. "We need to talk." He whips out his badge. "I'm with the F.B.I. I have a couple of questions I need to be answered."

F.B.I.? What would he want with me? The tax return. It's got to be that. "Shoot, but I don't mean literally," I say trying to lighten the mood. He doesn't change his expression.

Larry Kramer has been pursuing Donald Nostick for ten years. Donald was good at his business. He never left himself open for mistakes. He ran a crooked business, but he covered his tracks. Larry was able to arrest some of the fringe gangsters, but couldn't get Don. He started admiring the way Don was able to keep clean, but he tried his best to nail him. When Don was gunned down, Larry felt sad and also felt cheated. He wanted to be the man to bring him to justice. Now that opportunity was gone. He knew Jimmy Esposito since he became Don's, right-hand man. He also knew that Jimmy was the one who put the hit out on Don. Jimmy was not like Don. Jimmy was ruthless. He might look like a gentleman in his tux, but he would kill his mom if she took five bucks from him. Larry didn't like Jimmy and wanted him badly. He just never thought it could happen so fast. Jimmy has already made mistakes Donald would never make, and he's ready to bring him down.

"Jimmy Esposito is the head of the Luccio Crime Family. He ordered the hit on your old boss, Donald Nostick. He is a ruthless killer. No one gets in his way and sees him the next day. You have now joined his enterprise. We know that Jimmy has been laundering money here at the Jailhouse Rock Inn, and you are the one doing it for him. We also know that you are guilty of income tax evasion. Somehow, every week you are putting more money into your bank account than you claim to be making. You also have collected unemployment insurance while working here at the Rock. We also know that your girlfriend, Maryjane has filed a false tax statement. Needless to say, you're in big trouble. At best you and Maryjane will spend ten years behind bars."

I have never been in trouble with the law. I am hearing Larry tell me these things but it's like watching a movie. The sound of his voice seems to come from far away. I feel the room spinning, and at the same time closing in on me. I guess I really knew things weren't kosher around here, but I closed my mind to it because the money was outrageous. They say in near-death experiences, people see their lives flash before them. That's what's happening now. I am bringing Mj down with me. I won't see my family or friends; I'll be old when I get out. I imagine being a cellmate of Bubba and having to toss his salad, daily. Maybe this is a cruel joke Mike is playing on me.

"Did you hear a word I just said?! Larry states firmly.

I come out of my haze and search for the right answer. I've had friends that, when faced with similar situations just lie. Should I play dumb? Should I ask for a lawyer to be present, I decide to stay mum.

"I'm not here to put you in jail. I have bigger fish to fry. I want Jimmy and his band of thugs. I need your help. If you cooperate, I'll see to it that you don't spend a day in jail and we'll wipe the record clean. If you do the right thing. I know you're not one of these wise guys. I've been checking you out. I know you just got into something over your head, but that doesn't mean that you didn't break the law. Can I count on you?"

"Are you recording this or is this off the record?" I ask.

"No recorder. Just me and you. Whatever you tell me now won't be held against you."

"What about Maryjane?"

"We don't want her, we want Jimmy. We won't even tell her. If you cooperate her slate will be wiped clean, and she can even keep the money. I have here the income tax checks you both cashed." He reaches into his notebook and hands me copies of the checks. "Once you cashed them, you were guilty."

'So that's why we got the checks back so soon! Before I do anything, I want it in writing that our records are clean and there will be no jail time. And what about Jimmy? You tell me he's a ruthless killer. If he finds out about this I'm dead. And what about if you do convict him? Then he'll put a hit out on me."

"If he catches you in the act' you'll be in danger. We will always be close by. We'll do the best we can to protect you during this. After the trial, we'll give you a new identity and place you in the Witness Protection Program."

"Great, a lose, loss situation. If I do this, I don't want MJ involved in any of this! She has to remain clean. I don't want them after her."

"Deal. We need to get started soon. Are you in?"

"Like I have a choice. First I want everything in writing. Then what's the next step?"

"I'll have it in writing tomorrow. Then I'm going to come here with a couple of my men and place cameras and bugs in this office. We will come after you close the bar so no one will see us. We need to see him hand you the cash. These devices are so small, they will never be detected. We will monitor the office from our place around the block. Anything goes wrong and we will be here in minutes. We will do this till we get him to do it two times, then that will be it. You'll be done, except for testifying."

I've seen enough gangster movies. The snitch never makes it out alive. Those stupid bastards at the milk company. I hope all their cows run dry. The Witness Protection Program is great! I'll probably be living next store to Sammy "The Bull" Gravano and Henry Hill. I hope Steve Martin is still there, My Blue Heaven. I'm screwed.

"I hope those bastards that brought Jack Ruby into the court are no longer working."

"I'm sure they are gone. We'll protect you, I promise."

"Anything else? You sure you don't want to tell me I'm adopted or something?"

"That's for another day." He gathers his things and heads for the door. "I'll see you tomorrow morning with the paperwork. I'll need you to show me the books tomorrow, both sets. I know they're in the safe so don't try anything foolish. And don't try to run, we'll find you. Tomorrow night, we will install the bugs and then we'll wait for Jimmy."

"Do I at least get a gun?" "Have you ever fired a gun?"

"No, but it doesn't look that difficult."

"You would do more bad than good with a gun. Besides, if Jimmy finds a gun on you he would be very suspicious. Leave the guns in the proper hands." "Yeah, like Jimmy and his thugs. How about a Swiss Army Knife?' "I'll see you tomorrow morning." He heads out the door.

I reach into my desk drawer and take out my bottle of Bacardi Rum and pour myself a large glass, just like I've seen them do in the movies. I take a big gulp. It goes down like swallowing broken glass. I choke till I can't breathe, then run to the bathroom to vomit. Bad move, but it always works on the big screen.

I recover a little and wash my face. I look in the mirror and I look like shit. MJ is going to notice immediately. I'm going to have to make an excuse and leave it out the back door. I run down the stairway and head out the back door.

"Mj, I gotta run home quickly. I think I left the stove on. I'll be right back!" I say as I exit the back door.

"But Patrick, wait…." She says, but I'm long gone.

I jump into the car and head back to the house. I need some time to think this through. My mind is racing as I drive the short ride home. A million thoughts a second. What does it feel like to be shot? Will I ever get to see my kids again? No more of Mj's great blow jobs.

I'll be looking over my shoulders all the time. A car will backfire and I'll be hitting the deck. I'll be afraid to start my car every day. I guess I'll buy a remote start, or have my ex-wife start the car for me. Finally a good thought. I guess life as I know it is over. Tomorrow will be the first day of the rest of my life, however long that is.

The phone rings and it's MJ.

"Hi, sweetheart. I didn't leave the stove on."

"I tried to tell you that, but you just rushed out the door. I always check the stove before I leave."

"Well, I feel better that I checked it. I will be there in a while. I feel a little tired. I think I'll take a nap."

"Are you all right?" "Yeah, just a little tired."

"You want me to come home?"

'Nah, I'll be there soon. Thanks anyway, I love you." "I love you, too."

I want to get my shit together before I go back. There's no place I can go; nobody I can talk to. I'm on an island, all by myself. alone.

The next morning I get a knock on the office door. It's Larry, but he's not.

"It's Larry. Can I come in?" "It's open."

Larry enters the room with two other men, David and Joey, the jeans brothers.

"I think you know them." He says as they flash their badges at me. "Oh, so you've been at this a while, great," I say.

"We're sorry about this. We know you're a good guy, but you only have yourself to blame for this.' David says.

"We weren't here to get you. You just fell into this mess, and now we need your help." Joey says.

"Check around so we know what we need to bring tonight," Larry tells the others. card, first."

"Wait a minute. Before you do anything, I want my "Get Out of Jail Free" Larry reaches into his briefcase and hands me a document that says I will have full immunity if I cooperate, signed by Chief Justice Burger.

"Here, read it over and sign on the bottom. There's one copy for you and one for us." Larry states.

I read the whole thing, but don't understand all the legal mumbo jumbo. I add my little piece to the bottom. I write, "If this means that Maryjane and I won't go to jail and I will be placed in the witness protection plan then I give my signature." I sign it and hand it back to Larry. He looks it over and places it in his case. The other two are going over to the office with a fine toothcomb.

"We got what we need. We'll be back after closing tonight." Larry says. "Do you want me to leave the doors unlocked?" I ask.

They all giggle.

"No, we'll be all right," Larry says, as they leave the office.

I make my way back to the bar. Another slow day, only two patrons, or are they F.B.I. or C.I.A. or K.G.B. Every new face in here will be scrutinized by me. MJ spots me and gives me a quizzical look.

"What did Larry and the others want?"

"They enjoyed the hunting season so much they wanted to book their rooms for next year. They liked the ambiance of the Jailhouse Rock Inn."

"Larry didn't even hunt."

"He just liked being around all the excitement of the season." "Everything all right with you?"

She can read me like a book. I hope Jimmy doesn't, although I don't think he's read too many books.

"I'm fine, I think I'm getting a little cabin fever."

She leaves it at that, but the look in her eyes says differently.

We close the bar and head home, and that's when the "Watergate" break-in occurs. They go around to the back door and open the lock with ease. They head to the office and place cameras and microphones, so they can see and hear everything going on. When they finish, they place some cameras and mikes around the bar, especially around the table Jimmy and the suits frequent. They are in and out in no time, and now my every move will be recorded. Maybe it will make a good reality show, like Ozzie Osborn and his family. The clock is now ticking.

The first couple of days I am conscious of every move I make. I am afraid I will pick my nose or fart or do something stupid. I search the room to try and locate the equipment, but I can't spot anything. Maybe this is just for a T.V. show like Candid Camera or Punked. In the end, Jimmy and Larry and the rest will jump out of a closet and say "You've Been Punked" I wish.

After the initial days, I start to relax, as if the cameras are not even there. Life seems to be back to normal. I even grab Mj's ass behind the bar. I also rub my penis on her while making my way around her behind the bar. She gives me a look that says "do me here and now." It seems with my "cabin fever" we haven't been having a lot of sex. There is only one customer in the bar. MJ looks his way to make sure he's not looking and then grabs a handful of my crotch.

"You do this to every guy that grinds on you?" I ask. "Only if they let me."

"I can't wait to get home," I whisper to her. "Me, too.

I give her a peck on her lips. I want to go to my office, but I have to wait till my crotch tent subsides, but it's not cooperating and the looks Mj's giving me aren't helping and she knows it. If it stays like this for four hours, do I have to see a doctor? It finally retracts into its shell and I head to the office.

I am just about to sit on my chair behind the desk when there is a knock on the door. I go over to the door and open it. It's Maryjane, with her breasts exposed.

"Got a spare minute?" she asks.

"Mj, what are you doing? Someone is going to see you?"

'There's no one up here except me and you, and only one guy downstairs and Molly is taking care of him. Are you going to ask me in?"

She looks beautiful and with her breasts exposed I am immediately at attention, but the cameras and mikes are on. If I say no she certainly will be suspicious. I guess the jeans guys are about to get a show. I grab her arm and pull her into the office and start kissing her, trying to cover her boobs with my body. We work our way over to my desk. MJ unstraps my belt and pulls down my pants. I realize I can either be camera shy and not enjoy this or I can say the hell with it. I chose the latter. I undo her belt and drop her pants and panties. I push everything off the desk, place her on it and penetrate her warm, wet vagina. She groans as I thrust my penis in and out. It's been a while since the last time and I can't hold back. I unload in her as she is panting and groaning, having her climax. Once again, she pleases me like no other, but as I start to come down I realize my ass is on T.V. We get up and Mj heads to the bathroom.

"Thanks, big boy, you know how to satisfy my needs." "It's my pleasure. Literally."

She heads out of the office and down the hall.

"I hope you bastards enjoyed that," I say looking around the room trying to find a camera.

"You say something to me?" MJ yells from the hallway. "No, no, just talking to myself," I tell her.

"This better not be on YouTube," I whisper to the room.

It's the end of the month and it's time for the big show. Jimmy's coming this afternoon. He called ahead to make sure I would be here because he wasn't going to stay very long. He had some other business to take care of and he said he wanted to be in and out. The F.B.I. guys know of this because they have bugged my phone and the Rocks' phone. Bastards. They come over to the Rock to give me last-minute instructions. Act naturally, they say. Yeah, right. Don't do anything out of the ordinary. Then they leave me out to dry.

"I'll only be around the corner. If anything goes wrong, I'll be here in an instant. I am also leaving David and Joey in the bar, so you're as safe as can be expected." Larry says.

"Would you feel safe leaving your mother in this situation?" I ask. "My mother didn't break the law," Larry responds. Bastard.

It's now waiting time and the clock feels like it's going backward. I look at the clock every ten minutes and only a minute has gone by. I go up to the office and pour a glass of rum, this time only a small glass. I sip it and it starts to relax me immediately. After another half an hour, I hear a rumbling on the stairway. It's Jimmy and he's got his driver, Sammy, with him. They open the door without a knock.

"Hey, what's up? I'm sorry to be in such a rush, but I bought more property and Harvey the banker wants to close it out today." Jimmy says.

"What did you buy this time? Pretty soon you're going to own the whole county. They'll have to rename it Jimmyville."

"Hey, I like that. It has a nice ring to it. The place looks a little different to me. You change anything?"

I almost shit when he says this but I keep my smile on.

'Yeah, I moved my coffee cup from the left side of the desk to the right side. You like it?"

"You're a pisser. O.K. let's get this done." He reaches into the bag and pulls out a wad of cash, but not as much as usual. Twenty grand to be exact. He hands me a five hundred.

"Only twenty grand this month. I guess the economy has started to hurt the Rock." I say.

'Yeah, nobody goes out when it's fucking cold. Even the whores don't like walking the streets." Sammy whines.

"All right. You know what to do. We got to get going. How is the place doing? I miss it."

"Slow, dog slow. I don't think we made enough to cover the bills." "What do you mean, we made twenty grand!" Jimmy states.

"Oh yeah, I forgot my best customer came in today." I say "We gotta get going. I'll see you next month."

"All right, I'll see you then."

They leave the office and I want to collapse on the floor, but I have to wait till they're long gone. I look out the window and watch them pull away. I fall back in my seat and pour myself another rum. Aargh. All I need is an eye patch and I'll be an official pirate. Then there's a knock on the door and I almost shit my draws. I place the bottle back on the desk.

"It's open, come in."

MJ comes through the doorway, a sight for sore eyes.

"I saw Jimmy and Sammy leave in such a hurry. Is everything all right?" "Yeah, just the monthly "State of the Rock" address. They had to leave so fast because they had to get to the bank. Jimmy bought some more property and Harvey was waiting on them to close the deal."

"How did the Rock do this month?" "Twenty grand."

I shakes her head.

"Twenty grand! We didn't have twenty people this month. I don't like the feel of this. I think we should consider getting out of this business before it's too late."

[It is too late. Why didn't you say that last month? Oh, maybe you did.] "You're right. Let's think this over, but don't tell anyone."

MJ comes over and wraps her arms around me and gives me a big hug and kiss.

"You're the best." She says. "No I'm not, but you are."

We break it up before getting into another sex show for the boys.

"I have to head back to the bar. You want me to bring you something to eat?"

"No thanks, I have to cook the books first. I'll be down when I'm done." I go to work "laundering money" so they tell me. It takes about an hour to handwrite all the receipts. I'm just about done when I get another knock on the door. Who can it be now? I'm starting to feel like Soupy Sales, except I don't have Frank Sinatra at my door.

"Who is it?"

"Larry, mind if I come in?" "It's open."

Larry enters with David and Joey.

"We have to start meeting in a different place. MJ already questioned why you guys came last time. I told her you wanted to book rooms for next year. I can't keep lying to her."

"Mj is the least of our problems. We're trying to bring down a big-time mobster. You just handle her."

Bastards!

"What now?" I ask.

"You did a good job. You didn't look at all uncomfortable. We got what we need, but we need at least one more time to show this was not a one-shot deal." Larry says.

"Yeah, you did great! David says. "That was your second-best performance in this office."

"Second best? What do you mean?   oh, you son of a bitch." I get up off my chair and head toward David. Larry and Joey intercept me.

"David, you're an asshole! Sorry about that Patrick. We destroyed the tape, I swear." Larry says.

"I don't care F.B.I. or not, I'll kick your asses if I find out that there are copies of that. MJ would be horrified." I say.

"Back to business. If we can get him on tape next month, that should do it.

How often does Ira Erwinski come by?" Larry asks.

"He's only come by twice so far. Once to show me how to do the books and the second time to do the income taxes. I don't think there are any plans for him to come back. He did say to call him if I needed him."

"No, let's not blow this. We can get him later with your testimony." Larry says.

"How long will the trial last and how will you protect me during the trial?" "It could be months. We will keep you under wraps during the trial." "What about Mj and my family?"

"We will protect them. We will assign guards twenty-four hours a day. The one thing about the mob is that they usually only go after the informant. They respect families. If this were the Columbian mob, they would go after your third-grade teacher to get back at you." Larry says.

"Mrs. Simbetta? I say.

"You remember your third-grade teacher?" Joey asks.

"She was hot. She might be the first woman I made love to when I was by myself. Why couldn't teachers when I was growing up be more like the teachers are today? I would have loved to be molested, especially by my high school English teacher, Mrs. Tunis. I would never have had her brought up on charges."

"Yeah, Ms. April, science teacher. Whenever she dropped the eraser and bent down to get it, I would pop a boner." David says.

"You guys are perverts. Although I do remember my health teacher, Ms. Barbara. When she bent over in front of the class..... enough of this!" Larry barks. "Let's get back to business."

"We're going to need that five hundred he gave you. That is evidence. We won't take the twenty grand now but we will take it later."

Bastards!

"We're done for now. Before he comes next time, we will go over everything again. One more performance like that and he's a goner." Larry says.

"You'd better protect MJ!" "Don't worry. We will."

Again, time seems caught in a vacuum. The days are creeping along. I want this to be over, yet I know when it is over, I won't see MJ anymore. I am filled with more questions than answers. You would think moving to a quiet little town like Summit would isolate you from all the bad in the world, but it seems to be everywhere. What will happen to the Rock when all is said and done? Where will all the locals go for a beer?

Where will Mj earn a living? Where will I get sex?

Jimmy is due here next Friday. I'm starting to feel nostalgic about the Rock and its patrons. I've grown to enjoy Mike and his wit. He can match me tit for tat. Then you have Sgt. Bill Koe. He is a mix of Archie Bunker and Bill Cosby. Mike's brother Michael makes me laugh just watching him be himself. I think about Lucky

Louie, talk about an ironic nickname. Then there is my cook, no he's earned the title of Chef, Phil Boyardee. His pizza turned this place around, but his pasta turned stomachs. I'll miss the crooning of Turk Roberts. I hope that crazy artist, Mitch Henderson, becomes famous and shows his dad. And let's not forget Libby. Maybe I'll take her with me wherever they send me. At least I'll still have sex. NOT! I wish her luck and plastic surgery and lipo suction. In such a short time I've fallen in love with this place and the people. It would have been a great place to live out my life with Mj, even with the harsh winters. She always kept me warm. I think it's getting time to click my heels. Where going home Toto, wherever home may be.

Thursday rolls around and the Jeans and the Mean are at my office door. "Come in, no need to knock," I say.

"How's it going? Have you heard from Jimmy? Is he coming tomorrow?" Larry Asks.

"You know darn well he's coming tomorrow. You listen to every conversation I have! Let's cut the bullshit. I want this over as much as you do." I say. "If you do your job tomorrow that will be it," Larry says. "You just make sure you don't screw up your end."

'We got it covered." David says.

"And after you get Jimmy, someone else will just take his place and it will be business as usual, so what's the point?'

"And then I'll get that guy, and the guy after that until there are no more bad guys. To turn the forest into a plane you take it one tree at a time." Larry says.

"Oh, the Green Peace people must love you, taking down their trees." "You're such a wise ass! You're in this situation because of no one but yourself! You became the bad guy and now you're paying the price! Do your job tomorrow and we'll be done here." Larry spouts out. He gets up from his seat and heads out the door with the jeans following.

Chapter 23
Fair Farren

I wake up and realize it's Pizza Friday, probably my last, one way or another. I roll over to coax Mj into maybe our last sex act and she's not there. I forgot she was opening the bar today. I go into the bathroom to do the three s's shower, shit, and shave. I grab a cup of Jo and head over to the Rock, even though I'm not due there for another hour. I want to take it all in today. Surprisingly, I am as calm as I've been since this whole thing began. It's like the last day of school. You take your final exams, hoping you are prepared, and then the summer begins.

I walk through the front door of the Rock and I'm greeted with the familiar voice of my buddy Mike, and he's doing some early drinking.

"What's a man have to do to get a free beer around here?" He says. I start walking toward him while unzippering my fly.

"No thank you queer, I guess I'll just have to buy another." "Mj, give that crybaby a beer, and I'll have one with him," I say. "At eleven in the morning?" MJ inquires.

"It's midnight somewhere in the world," Mike says.

MJ gives Mike his tin of Bud and pours me a Genny from the tap. She looks deep into my eyes to see what I'm up to, but can't figure it out.

"What's the matter, Patricks is not allowed to have a beer." Mike says "Zip it, dickhead." MJ barks.

"Mike got yelled at, ha ha." His brother laughs. "And you zip it too, smuck." MJ says to Michael. Michael bows his head in shame.

MJ wants to inquire more about my behavior but leaves it for later. There are only four people in the bar but I raise my glass to them and make a toast.

"To the best bar group of drinkers of any bar in the world." I toast. "Here, here." Mike chips in.

MJ even pours a little bit of Genny and joins us. She makes a face while drinking the beer.

"Does beer always taste this bad? I guess it doesn't mix with toothpaste." She ponders about her pre-noon drink.

"That's why I don't brush my teeth!" Mike jokes[I hope.]

I finish my beer and Mj takes the glass ready to refill it while eyeballing me.

"No more, for now, thanks," I say to her delight.

"I'll take it if he doesn't want it," Mike says, never missing a chance at a free beer.

"Beat it loser," MJ tells him. She looks toward Michael and gives him a "don't you dare" look and he shies away.

Boy, I'm gonna miss this place.

I make my way to the office awaiting the big showdown. It's closing in at noon and Jimmy usually shows up around five. By then Mike will be two sheets to the wind. Pizza Friday has begun to pick up again, so we might have a good crowd tonight for my bon voyage. I look around the office and realize that I will miss this place. I'd never run a business before and I kind of liked it. I think I'd like to try it again, sometime, if I'm alive to do it.

I always enjoyed movies and books about the mob. My favorite book and movie were The Godfather. The mob didn't have offices of the F.B.I. There, they will take statements from me and my new hurt innocent people. They only went after the ones who betrayed them, and I always like to see these betrayers dealt with. They say life imitates art and I am proof of it. Now I'm the snitch. I-combines.

I think of calling MJ up to have maybe our last sex act, but the bar is getting busy. I think of having sex with myself, but not with an audience. I'm starting to get fidgety so I make my way down to the bar.

It's t-minus two hours and counting. The Rock is starting to fill up. Happy hour is approaching. Mike is holding up rather well. He hasn't started to slur his words yet. I look around and see a lot of familiar faces, and as I'm doing this I notice Mj is keeping a wary eye on me. I would love to let her in on what's happening, but that would put her in danger. I see David and Joey in their usual spot. They give me the "hi" sign. I sure hope I don't need them. I go into the kitchen to pat Phil on the back.

"Best damn pizza around. This stuff is so good you could probably start a franchise." I say.

"I've been thinking about opening my pizzeria. Sell just pizza. Whatta ya think?" Phil says.

"I think it's a great idea, but what would we do here?" I question.

"You can get someone new. I'll give him the recipe. Then I'll go back to Brooklyn and show them!" He states.

"We'd sure miss you around here."

"Thanks. You believed in me when no one else did. I owe you for that"

"I owe you for making the Jailhouse Rock Inn a success." I shake his hand and head back to the bar.

Mike has started to do shots, something he rarely does. I approach him and ask what the celebrations are all about.

"My divorce was finalized today! I'm a free man!" He says.

Mike's wife left him for another man. She moved with him to Florida. Mike took it hard. She was the love of his life. He might be celebrating on the outside but he's crying on the inside.

"Well, congratulations! MJ gives Mike one on the house." I say. She throws me a look that says he doesn't need another.

"All right, MJ! Make it a double scotch, neat." He says.

"What are you giving away all the profits?' A voice from behind me states.

I turn around and see that Jimmy has arrived. He laughs at his joke. "I'm only kidding. Maryjane, give him another two."

Mike lets out a shrilling hoot.

"I'm gonna get drunker than I've ever gotten drunk tonight!" He slurs. "I'll be down to join you in a bit," Jimmy says and gives me the nod to

head upstairs. He is brown-bagging it again and it looks pretty full. I guess the Rock has had another good month. Let the last act in this story begin.

I lead the way as Jimmy and Sammy follow me to the office. Sammy gets to the top of the stairs and heads to the bathroom.

"I got to take a piss, I'll be right in." He says.

Jimmy and I continue to the office. I sit down behind the desk and Jimmy hands me the bag. I count the money, sixty thousand plus. He grabs about two grand and hands it to me. I cringe that I have to give it to the Feds.

"You're doing a great job. You keep this up and I might have something else in mind for you, make this money look like peanuts." Jimmy says.

I know that what he does for a living is wrong, but I am feeling bad being part of his demise. Sammy knocks on the door and enters the room. He sits on a chair against the wall.

"I think I would like to retire up here someday. It's so peaceful and everyone is so nice. Yeah, someday." Jimmy looks annoyingly at Sammy. A beeping noise is coming from him. "Is that your phone, answer the damn thing."

"No, I left my phone in the car." He replies. Then he reaches into his shirt pocket and takes out what looks to be an iPhone and its beeping. "Oh, it's just the bug scanner. I never turned it off after we checked your office in Brooklyn before we left."

Sammy says.

"Well turn the damned thing off, it's annoying," Jimmy says. "So, you take care of the books and I'll see you down….." He stops in mid-sentence. "Sammy, on second thought, why don't you turn on the scanner."

"But boss, you just said it was annoying you," Sammy says. "Just put it on and give it to me," Jimmy tells him.

My heart is about to stop. I thought that Larry said these were undetectable. Sammy turns on the device and hands it to Jimmy. It immediately starts beeping. Jimmy gets up from his chair and starts walking around the room, scanner in hand. As he approaches the lamp the device starts beeping louder and faster, until it's almost deafening. Jimmy reaches into the lamp and pulls out a tiny camera, the size of a flea. He inspects it and hands it to Sammy, who's an expert on such things. He examines it and immediately throws it on the ground and stomps on it.

"It was a camera and a microphone, state of the art. Someone is watching us. Give it to me, I'll check around for more." He searches the room and finds four more. I'm trying to keep calm, but Jimmy's giving me a look I've never seen before in my life, a combination of rage and calmness. He pulls a revolver from his belt. Sammy follows suit.

"You have ten seconds to tell me who bugged this joint." He says, pointing the pistol at my head.

"I have no idea! Why would anybody care about a little town bar like this?" I say.

"Sammy makes him talk," Jimmy says.

"I don't know anything. Wait a minute. One time Mj and I fooled around on the desk in here. The next time Donald came here he went into the office and I hear him cracking up, you know that coughing, choking thing he used to do. Later on, he comes out and tells me that the desk should be used for work purposes only, then cracks up again. I had no idea what he was talking about. Now I see. He must have had this place bugged for some reason, and he must have seen us fooling around.

"Maybe you're right, at least you better be right!" Jimmy says.

"Boss, I don't think so. Donald not only didn't have a computer or a cell phone, he still had a rotary phone in his office. He hated all the new technology. Not only that, but this stuff is so new, I don't think it's on the market yet. That means government, F.B.I." Sammy says.

Larry is scurrying around his room. He grabs his cell phone and calls David to let him know what's going on.

"They found the bugs. They were about to ruff up Patrick when the last bug was destroyed. Keep your eyes out for them. One of you goes to the back of the bar and one stays in the front. I'll be there in a minute. Don't do anything until I get there." Larry says.

Sammy cocks his pistol and points it at my head. "You have five seconds to talk. One, two.."

"Not here. We have to get him to the limo and take him for a ride. Then he'll talk. Sammy will have his gun on you the whole time. Don't try anything funny because he'll kill you. Let's move it." Jimmy says.

We walk down the stairs with Sammy right behind me, gun in the coat pocket, like something out of a Humphrey Bogart movie. I know if they get me into the limo, I'm a goner. I have to make a move, but I can't do it in the bar; too many innocent people, especially Marjane. If they get me in the limo, I fear ending up like Abe Vigotta in the Godfather, strangled to death, feet flailing. It didn't look like a great way to go. I hope Larry has a good plan.

Larry enters the bar and moves over toward Joey. "Any sign of them yet?" He asks.

"No. What's the plan." Joey asks.

"I don't know. Too many customers to encounter them here. Let's play it by ear." He says.

We enter the bar area and Sammy sticks the gun in my back as a reminder.

I spot David first, then see Larry and Joey. I move through the bar.

"Maryjane, I'll be back in a little while. I'm going to check out a house Jimmy wants to buy. I'll see ya soon." I say.

MJ knows something is wrong but says nothing.

We head to the front door. As I pass Mike, he grumbles some unintelligible words. He attempts to get up from his stool and his leg gets stuck in the stool. He stumbles forward and lands on Sammy. They go down like a ton of bricks and the pistol discharges. The place went from a roar to silence in a second. Larry seizing the moment grabbed Jimmy and threw him to the floor. David and Joey pulled out their guns.

"Everybody down," David screams. Joey rushes over to Sammy and points the gun at him.

"Drop it." He tells Sammy. Sammy thinks for a second, then complies. "Don't move." Joey grabs the gun and tells Sammy to lie on his belly. He looks over and sees Mike bleeding from his gut. "Call an ambulance. Man is shot."

Mike looks at Joey. "Who's shot? We better help the guy." Mike says, oblivious to the pain.

I look over and see Mike bleeding.

"Mj, quick, get me the first aid kit. She reaches behind the bar and pulls it out and brings it over. I take off my shirt and hold it over the wound, keeping pressure on to slow the bleeding. I look over at the floor and see that Larry has Jimmy in cuffs.

Jimmy spits in my direction.

"You better be quiet, if you know what's good for you." He says. "Shut up and stay still," Larry says.

"I need a drink," Mike yells.

The ambulance pulls up to the front and the paramedics rush in.

"Stand back, let us in." Cheryl, the first paramedic on the scene says. She checks out the wound and calls ahead to the hospital, informing them of the situation.

Several cars come wheeling down the block and pull up in front of the Rock. The local police along with a backup team of F.B.I. agents pile out of the vehicles. No one at the Rock knows what the hell is going on. MJ comes running over to me and gives me a big squeeze.

"Are you alright?" she asks. "Yes, I'm fine," I say.

"What's this all about?"

"Your boyfriend is a scumbag," Jimmy says.

"I told you to top shut up!" Larry says whacking him on the head. 'You'll have plenty to talk about back at the station."

"I want my lawyer" Jimmy complains.

"Don't worry, you'll be needing him," Larry responds.

The other agents come in and assist Larry in bringing Jimmy to the police car.

"Patrick, I'm going to need you to come along. You have to make a statement." Larry says.

"Are you in trouble?" MJ asks.

"He sure is. He owes me a lifetime of free drinks." Mike says while being taken out on a stretcher.

"I'll tell you whatever I can when this is over. I love you." I say. "I love you, too!

I head to the cars, never to see the Rock again.

They take me to the local precinct along with Jimmy and Sammy. They arrest all of us. Larry tells me this is standard procedure, I hope. They book us in this station because the shooting took place here, but as soon as they cut through all the red tape they will take us to the Manhattan offices or the F. B . I. There, they will take statements from me, and my new life will begin.

The arraignment of the three of us takes place a week later. They have to charge me on record, and if I cooperate they will drop the charges. I am not kept in prison with the others, thank God. I am kept under protective custody, somewhere in Queens.

Two F.B.I. agents watch me day and night. I was allowed to talk to my family and Maryjane one time but could tell them nothing. MJ is crushed and she's missing me. She wants to come to see me but they tell her that she may be followed and they can't take the chance. Boy that makes me feel secure. She also tells me that Johnny Scarpinto and some of the suits have been seen around town. I tell her to stay clear of them.

The Jailhouse Rock Inn is closed and there is crime scene tape around the outside perimeter of the place. They told Mj that the place was going to be closed for the foreseeable future. Since Jimmy is the owner on record, and this is where the money laundering took place, they are keeping it closed until after the trial. If they convict Jimmy, the government will take ownership of the Rock. I can see it now, Dave and Joey behind the bar and Larry in the back making the pizza.

The trial takes place three weeks later after Jimmy and his attorney try every legal maneuver to get the charges dismissed. The government tries Jimmy and Sammy separately. Jimmy goes first. They bring me to court surrounded by F.B.I.Agents. They make me wear a bulletproof vest. One day on the way to the courthouse, the unmarked car bringing me to the court is under attack. I almost shit my draws when, what sounds like bullets, start pelting the car. The agent beside me covers me with his body.

Guns are pulled, only to find some little kids throwing rocks at the car. I guess a little payback for when I did the same thing as a kid.

I am on the stand for five grueling days of testimony. The defense attorney tries everything in his power to discredit me. He finds things about my past I didn't remember happened, even bringing up my lust for my third-grade teacher. Luckily, since I never did anything "so" bad, he couldn't shake my character. They even brought in my ex-wife to testify what a bad guy I was, but after five minutes of cross-examining by the prosecutor, they deemed her "certifiable" and took her screaming, yelling, and kicking from the courthouse ranting something about how I was the devil himself.

The defense attorney somehow even found the tape of me and Mj making love in the office. The judge wouldn't allow it to be seen, thank goodness. I can imagine the front page of the "Post" showing a photo of the lovemaking, a thimble superimposed over my penis with the headline "Big Italian Mobster brought down by Small Irish Spud."

After four months of trial and one juror being dismissed for taking a bribe from none other than Johnny "The Lip" the jurors deliberate only two hours and convict Jimmy of the charges. When he comes in for his sentencing, he is in an orange prison jumpsuit, the first time in years he has been in public without his tuxedo. The "Post" has this photo on the front page with the headline; Jimmy "The Dux" will pay his Bill. He gets twenty to life, no parole before twenty years. A couple of weeks later Sammy gets twenty-five to life, because he used a gun and because he shot Mike, who testified in Sammy's case.

Mike had everyone in the courtroom cracking up. He was showing his gunshot wound on his belly, sticking his finger into the hole the bullet made and saying he felt like Swiss cheese. The judge told him to put his shirt back on. He said one more witty remark and he would be held in contempt. Mike then made a zipper-closing move with his finger over his lips. The courtroom howled.

A week later, Johnny Scarpinto is convicted of jury tampering and is given twenty to life. Ira Erwinski escapes jail time. Too many friends in high places.

After the trial, I am brought before the trial judge, Judge Roger Herbst, in his chambers. Larry tells the judge of the arrangements made by the F.B.I. before the trial and okayed by a federal judge, to place me in the witness protection program. The judge rips me a new asshole and says if it were up to him, I would be going away for twenty years, too! He says he disagrees with letting someone get away with committing a crime and if I ever so much as jaywalk, he would throw the book at me. I nod and get the hell out of there.

Larry brings me to his office and goes over the details of the protection program. They set me up with a house, paid for, and a monthly income, enough to barely survive. They give me the money that I had in my bank accounts. I signed over the deed to my upstate house to Maryjane.

I have to report to them if I suspect anything suspicious, and if I were to move from the house they gave me, they would no longer help keep me protected.

"You'll need a new name. We can issue you one or you can pick your own.

Just make sure the name has no significance, something to give them a clue to find you. You have one in mind?" Larry asks.

"I have been thinking of names. I like Alexander, Alexander Douglas." I say.

"All right, Alexander. Where would you prefer to live? The choices are Texas, New Jersey, or Arizona."

"Hawaii!" "Not a choice."

"Neither is New Jersey or Texas. Arizona by default." "And will you be traveling alone?"

"Yes. What about the Jailhouse Rock Inn?" I ask.

"The case is over. The government has no use for it. It will be auctioned off." Please."

"Use your connections and my money and buy the place for Maryjane.

"O.K, It's a done deal."

"Thanks." I get up and shake Larry's hand. "You're not such a bad guy," I say. "Neither are you."

I spoke with Maryjane yesterday. I told her I would be leaving soon. "Patrick, take me with you, please." She pleaded.

"I would like nothing better. You would have to change your name, rarely see or talk with your family, and be looking over your shoulders for the rest of your life. I wouldn't ask you to do this. I also won't stop you from joining me. It's up to you. Whatever way you choose, I will understand." I say.

I can hear her sobbing on the other end of the phone.

"Patrick, I love you so much, and I would live in fear every day if it meant staying with you. But I can never just leave my kids. Isn't there some way I could still see them?"

"They would case out your kids and then follow you back here. It won't work."

"I'm sorry, Patrick. I can't do it. How am I gonna live without you?" "You're a beautiful and bright woman. You'll be O.K. just don't forget me.

And don't be surprised to find me under your sheets one night."

"I'll be praying for that every night. I love you." MJ sobs "I love you, too." And I sob.

I am leaving the F.B.I. offices with a set of keys for a Hyundai Sonata, in my name, Alexander Douglas, given to me by our government. No wonder the American auto industry is having problems. As I go to open the door to leave I hear an old familiar voice. It's Mike. He had to sign some paperwork and was headed back upstate.

"Patrick, can I hitch a ride with you?" he says, always looking for a free ride.

"You don't want to go where I'm going." "You" re not heading back to Summit?"

"No. it's not safe for me there. I'm on the run."

"What's going to happen to the Jailhouse Rock Inn and Maryjane?"

"I bought the Rock for MJ. And you look after her. She's the best." "This ain't fair. Too bad what happened to you."

"And too bad what happened to old Jeb Potter. What did happen to him anyway?"

"Look at the time. I've got to catch the train. It's been great knowing you." Mike says on the run.

I see him disappear, hurrying down the crowded city street. Goodbye Mike, I whisper to myself. Goodbye MJ. Goodbye Summit. Goodbye Patrick Hunnewell.

Made in the USA
Middletown, DE
12 June 2023

32128651R00119